# Where Is Papa's Shining Star?

by

Judy Nickles

**Where Is Papa's Shining Star?**

COPYRIGHT © 2008 by Judy Nickles

Cover Art by *Rae Monet*

The Wild Rose Press
PO Box 706
Adams Basin, NY 14410-0706
Visit us at www.thewildrosepress.com

Publishing History
First Vintage Rose Edition, 2010
Print ISBN 1-60154-674-2

Published in the United States of America

**He twirled the dial until he caught the strains of Guy Lombardo's orchestra.**

"That's one of my favorites," Alan said, leaning forward in his chair, his feet moving in time to the music. "Do you dance, Miss Seldon?"

"Oh, yes, all my friends danced at school parties."

"I haven't danced in years. I don't suppose you'd indulge me?"

"There's hardly room in here, Mr. Ashley."

"We could turn up the radio and go into the foyer."

"I'm not sure I remember how."

"Neither am I, but I'd like to try, wouldn't you?"

"Perhaps."

He stood for a moment in the middle of the foyer to orient himself, then held out his arms and was rewarded with the feel of Lenore Seldon stepping into them. Careful not to hold her too closely, he said, "All right, on the next beat." They moved off, not quite in time to the music.

"Is it coming back to you?" he asked.

"I think so."

"The tempo is nice, but I believe we're a bit behind. Shall we pick it up?" He quickened his steps as he spoke. "Are you keeping watch for obstacles?"

"Yes...oh, Mr. Ashley, the stairs." She finished her warning as his heel met the bottom step, and he toppled, pulling her down with him into his lap. For a long shocked moment they sat still, breathing harder than the exercise warranted. She was lighter than he'd supposed, but her hair, when he reached to touch it, was as silky as he'd imagined. Sliding his hands to her cheeks, he brought her face forward until their lips touched.

He thought she responded briefly, but, before he could speak, she jumped from his arms and ran up the stairs.

## Dedication

For KatieBee,
who has loved Alan and Lenore from the beginning

## Prologue

*France*
*September, 1918*

He remembered a flash of light. Blinding brilliance like the sun reflecting off the snow in the mountains where he'd skied with his college fraternity brothers. Searing heat. A burning more intense than he'd ever felt from the early afternoon sun on the sandy beach where he'd frolicked as a half-naked boy. He forced his eyes open in the light of midday, but there was nothing. The darkness, blacker than any he'd ever experienced, terrified him. His mouth felt full of cotton. "Water," he begged hoarsely. "Please...in God's name... water!"

The tin cup pressed against his lips was warm, and so was the water that trickled onto his tongue. "Who is it?"

"Rycroft, sir."

"The others?"

"Dead."

"My God." Shock gave way to pain. He groaned.

"I thought you were, too, but then you moved. Rest easy, Captain Ashley. Help's on the way."

****

*Brookston, New York*
*November, 1918*

She sat unmoving, her rigid back pressed against the wooden slats of her mother's low sewing chair. Her father caressed her small, delicate hands. "I'm so sorry, Lenore. I wish I could tell you that it's

1

a mistake, but here's the telegram Mrs. Broome sent over."

The young woman shook her head, gently at first, then so vigorously that her glossy black hair loosened from its pins and fell over her shoulders. "No. No!"

She had been nineteen a few minutes ago when her father led her to the chair. Now, though she rocked her body rhythmically, reminiscent of her early childhood, her youth had fled.

****

*Barnwell, Texas*
*May, 1920*

"She's a beautiful baby, Roberta. Just look at her."

"I don't want her. I never wanted her! I thought I was going to die. The pain was terrible!"

The man transferred his gaze from his new daughter to his wife. "Dr. Smithwick said you did very well."

"Dr. Smithwick wasn't lying here being ripped apart, and neither were you." The woman's attractive face twisted in anger.

"Roberta..."

"Get out, Albert. Get out and take her with you. And send in the nurse."

He did as he was told. Cradling the infant in his arms, he walked into the nursery he had furnished alone and laid her in the white wicker bassinet. "You're my best little girl, you know, my shining star. Never forget that, sweetheart. Never."

The doctor paused at the door. "She's a fine, healthy girl, Rycroft. Your wife's all right, too."

Albert Rycroft didn't look up. "Thank you."

"I'll be back tomorrow to check on both of them. Meanwhile, the nurse can handle things. Roberta says she doesn't want to feed the baby."

2

"No, I'll take care of it."

The doctor sighed. "Well, it would be better if...oh, maybe not. I don't know. I'll see you tomorrow."

He watched the new father bending over the cradle. "My beautiful little girl, my best little girl. You're my shining star, you know. You're Papa's shining star."

\*\*\*\*

*Brookston, New York*
*1921*

Judge Amos Sutherland, recently retired from the New York State Supreme Court, turned the pages of the thick file on his desk as he contemplated his first case since returning to private practice. The will he had just finished reading for the second time was straightforward; the pending litigation seemed without merit.

He had known Alan Ashley, Sr. and disliked him intensely. He wondered if the son, to whom everything had been left, was anything like the father, though it didn't really matter. It was for Samuel Bernard, a former student and clerk, now counsel for the son, that he had agreed to serve as co-counsel when Ashley Senior's nephews decided, belatedly, to contest the will. "I won't argue the case for you," he told the younger attorney. "Turning this over to me would be a clear admission that you don't feel competent to represent your client."

"I don't. Frankly, I'm terrified at the idea of going up against Trotham and Dunbar."

"All you have to do is prove your case."

"I'm not in their league. I didn't even go to law school."

"You read law with me and passed the bar on your first try. Don't sell yourself short, Samuel."

"I'm just being realistic."

"The will is straightforward. Everything belongs to the son."

"I know that, but they're saying he can't successfully assume the directorship of Ashley Enterprises because he's blind."

"Can he?"

"Of course. He studied business at Harvard and graduated *summa cum laude*, then took an advanced degree before enlisting in 1918. He's spent the past two years at the Institute for the Blind, learning Braille and every other method that's available for adapting to a sightless world." Sam pounded his fist into his palm once, then again.

"Is he as angry as you are?" The judge sat back in his cracked leather chair, his faded eyes boring into Sam's.

"I'm sorry. I lost control."

"Not a good thing to do, especially in the courtroom."

"I know, and to answer your question, yes. Yes, Alan's angry about everything. His blindness, the fact that his fiancée broke their engagement because of it, how my father has betrayed him...and I don't blame him."

"Perhaps not, but you'll counsel him against displaying his emotions, won't you?"

"Yes, of course."

"All right. I've looked at the will. Now tell me why they think it can be broken almost ten years later, and how they plan to do it."

"Percy's and Geordie's father was Alan's uncle and a partner in Ashley Enterprises until 1910, when he sold his interest to his brother. My father moved up as second-in-command. Two years later, when Mr. Ashley and his wife were killed, Father took charge because Alan was still in school. He was also Alan's guardian. That was eight years ago. But he should have known that Alan would step up as soon as he could."

"Perhaps he didn't want to know."

The quick mottling of Sam's neck crept into his face. "My father has always liked being in charge of everything and everyone."

"He opposed your marriage, I understand."

"That's putting it mildly.

"But you married Ellen despite the opposition."

"I have no regrets. She's everything to me."

"I'm pleased that you're happy. Now about the cousins."

"Their father died two years after Alan's parents, and they ran through their inheritance within a few years. Now they see an opportunity to recoup their fortunes. They told my father that if they were in charge, he could remain in the directorship, but they'd draw the lion's share of the profits after expenses."

"Those profits are considerable?"

"Ashley Enterprises is worth several million dollars—without the subsidiary holdings."

"How do you know?"

"Alan requested the books when he came back, and Jerome Vannoy, the comptroller, thinking that Alan was going to step in immediately, produced them. Alan and I went over them carefully before my father found out and told Jerome to get them back."

"Were there any irregularities?"

"I'm not an accountant, but they seemed in order to me."

"Tell me about Jerome Vannoy."

"He's a few years older than Alan. In fact, they knew each other slightly at Harvard. Alan seems to think he's honest. I suppose I trust him as much as I trust anyone at this point."

"So your father and the cousins are going after Alan on the grounds that he's incompetent because of his disability."

"I don't want it to come to trial for a number of reasons, among them the fact that it would be an additional humiliation for Alan, in view of everything he's experienced already."

"I don't think they have grounds to bring it to trial."

"Their attorneys, Trotham and Dunbar, seem to think so."

"Well, the legal-beagles will profit, in any case. What do they bill an hour?"

"I couldn't begin to guess. More than I do." Sam ran his hand through his hair. "I really need your help."

"Young Mr. Ashley is willing to fight?"

"To the death, he says."

"All right. I'll speak with him. But remember, this is your case. Because of the Ashley name, it will get a great deal of notice all over the state. When you win it, your career will be assured."

"Don't you mean *if* I win it?"

"Unless these men know something we don't, they haven't a prayer." He glanced at the young woman sitting a few feet away with her stenographer's pad. "Did you get all of this, Miss Seldon?"

"Yes, sir, I believe so."

"Make a typewritten copy and a carbon. I'll want you to go with me to Rumers Crossing tomorrow. If your mother is concerned, assure her that Mrs. Sutherland will make a proper chaperone and that you won't have time to get into any trouble."

Lenore Seldon's normally pale face took on more color. "I'm sure Mother won't have any concerns, sir. How long will we be there?"

"A week, perhaps. I don't think it's going to take that long, but we'll prepare for all eventualities." He lifted his spare frame from the chair and addressed himself to Sam again. "Go back and tell young Mr.

Ashley that he needs to decide on something for your father, whether it be a settlement or outright dismissal, and I'd advise you to learn whatever you can about where the loyalties of the others in the executive offices lie. If Ashley Enterprises needs to be restructured, it will fall to your friend to do it. He'll need an independent audit of the books immediately. I'll subpoena them if necessary."

"I can't tell you what a relief this is, sir. I was in well over my head."

"Up to your eyebrows, perhaps, but not completely over your head." The judge chuckled. "Don't worry, Samuel. You were one of my brightest clerks on the court. I was sorry to lose you. Your practice is going well, I take it?"

"Ellen grew up poor, so she knows how to manage. We aren't starving."

"You'll appreciate good times more, having experienced the lean ones." He extended his hand. "All right. I'll see you in Rumers Crossing tomorrow. There's still only one hotel, I suppose."

"It's not elegant, but you'll be comfortable enough. I'll make your reservations as soon as I get back this afternoon."

**\*\*\*\***

*Rumers Crossing, New York*
*1921*

"I've heard the situation from Samuel. Now I'd like to hear it from you." Judge Sutherland motioned for Lenore to sit down near the broad mahogany desk in Alan Ashley's study. "My secretary will take down what you say, and we'll compare stories."

"I assure you, Judge Sutherland, there is no story, only the cold, hard fact that Sam's father, my erstwhile guardian, is in league with my profligate cousins to take control of Ashley Enterprises."

Lenore glanced up from her stenographer's pad.

7

The auburn-haired man across the desk from her was strikingly handsome despite the dark glasses that hid his eyes. His military posture suggested a degree of physical strength, and she judged, from where his shoulders rested near the top of the chair, that he was tall. His very white, well-manicured hands rested on the desk in front of him. In a burst of emotion, not reflected in his face, he clenched his fists, making the snake-like scars on the backs of his hands more prominent. From the hard set of his jaw, she had the fleeting impression that it had been a long time since he smiled.

When he turned his head as if looking for her, she said, "I'm on your right, Mr. Ashley, close enough to your desk that I'm touching the corner with my elbow."

His lips twitched. "Thank you." He swiveled his chair so that he was facing her. "All right, here are the facts."

Later, a woman he introduced as Mrs. Swane, his housekeeper, brought coffee and plates of walnut cake with cream frosting. "If there is a typewriter, I can transcribe my notes now," Lenore said to her.

"It's..." the housekeeper began.

Alan Ashley's palm came down on his desk, startling everyone. "Miss Seldon. If you need something in my study, kindly address your questions to me."

Lenore's face grew hot.

"There was no need to snap at her," Judge Sutherland said mildly. "Mrs. Swane is standing right here." He glanced at Lenore and shrugged.

Lenore squared her shoulders. "I'm sorry, Mr. Ashley. Please direct me to the typewriter." She sounded more polite than sorry.

"There is a typewriter on a stand to the left of the ell on my desk." His tone was as unapologetic as hers.

"Yes, I see it now. Thank you."

"And there is a box of paper in the upper left-hand drawer of the desk and a box of carbon paper beneath that."

"Thank you, Mr. Ashley." Lenore uncovered the machine and positioned a straight-backed chair in front of it.

While she was typing, Sam Bernard arrived and helped himself to coffee and cake. "I heard from your cousins' attorney. He said they would like to settle this out of court. I guess the word is out that Judge Sutherland is involved."

"What sort of a settlement do they propose?" the judge asked.

"My father will continue as co-director of the company, and they will sit on the board with Alan."

"Well remunerated, of course."

"Of course. I told Mr. Dunbar that wasn't acceptable."

Alan leaned across the desk. "And?"

"It seems that he's spoken with some of the doctors who treated you at the hospital in Massachusetts and also at the rehabilitation hospital. Two of them are prepared to testify to your... mental... instability."

Out of the corner of her eye, Lenore saw Alan's long fingers form angry fists again, but his shoulders slumped a little, signaling his hurt.

Judge Sutherland poured himself a second cup of coffee. "For a fee, I'm sure."

"Sam had me sign a release for my medical records," Alan said. For a moment, Lenore felt almost afraid of the barely-controlled anger in his voice, as if he might turn and strike out at whoever was closest to him. "There's nothing damning in them."

"Yes, I just received them," Sam said, opening his briefcase. "That's the other reason I came, to give them to Judge Sutherland." He handed over a thick file tied with twine. "And I spoke with Rolf Sims, Alan. He said he'd be glad to meet with the judge to interpret them."

Judge Sutherland laid the file aside. "Who is Rolf Sims?"

"Sam and I grew up with him," Alan answered. "He practices medicine here, but he's not just a small-town doctor. He's a skilled surgeon with privileges at several hospitals in the area. After the war, however, he decided he'd had enough excitement and came home."

"So his credentials are good."

"The best," Sam said. "Rolf had an offer from Johns Hopkins, but as Alan said, he was ready to come home and live quietly."

"Then I should speak with him."

Lenore typed steadily, aware that the conversation continued and that Alan Ashley participated only occasionally. Finally she rolled the last sheet of paper from the carriage, laid it atop the others, and replaced the cover on the machine.

"Are you finished already? Are you sure everything is accurate?" Alan turned his head in her direction.

"I can assure you that it is," Judge Sutherland said. "Miss Seldon knows her business."

Lenore tapped the sheets into a neat pile. "I'll put these in your case, Judge Sutherland."

"Did you find any discrepancies?"

"No, sir, though Mr. Ashley gave additional information."

"You can do a thorough comparison this evening after I meet with Dr. Sims." Judge Sutherland got to his feet. "We'll go back to the hotel now. Samuel, please arrange for the doctor to see me this evening. And, of course, let me know if Mr. Dunbar contacts you again."

He approached the desk and extended his hand to Alan, then dropped it as he remembered the man couldn't see what he was doing. "I'm confident the case won't go anywhere. It's what is termed frivolous. Your father's will is solid, your education and preparation for the directorship of Ashley Enterprises is undisputable, and short of being locked away somewhere, which you aren't, there is no reason that you shouldn't step into the position."

"Except that Percy and Geordie want their greedy fingers in the pot."

Sam's shoulders sagged. "And my father."

"They'll be disappointed, I'm afraid. Come, Lenore, we'll go now."

****

Lenore slid behind the wheel of the car parked under the porte cochere. "It must have been a terrible blow to lose his sight that way and so young, just when his life was beginning."

"You're excusing his rudeness?"

"No, sir, just thinking aloud."

"His father was insufferably arrogant. I'm afraid young Ashley isn't much different. He's better-looking, however."

"The lawsuit is really frivolous?"

"Well, I find it dangerous to be overconfident with any case, but unless Bernard's father and the cousins can produce evidence to the contrary, I see no way they can gain control of the company."

"What about the doctors?"

"It could have been a smoke screen, leverage to get an out-of-court settlement. Of course, I'll see to it they don't get a penny." Judge Sutherland patted Lenore's shoulder. "You handled yourself well in there."

"I tried to put myself in his position. What must it be like to talk to people you can't see and have to trust them?"

"We'll collect Emma, have an early dinner, and be ready to interview this Dr. Sims. Stop at the desk and see if they have a typewriter available and have it sent up. It may be a long evening."

****

Lenore often accompanied Judge Sutherland into court, so she was knowledgeable of judicial proceedings and comfortable in that setting. Alan Ashley, however, was not. His barely-concealed anger on the first day of the lawsuit interfered with his carefully cultivated authoritative demeanor. That fueled the fires of his anger to burn even hotter.

"Would you like to walk out and stretch a little?" Lenore asked during a recess at midmorning.

He jumped at the sound of her voice near his ear. "You startled me. Be kind enough to announce yourself before you speak."

"I'm sorry, Mr. Ashley. I did tell you before we began that I was sitting next to you at the table." She hesitated. "I was thinking of going to the porch at the end of the corridor. Courtrooms are rather stuffy sometimes."

"Yes, all right." He rose. "I'll have to take your arm."

"Certainly." She offered a slender arm. "This way."

"Perhaps you're wondering where my white cane is," he said abruptly as they exited the courtroom.

"I didn't know you had one."

"Every blind man has a white cane."

"I see." She pushed open the door at the end of the hall. "We're at the porch. There isn't a step down."

They moved outside into the warm autumn sunshine. "We're on the west side of the court house. Are you familiar with the large red brick building across the street?"

"It's the bank," he said promptly. "My great-grandfather founded it."

"So the Ashleys have been in Rumers Crossing for a long time."

"Since before the Revolution."

"How interesting."

"Is it, really?"

"Oh, yes, I love history. My father used to read aloud from *A Child's History of the World* when I was a little girl. I always wanted to travel and see the places he read about."

"But you didn't."

"Not yet, but I hope to someday."

"Travel requires money."

"Have you traveled widely?"

"I spent six months on the continent before entering Harvard in 1913."

"Were you in Greece, by any chance?"

"Yes, I was."

"Is the Acropolis as magnificent as it appears in pictures?"

"More so, actually."

"I should love to stand there and soak it all in." Lenore sighed. "The sun is nice this time of year, isn't it?"

"A hard winter is predicted."

"Yes, but until it comes, we have this lovely weather to enjoy."

"Are you always so optimistic?"

She laughed. "My brother Teddy calls me Pollyanna. That's the name of the title character in a children's book for girls, so I'm sure you're not familiar with her. She always looked for the good in everything."

"And you follow suit?"

"Not always, Mr. Ashley, but I'm happier when I try to find some good in every circumstance."

"I suppose you think I should try to find some

13

good in my blindness?"

"Not at all, but you have a great many advantages despite that, and Judge Sutherland feels that this lawsuit will be thrown out."

Sam Bernard put his head out the door. "It's almost time to reconvene," he said. "I'm going to find the facilities, Alan. Would you..."

Alan dropped Lenore's arm. "Yes, thank you, Sam. I'm sure Miss Seldon would be mortified to lead me there."

"Alan..."

Lenore smiled at Sam and shook her head to stall his defending her. When the men had gone, she closed her eyes and turned her face to the sun, breathing in its warmth.

****

"The first day is just preliminary business," Judge Sutherland said as they left the courthouse at four o'clock. "Tomorrow we'll get to the heart of the matter."

"My housekeeper is preparing dinner for everyone tonight," Alan said. He sounded more resigned than hospitable.

"I can vouch for her culinary talents," Sam said. "Unfortunately, Alan, Ellen and I have another engagement."

"Of course."

"My wife and I will be delighted to join you," Judge Sutherland said. "Hotel food is adequate at best."

"Miss Seldon?" Alan didn't even pretend to speak cordially.

"Thank you," she said. "I'd love to come."

****

Awed by the formal dining room and the long table with its expensive linen, china, and heavy silver, Lenore almost forgot to eat. When dinner was over, she offered to help Mrs. Swane clear away.

"That's not necessary, Miss Seldon," Alan said.

"Oh, please, I always do at home."

Mrs. Swane looked her up and down. "Come along then. I won't mind the company."

The kitchen was almost as overwhelming as the rest of the house. "You have all the latest conveniences," Lenore observed.

"Mr. Alan had everything replaced when he returned after the war." She patted the gas range as if it were a child. "I've always liked to cook."

"Dinner was wonderful, Mrs. Swane. Thank you."

"You don't look like you eat much."

Lenore laughed. "I'm like my father. He was a hearty eater and never gained a spare ounce."

"He's no longer living?"

"No, it's just Mother and me now. My brother lives in Texas."

"That's a long way."

"We miss him, but he gets back to visit as often as he can. Shall I put the glasses in the pan now?"

"Yes, the water's ready. What do you think of Mr. Alan?"

"I'm not sure I should express an opinion, Mrs. Swane."

"He was a sweet little boy. Lonely, though. Mr. Richard and Miss Caroline ignored him. They were too busy with other things."

"That's very sad."

"I was more like his mother than his own mother was. He still looks on me that way."

"I'm sure he needs you."

"He doesn't want to need anybody."

"It must be difficult for him to be...dependent."

"Oh, he can do for himself well enough. It's people he needs."

"A wife, you mean. Surely there are dozens of young women who would be pleased to have him

15

come courting. He's very handsome." Lenore's hand flew to her mouth, scattering soapsuds from the pan. "Oh, dear, you won't tell him I said that, will you?"

Mrs. Swane laughed. "He's too handsome for his own good. Always was. But the kind of girls in his set weren't any good for him. He was going to be married, but she didn't want him after he went blind."

"How callous! He's not only his eyes."

"She wasn't good enough for him."

"Tell me about the house, Mrs. Swane," Lenore said, feeling an urgent need to move the conversation to less personal topics. "It's very old, isn't it?"

****

The litigation turned nasty on the second morning. Out of the corner of her eye, Lenore watched Alan Ashley squirm as he listened to Aubrey Trotham present evidence that Alan was incapable of leading Ashley Enterprises. When the judge declared a recess, she asked Alan if he'd like to walk out on the porch again.

"I'd like to throw that shyster off of it," he muttered.

"I'm sure you would, but wait until Judge Sutherland refutes the evidence later. I think you'll find that even better than going to the trouble of throwing someone off the porch. Besides, this is only the second floor."

Alan's head swiveled toward her. "You surprise me, Miss Seldon."

"Why?"

He took her arm. "I wouldn't have thought you had a sense of humor."

"Oh, dear, why not? Am I sour?"

"No, but you seem all business most of the time."

"I'm here with Judge Sutherland on your business. You don't want me to be less than serious about it, do you?"

"No, of course not," he snapped. "You misunderstand me."

"Humor sees us through many situations, don't you think?" she said, ignoring his ill temper.

"I wouldn't know...Pollyanna."

She laughed again. "Would you like to stop at the facility? We're at the door."

When he came out and took her arm again, he said, "Did you enjoy your dinner last night?"

"It was delicious."

"And your visit with Mrs. Swane? I suppose she told you all about me?"

"A little, but we talked mostly about the house."

"Would you like a tour of it?"

"Why, yes, I would."

"Perhaps you'd come for dessert tonight. I could send my chauffeur for you."

"You're not including the Sutherlands in your invitation?"

"No, I'm not. I find them rather dull. It's you I want to visit with."

"I see."

"Are you rejecting my invitation?"

"No, but I must see if Judge Sutherland needs me for anything and ask Mrs. Sutherland for her approval."

"It's necessary to have her approval?"

"Well, she did come along partly to chaperone me, for my mother's sake, you see."

"No, I don't, really. You're a grown woman, aren't you?"

"I'm still my mother's daughter and owe her the respect of feeling at ease over my whereabouts."

"So you're an old-fashioned girl?"

"There's nothing wrong with that."

"Mrs. Swane lives in. She'll be around."

"I'll discuss it with the Sutherlands," Lenore

said. "Here's the porch, and it's another beautiful day."

****

Amos Sutherland wasted no words when court reconvened after lunch. His determined attack, cloaked in courteous but irrefutable logic, left Aubrey Trotham reeling, Claiborne Bernard and Alan Ashley's cousins in a state of confusion, Sam Bernard beaming, and Alan Ashley almost licking his lips with satisfaction. After the judge announced he would render his decision the next morning, the courtroom emptied without delay.

"I don't like to be without definite plans," Alan said to Lenore as they left the building.

"I'll telephone Mrs. Swane as soon as I've spoken with Mrs. Sutherland. It won't be necessary to send your car, either. I'll drive myself."

"I'll expect you at eight o'clock."

"I'll telephone."

At the hotel, Lenore wasted no time discussing Alan's invitation with Emma Sutherland. "I told him I'd need your permission since you're acting as my chaperone."

"An old-fashioned notion these days," Emma observed. "I wonder you don't rebel against it the way other girls are doing."

"I don't want to, Mrs. Sutherland."

"No, I know you don't. Your mother brought you up well."

"Thank you."

"You said the housekeeper lives in?"

"Yes. I should think if I'm going for dessert that she'll be in evidence."

"How can he give you a tour of the house?"

"I'm sure he knows it well, since he grew up there."

"To tell you the truth, Lenore, I don't like him very much. He's quite abrasive."

18

"I think he hides behind that attitude, don't you?"

"Are you interested in him?"

"Not in the least, but I'd like to see the house. Mrs. Swane told me some of its history last night."

"I don't see how any woman could be interested in someone as rude as he is, much less a refined young woman like yourself. Amos isn't that way. Neither was your father. He always treated your mother as if he were still courting her."

"Yes, I remember."

"David Broome treated you that way, too."

"Yes, he did."

"Someday you'll meet someone else like that."

"I hope so, Mrs. Sutherland."

"Well, I don't suppose I have any objections to your going tonight. You'll be driving yourself and can leave any time you've had enough of young Mr. Ashley's bad manners."

Lenore laughed. "I hope Mrs. Swane made walnut cake again. That buttercream frosting melts in one's mouth."

****

"The secret room that was used when this was a safe house for slaves escaping to Canada is off the attic," Alan said as they finished their tour of the third floor servants' quarters no longer in use. "But we won't go up there because it's not well-lighted, and it's quite dusty. There's nothing much to see, really. It's behind a sliding panel in a cedar closet, and a tunnel runs through a man-made hill that abuts the house."

"It sounds fascinating."

"I thought so as a child. Shall we go downstairs and see what Mrs. Swane is serving?"

"You speak of the house almost as if it's a person," Lenore said as he took her arm on the stairs. "I find that very nice."

"It has been the only constant in my life. My parents spent much of their time traveling."

"You traveled, too, you said."

"Not with them. We'll have our dessert in the drawing room." He reached to open the door.

"How do you orient yourself?" Lenore asked. "I hope my curiosity doesn't offend you."

"I find it refreshing that you don't ignore my blindness as some shameful secret. I count steps sometimes. Other times I just feel where I am. I know this house intimately. Please take the blue chair by the fireplace."

"I hoped you'd serve this again," Lenore said as Gladys Swane brought in plates of walnut cake.

"It's Mr. Alan's favorite, except for my butter cookies, which I have to hide from him."

"Thank you, Mrs. Swane," Alan said, "for the cake and for sharing my evil ways."

She winked at Lenore. "Enjoy your dessert. The coffeepot is full, and it's hot, so take care."

Lenore poured coffee from the silver pot, being careful not to fill Alan's cup full. "It's quite hot, as Mrs. Swane said."

He took it unhesitatingly. "How did you know not to fill it full?"

"I noticed last night that Mrs. Swane didn't fill it. Actually, I'm not sure why the rest of us risk spilling."

"Do you like music, Miss Seldon?"

"Very much."

"You might go to the record cabinet and find something while the coffee cools."

"Is there anything in particular you'd like?"

"Suit yourself."

Lenore selected Mozart and started the phonograph. "You have a large collection."

"It's one of the few things I can enjoy now. Tell me, Miss Seldon, do you intend to work for Judge

Sutherland forever?"

"Why not?"

"I thought you might have other ambitions. Marriage, perhaps."

"I believe that's more in the category of a wish or a dream, not an ambition."

"You were right about Judge Sutherland. He struck down every foolish argument that Sam's father and my cousins put forth."

"The entire lawsuit was foolish. I was watching the judge while Mr. Trotham presented his case. He looked rather bemused over the whole thing."

"Sutherland made mincemeat of that stuffed-shirt shyster."

"He did, didn't he?"

"I hope I wasn't premature in reserving a table at Le Monde for our victory celebration tomorrow night."

"I doubt that you were."

"You'll be there, of course."

"Of course."

"I don't suppose you've ever dined in an elegant restaurant like Le Monde."

"I've heard of it. It's French, isn't it?"

"The chef is straight from Paris. What kind of education did you have?"

"I attended the public schools in Brookston and enrolled in business school."

"Do you consider yourself well-educated?"

"I hope so."

"Judge Sutherland seems to trust your business ability."

"He's taught me a great deal."

"I can't move you, can I?"

"How are you trying to move me, Mr. Ashley?"

"Out of your Pollyanna world, I suppose."

"I like it there. I'm quite happy and content as I am."

"I am not, as you can see."

"Yes."

"No words of sympathy?"

"Of course, I'm sorry for the loss of your sight, Mr. Ashley, but you seem to manage quite well. I'm not sure I could do the same."

"I spent two years learning how to live in a dark world, and yes, I do it well. That doesn't mean I have to like it."

"No, it doesn't mean that you have to like it."

\*\*\*\*

At nine-thirty, despite Alan's protests, Lenore thanked him for a lovely evening, got into the car, and drove back to the hotel. She knocked on the door that joined her room to the Sutherlands'. "I'm back, Mrs. Sutherland."

The older woman opened the door. "Did you have a pleasant evening?"

"Very. There was walnut cake with buttercream frosting again."

Emma patted Lenore's cheek. "You're a good girl, Lenore."

"Mr. Ashley was a perfect gentleman."

"As he should be."

"Goodnight. Tomorrow is going to be either a very long or a very short day."

"Amos says that the judge will render his verdict and adjourn in short order."

"I hope so."

\*\*\*\*

The following evening, Lenore sat between Judge Sutherland and his wife at Le Monde and listened as Alan Ashley ordered dinner in fluent French without benefit of the menu. Sam Bernard and his wife Ellen, a blonde, blue-eyed woman with a healthy complexion devoid of makeup, sat across the table. The case was over, decided in Alan's favor as Judge Sutherland had predicted.

Alan felt for his wine glass, filled with an expensive vintage despite the constraints of Prohibition, and lifted it. "To a successful outcome," he said, but Lenore thought he didn't sound particularly elated. She pretended to sip from her own glass out of courtesy.

"Your mother wouldn't approve," Emma Sutherland whispered to her.

Lenore flushed and replaced the glass on the table.

Alan turned toward her. "You don't drink wine, Miss Seldon?"

"No, sir, I don't."

"We are *in loco parentis*," Judge Sutherland said. "Her mother is quite particular with her, as you may have concluded."

"I see." The chill in Alan's voice made Lenore shiver. He had seemed more pleasant earlier today. "Well, I'll have the waiter serve water with your meal, Miss Seldon."

"Now, Alan, don't be mean." Ellen Bernard's voice was a cheerful interruption. "You can't corrupt everyone as you've corrupted me." She turned to Lenore with a tentative smile. "Even though I came out of the hills of Kentucky, I'd never had so much as a drop of moonshine, and the first time Alan took Sam and me to dinner, I almost choked on the wine."

Alan toyed with the fluted napkin in front of him. "You enjoy it well enough now."

"So I do," Ellen agreed, "but you don't want Miss Seldon carried out as I almost was, do you?" She reached for Alan's hand. "You've won the day, Alan. Be nice."

Lenore thought he was making a conscious effort in that direction as he opened his mouth, then closed it without replying.

As they waited for dinner, Lenore listened to the conversation with interest. She'd been transplanted, however temporarily, into a different world from the one in which she'd grown up, and it fascinated her. Alan Ashley fascinated her most of all, the way he handled his eating utensils with ease and curled his fingers around the slender stem of his glass without hesitation and lifted it gracefully to his lips. A casual observer wouldn't know that he was blind, not in the beginning. It was his bitter spirit that disturbed her more than she wanted him to know.

She thought perhaps she enjoyed the luxurious restaurant and rich food too much and felt both relieved and disappointed when dinner was over. Watching Alan sign the check at the place where Sam placed an unobtrusive finger, she wondered what it might be like to have plenty of money to spend on whatever one wanted.

"You'll send me your charges, of course," Alan said to Judge Sutherland while they waited for the cars to be brought around.

"I bill at the same rate as Samuel. Send me a check for whatever you pay him."

"You did the lion's share of the work, Judge Sutherland," Sam said.

"It was your case."

"Not really."

"I'm not concerned about it. This is our car. Goodbye, Mr. Ashley. I wish you success."

"Miss Seldon," Alan said.

Lenore turned back. "Yes, Mr. Ashley?"

"I don't suppose you'd be interested in making a change when I reorganize my office?"

"No, sir, I wouldn't."

"I'll give you twice your present salary."

"It's a generous offer, Mr. Ashley, but I'm quite satisfied where I am."

"I supposed you might be."

"Thank you for the compliment, however."

Alan nodded curtly. "Goodbye, Miss Seldon."

"Goodbye, Mr. Ashley. Good luck." She joined the Sutherlands in their car.

"Call on me anytime, Samuel," Judge Sutherland said through the open window. "I shall follow your career with much interest."

Lenore shifted gears and accelerated. "I'm glad everything turned out for the best, but Mr. Bernard is right. You did do most of the work, Judge Sutherland."

"I've had my success, Lenore my dear. Emma and I are comfortable. I expect there will be an additional bonus for you in my fee. Emma says I've driven you these past few days."

"Oh, no, sir, that's not necessary. It's been...very interesting."

"I'm curious to know what young Mr. Ashley will do about his friend's father. He should be summarily sacked for his disloyalty."

Emma Sutherland leaned forward. "If, as you say, Alan Ashley is anything like his father, he'll get rid of the man. Lenore, dear, I hope that man didn't hurt your feelings over the wine."

"Of course not, Mrs. Sutherland."

"He's very rude."

Judge Sutherland patted her knee. "Now, Emma, I've spoiled you with my old-fashioned charm."

"He had the audacity to try to take Lenore away from you within our hearing."

"I think he knew I wouldn't accept, Mrs. Sutherland. I'm quite happy where I am. I think Mr. Ashley will be nearly impossible to please, and I wouldn't even want to try."

Chapter One

Alan Ashley gripped his white cane and stepped from the car as the uniformed chauffeur opened the door. "Thank you, Rod."

"Would you like for me to walk upstairs with you, Mr. Ashley?"

"I think not. I suppose if I get lost someone will show me the way." The corners of his mouth turned up slightly, then fell into their usual tight line.

"We did this four times yesterday, sir. You know the way."

"Yes, thank you, Rod, actually I do." He took a deep breath and started forward murmuring, "Five steps to the door."

"Good morning, Mr. Ashley."

"Good morning. James, isn't it?"

"Yes, sir, I've been the doorman here at Ashley Enterprises for five years now."

"Do you have a family, James?"

"A wife and two children, a girl and a boy."

"Do you get by all right on your salary?"

"Oh, yes, sir. Everybody sure appreciated the raise. Mr. Young said it was your idea."

Alan dismissed the thanks with a wave. "The workman is worthy of his hire."

"You read the Bible?"

"Not lately. Is that where the quote is from?"

"Yes, sir."

"Well, I'll be on my way, James. The elevator is still straight ahead where I left it yesterday, I presume?"

Straight ahead, sir." He stepped aside.

"Welcome back, Mr. Ashley."

"Twelve steps to the elevator," Alan muttered, moving the cane from side to side and wondering who was in the lobby to stare at him.

He heard the elevator doors open. "Good morning, Mr. Ashley."

"Jackson, is it not?"

"Yes, sir, I'm Jackson."

"How long have you been with Ashley Enterprises, Jackson?"

"Fourteen years, sir. Your father was here then."

"Yes. My father."

There was a short silence. "But you'll pardon me saying so, sir, he never knew my name."

Alan's mouth twisted slightly. *He barely knew mine.*

He felt the elevator begin to rise and finally come to a stop with a soft jolt. "Fourth floor, Mr. Ashley."

Alan stepped out into the corridor with more confidence than he felt. His office was to the right, barely a dozen steps. He listened for the sound of anyone else, but he was alone. Turning stiffly to the right, he began to count his steps.

"Good morning, Mr. Ashley."

"Mrs. Fenton?"

"Yes, sir. I left the office door ajar this morning so I could watch for you. I hope you don't mind."

He did mind, but he forced a brief smile that he hoped was sincere. "It was thoughtful of you."

Realizing that he hadn't removed his hat upon entering the building, he did so now. It caught immediately on the rack just inside the door. Encouraged, he extended a hand to find a hanger for his coat, wondering if the woman behind the desk was having to restrain herself from jumping up to help him. When he managed to get the hanger into the arms of the overcoat and back to the rack, he felt

27

gratified.

"Is my door open also, Mrs. Fenton?"

"No, sir. Shall I..."

"No. No, thank you." He started forward and collided with her desk.

"I believe you forgot to step left from the door," she said. "I did, too."

"Oh, so you tried this maneuver?"

"I felt...that is, I feel that I should...understand and be able to...to anticipate your needs."

He wanted to shout that his only need was to have his sight back, but what good would it do to lash out? The best doctors had told him that his blindness was permanent. "Quite right," he said. "I'm sure we'll work well together." He stepped left. "The first order of business is the hiring of my assistant. What time is the first applicant due?"

"Nine o'clock."

"I should like for you to announce him first, if you please. And bring your pencil and dictation pad when you show him in. I want careful notes about each person, including your impressions of their appearances and how...if they appear comfortable around me...around a *blind man*."

He started forward again, one hand extended to feel for the doorknob. Once inside his private office, he leaned against the closed door, drained with the effort. *Can I do this every day for the rest of my working life? Can I keep this business going without being able to look my clients in the eye...without being able to see the people I work with and have to depend on? Is it even worth the effort?*

## Chapter Two

*1924*

Lounging familiarly in the drawing room that had been off limits to him when he visited this house as a boy, Sam Bernard accepted a cup of coffee from Mrs. Swane and nodded his thanks. "You should get out more, Alan."

"Why?"

"Because it's good for you."

"It isn't good for other people. They're uncomfortable with me."

"Ellen and I aren't."

"You're my oldest friend, Sam."

"I'm also your attorney, and my best legal advice is to be more in evidence as the head of Ashley Enterprises. You fought hard enough to retain the position."

"The business is all right. Our profits have risen every year since I came back."

"Then let me be blunt. There are those in the business world who see you only as a figurehead. They believe that Trent Young has run Ashley Enterprises these past three years."

"He carries a great deal of responsibility. I was fortunate to acquire him."

"But he's not the company. You are."

"Sam, I don't care what anyone thinks, and my erstwhile relations are quite out of the picture."

"As is my father, thank God."

"He fulfilled his responsibilities as my guardian and in keeping the company going."

"You're generous not to mention the rest."

"We must go forward, Sam."

"That's precisely my point. Ellen says that you're too young to shut yourself up alone in this house. She's tried more than once to arrange introductions for you."

"To women like Elise?"

"Not all women are like Elise."

"Do you know what she told me, Sam? She told me that she could never marry half a man." Alan Ashley brought his hand down hard on the arm of his chair. "Half a man! That's how she saw me without my eyes."

Sam Bernard sighed. "I know what she said, and you know what you are. Elise was..."

"Elise is gone, and I don't wish to repeat the experience."

"All right. I'll say no more. Ellen is expecting you for dinner on Friday night as usual. And Bea asks specifically that you bring your 'bumpty book' to read to her."

Alan laughed. "She'll be reading Braille before she learns to read print."

"No doubt she will. It fascinates her. Shall I pick you up?"

"Rod will drive me from the office."

"Ellen has invited the new pastor of St. John's and his wife. I hope you don't mind."

"Actually, I do. You know that I don't like meeting new people socially."

"I said as much to Ellen, but it would please her if you'd come. She doesn't entertain often, you know."

Alan rose from his chair as he heard Sam get up. "All right. I'll come for Ellen's sake."

"I'll tell her. And don't forget..."

"I'll certainly remember the bumpty book."

## Chapter Three

"I don't suppose you remember me."

Alan sorted through the various voices stored in his memory. "How could I forget? You bedeviled me daily in the hospital in France and then had the audacity to turn up in the one I was sent to here in the United States." He put out his hand. "How are you, Thomas?"

"Just splendid, Alan. Like the bad penny, I've turned up again. I'm the new rector at St. John's."

"Indeed."

"I saw your name on the list of communicants."

"I don't attend anymore, but I do send a regular contribution."

"That's appreciated, I'm sure, but your presence would be more pleasing to the Lord."

"The Lord will have to get along without me."

"Ah, Alan, I'd hoped things had changed with you."

"Thomas, you were a good friend. You made me realize that I could live again, even in a dark world, and I'm grateful. But don't begin on me about attending church. I don't belong there."

"If you don't belong in God's house, where do you belong?"

"The matter isn't up for discussion."

"All right, but I won't give up. God spared your life for a purpose."

"It's unfortunate that He didn't spare my sight as well. Is your wife here?"

"I believe she's helping Ellen in the kitchen. I had hoped to speak with you before dinner about

31

filling the vacant position on the vestry. Your name came up in the last meeting."

"Out of the question, Thomas."

"Why?"

"I believe I just explained all that."

"Perhaps you'd at least consider it."

"No. Ah, Bea, how is my very favorite little girl?" Alan scooped up the child who was tugging at his trouser leg.

"I'm fine, Uncle Alan. Did you bring your bumpty book?"

"I did indeed. We'll read right after dinner."

"Mummy set your place by me so I can help you."

"Like you did the last time? By telling me that my potatoes were at two o'clock, and instead it was your unwanted broccoli?"

Bea giggled and patted his face. "I hate broccoli."

"I do, too." He set her down. "And if you try to fool me tonight, I'll eat you like the wolf ate Red Riding Hood."

"He ate the grandmother, Uncle Alan."

"Ah. I stand corrected."

Ellen came out of the kitchen. "Hello, Alan. I see that Bea has already taken possession of you." She kissed his cheek. "You must meet Janet Greer. She said that you already know Thomas."

Alan felt someone take his hand.

"I'm Janet, and it's a great pleasure to meet you, Mr. Ashley."

"Welcome to Rumers Crossing. Are you getting settled at the manse?"

"It's really too large for two people, but it's a beautiful old house. I understand that yours is large also and has quite a history."

"Yes, it does. Perhaps you and Thomas will join me for dinner one night soon, and I'll give you a tour."

"That would be lovely."

"All right, everyone come into the dining room and sit down now," Ellen said. "And Bea, don't let me catch you sneaking your vegetables onto Uncle Alan's plate again."

Bea reached for Alan's hand. "I won't, Mummy."

****

Ellen served coffee after Alan returned from tucking Bea into bed. "I tried to locate more Braille books for children this week but with little success."

"They seem to be rather scarce," Alan said, accepting the cup that Ellen placed in his hands. "However, I shall see what Mrs. Fenton can turn up."

"I mentioned to Alan that his name had come up in regard to filling the vacant position on the vestry." Thomas Greer glanced at Sam for support and instead received a frown and a slight shake of the head.

"This is a social occasion, Thomas," his wife said. "You shouldn't discuss business."

"I take advantage of my opportunities when they arise. Would you at least consider it, Alan?"

"If that will turn the tide of this conversation," Alan said, his irritation evident.

"I need an answer in two weeks."

"You shall have it. Ellen, dinner was delicious, as usual."

****

"May Janet and I run you home?" asked the rector later as they stood up to leave.

"Thank you, my chauffeur was instructed to be here at nine." Alan opened the glass on his watch. "It's almost that now."

"I hope you'll remember your promise to give Janet and me a tour of the house soon."

"I'll make plans for the first evening I'm free."

"The first evening you're free?" Ellen said after

the other guests had gone. "Alan, you're a fraud. You sit home alone every evening."

"Thomas Greer is irritating with his talk of my taking a place on the vestry and coming to church."

"Sam and I go every Sunday and take Bea."

"I'm pleased, but that has nothing to do with me."

Ellen sat down beside him and touched his arm. "Alan, you're depriving yourself."

"I don't see it that way, Ellen my dear."

"I know you turn down multiple invitations. I suppose I should be flattered that you accept mine."

"You're like family, Ellen, and, of course, there's Bea. I'm quite attached to her."

"There are others with whom you could establish similar relationships if you'd just..."

Alan stood, shaking off her hand more abruptly than he intended. "I believe I hear Rod at the door. Thank you for another pleasant evening and a magnificent meal, my dear."

He bent to kiss her cheek. "I'll see myself out."

\*\*\*\*

Alan took his pipe from the smoking stand beside his chair and used the heat of the flame from the lighted match to guide it to the bowl. "You saved my life, in a manner of speaking, Thomas, but my soul is another matter. Leave it alone."

There was a moment of uncomfortable silence. "You're wrong, Alan," the pastor said at last. "Your life is transient, as you above all should know. Saving it is only a temporary condition. But your soul...ah, my friend, your soul is immortal, and I'll never stop trying to rescue it."

Janet nudged her husband. "Thomas, you promised you wouldn't. It's been such a lovely evening."

Alan turned in the direction of Janet's voice and smiled. "Now you know all about the secret room."

"I'm going straight to the library in the morning and see what books I can find on the Underground Railroad and its history in this area."

"I don't think you'll find much. A magazine editor wrote to me several months ago wanting to do a story on the house."

"You accepted, of course."

"I told him I'd think about it. Actually, I'd quite forgotten it until now."

Janet sat forward with obvious eagerness. "Do write him back, Alan, and tell him you'll do it."

"Perhaps you'd like to play hostess when he comes. Mrs. Swane doesn't enjoy that sort of thing."

"I'd be delighted. I'll learn everything I can in the library, and the man will be quite impressed."

"So now the editor has an answer," Thomas said. "What about me, Alan? What about taking your place on the vestry?"

"You're very annoying, Thomas. We agreed that I had two weeks to consider your request."

"All right, all right. But you can't keep me dangling like the hapless magazine editor."

****

"What's bothering you, Alan?" Sam Bernard put down his attaché case and made himself comfortable in a deep leather chair in Alan's study.

"Nothing."

"Something."

There was no mirth in Alan's laugh. "Thomas Greer is annoying, and so are you. I don't like my mind read."

"We always knew what the other was thinking."

"I suppose."

"And Thomas and I are both your friends."

"I'm properly grateful, Sam. It's just that Thomas won't let me alone about the place on the vestry."

"You'd be an asset, and it shouldn't take up

much of your time."

"I contribute generously."

"Your money, not yourself."

"I'd have to attend church, and it would be, well, hypocritical."

"You no longer believe?"

"I don't know if I do or not. Sam, a blind man..."

"You run one of the ten largest companies in this country."

"That's different."

"How?"

Alan moved impatiently. "I can't talk to you."

"You haven't talked to me honestly in several years."

"What is there to say? I do what I have to do. Isn't that enough?"

"No."

"Why not?"

"Because you're a man, Alan, a better man than you were before. You've been through the fire, and it's refined you. There's not an employee in the building who doesn't think you can walk on water, who wouldn't do anything you asked them to do, and who wouldn't stand by you if the profits plummeted. You've treated them with a respect that your father never did, made an effort to know them, raised salaries generously, given them access to medical care through Rolf Sims...shall I go on?"

"I only did what was good for business."

"No, you didn't. You gave them the consideration that your father never accorded you, and if you'd followed him into business after Harvard without going to war first, you'd be like him. I almost think that you...that your blindness is a blessing."

"A blessing?"

Sam cringed inwardly at the iciness of Alan's voice, but he plunged ahead. "I think it has sharpened your vision. Alan, you're a brilliant businessman. You were a brilliant student. You pulled me through more than one exam in prep school."

"You're selling yourself short. Anyone who didn't go to law school and yet passed the bar on his first attempt isn't to be dismissed."

"We're not discussing me. As I said, you were inherently brilliant. Success came easily to you. But there was always something of your father in you, and the war changed all that. It changed you. You're a better man personally."

Sam leaned forward. "Alan, I love you like a brother, and I'm trading on the assumption of your affection for me when I say that the only thing left to be dealt with is your bitterness. You were always bitter in some ways, and I can't blame you. Your parents..."

"I'm no longer the neglected little boy, the dutifully produced heir."

"They denied you the love you deserved, and now I think you feel that you really don't deserve it. You resented their neglect, but now they're gone, so you've replaced them with your blindness. They made you feel unworthy, and now you truly believe you are unworthy because you are blind."

"You say the word easily."

"I don't pretend to understand what it's like, just as you can't understand what it's been like for me to be estranged from my family."

"It's their loss."

"It's mine, too, and Bea's. She's grown up closer to you than to my own brother and sister. She's a beautiful, intelligent child, and they don't care about her because of her mother."

"You know that I love Ellen, Sam."

"Because you see her, Alan, in a way that my family never did."

"If you hadn't sided with me about the business,

perhaps there would still be a chance for them to be part of your life."

"I did what I believed was right, and I've never regretted it."

Alan put the tips of his fingers together and considered Sam's words. "All right, Sam, your point is well taken."

"Alan, you deserve the best life has to offer. You've worked for it. Don't deny yourself."

****

Rod accompanied Alan to the church on Saturday afternoon. "The Ashleys have a pew on the right. See if you can find it, then count back to me." Alan fingered his white cane, lifting it and setting it down, as he waited.

"It's here, Mr. Ashley. Fourteen from the back."

"Count again. I'm not inclined to put myself in some fat dowager's lap on Sunday morning."

Rod's laughter echoed in the empty sanctuary. "That would be quite a sight. Yes, it's fourteen, Mr. Ashley."

"All right, I'm coming." Touching the first pew with his fingertips, Alan made his way down the aisle. "Here."

"Yes, sir, this is it."

He fumbled with the catch on the gate, closed it, then opened it again. "Is the kneeling bench down?"

"No, sir."

Alan stepped inside and closed the gate behind him.

"You want to try it again, Mr. Ashley?"

"I believe so, Rod. Are you sure I'm not keeping you from your family? It's Saturday, after all."

"No, sir, not at all."

"Is the car satisfactory?"

"We're all enjoying it, Mr. Ashley. You didn't have to give me a car, though."

"It was convenient for me to have you available

quickly. I do try not to impose on your free time, however."

'"You don't do that, sir. Shall I wait at the back while you try this again?"

## Chapter Four

*1931*

"Barrows is leaving."

"Retiring?" Sam poured himself a cup of coffee from the pot always sitting ready in the small kitchenette in Alan's office. "That's unfortunate. He's suited you well for ten years."

"I think it's a matter of his health, so I'm not inclined to press him to stay longer." Alan pushed his cup across the desk. "This is cold."

Sam got up and refilled the cup. "This is hot."

Alan's mouth twisted. "I'm being left sightless for the second time."

Sam ignored the remark.

"The only thing he never mastered was the Braille writer."

"Would you like for me to make inquiries about a replacement?"

"I thought I'd advertise."

"Is that a good idea? With so many people out of work these days, you're likely to be inundated with unqualified applicants."

"I'm going to interview from my house."

"Good heavens, why?"

"I want to judge how people handle themselves around me outside of an office. Barrows was discreet with his assistance. I don't want someone who's inclined to hover." His hand closed around the cup as if he could see it. "Or someone who's afraid I'll spill something or fall on my face."

"I'd suggest that you don't conduct your

interviews with that attitude. People mean well, Alan."

"I don't care what they mean as long as they do what I expect of them."

"You'll want another man, I suppose."

"Of course. Mrs. Fenton is an excellent secretary, but when I'm dealing with potential clients, another man in the proceedings seems to engender more confidence."

"I'm sure you won't lack for applicants, but having them in your house might be risky."

"Possibly, but it's a risk I deem prudent. I don't want to waste my time, so I plan to limit the interviews to a few hours on a single morning. Serious applicants will be there early, and I'll sift through them. The ones worth considering can be called back later."

\*\*\*\*

*Position available for administrative assistant to president of Ashley Enterprises. Dictation skills, typing, filing, accounting knowledge required. Experience and references. No exceptions. Apply One Ashley Road, Rumers Crossing, between 8:00 and 11:30 AM on Friday, August 4th. Salary negotiable dependent on experience.*

\*\*\*\*

Gladys Swane was halfway to the kitchen after seeing out the last man interviewed when she heard the knocker again. With her mind on the cold chicken waiting to be diced, she returned and opened the door. "Yes?"

"I came about the ad."

Mrs. Swane opened the door a little wider, squinting against the midday sun at the woman who stood on the broad brick veranda. Perspiration beaded her pale face and wilted the collar of the white blouse worn under a shabby suit. She looked vaguely familiar. "The interviews ended half an hour ago."

"Yes, I know. I'm sorry to be late. A tire blew on the bus, and...I'm sorry to have troubled you." The young woman turned away.

The housekeeper was about to close the door when she saw the woman stumble and steady herself against the nearest white column. "Did you walk from the bus station?"

"Yes, I did."

"Would you like a glass of water?"

"I...yes, please."

"You're welcome to sit on the bench and rest."

Alan Ashley stepped out of his study. "Who is it, Mrs. Swane?"

"Another applicant. I told her the interviews were finished."

"A woman?"

"Yes. I was about to get her a glass of water. She walked from the station and seems almost done in."

"I see. Is Rod still in the kitchen? Perhaps he'd take her back. It's quite warm today."

"I'll tell him." She started for the kitchen again.

"Mrs. Swane."

"Yes, Mr. Alan?"

"Ask her in. I'll speak with her."

"Are you sure? I was about to serve lunch."

"All right, serve it. She's probably hungry, too." He stepped back into the study.

Mrs. Swane found the woman slumped on the bench in the small patch of shade under the eaves. "Mr. Ashley says he'll see you."

The woman swayed as she got to her feet. "He'll see me?" As she looked up, recognition dawned on the housekeeper's face.

"Miss Seldon? Are you Lenore Seldon?"

"Yes, Mrs. Swane."

"Are you all right?"

"I'm just a little tired from the walk in this heat."

"Come in immediately. It's cooler in the house, and I'll be serving lunch. I suppose you could eat something?"

"Yes...oh, yes."

Mrs. Swane frowned at the eagerness in the young woman's voice. "Come in out of the heat. I never expected to see you here."

"I didn't expect to be here, Mrs. Swane, but Mr. Ashley offered me employment once, so I hoped..."

"Do you really want to work for him, Miss Seldon? He's not as hard as he was ten years ago, at least not in public, but he's withdrawn into himself more than ever."

"I need the work badly, Mrs. Swane. I have to try."

Mrs. Swane walked to the study door. "Here's the young lady, Mr. Alan."

Alan rose from behind his desk and extended his hand. "I'm Alan Ashley, president of Ashley Enterprises." The hand that grasped his was small and slightly damp.

"I'm Lenore Seldon."

"I know you."

"Yes, sir. I worked for Judge Sutherland."

"Of course. Sit down, Miss Seldon. There's water in the pitcher on the desk and a clean glass."

"Thank you."

Listening, he thought that her hand trembled as she filled the glass, and he knew that she drank the water in one swallow. "You walked from the station. That's a long way."

"Yes, sir."

"Judge Sutherland died three years ago, did he not?"

"Yes. I'd been with him for almost ten years."

"What have you done since?"

"I worked at whatever I could get."

"Are you currently employed?"

"I work for room and board at the Greenfield Children's Home."

Mrs. Swane pushed the tea cart into the room. "Where do you want this, Mr. Alan?"

"I believe we'll sit on the divan. Just leave it, Mrs. Swane. Miss Seldon will serve."

He walked out from behind his desk and negotiated the familiar path to the long leather couch with the low teakwood table in front of it. "Now, Miss Seldon, if you'll serve my plate and describe the arrangement of the food using the hands of a clock."

He heard her take the covers off the dishes. "Ah. Chicken salad?"

"Yes, sir." She filled his plate and set it in front of him. "Sliced tomatoes on a bed of lettuce at two o'clock, chicken salad at four o'clock, and a roll at eight. Would you like your roll buttered?"

"Yes."

She complied, then poured iced tea from a silver pitcher. "I've placed your tea beside your plate at two o'clock, and your fork is on a napkin to your left."

"Thank you. Now please serve yourself."

In the silence that followed, he wondered if she was watching him eat, but she'd witnessed his skill before, at Le Monde as well as here at his home. It occurred to him the silence meant simply that she was hungry. Very hungry.

"So, Miss Seldon, you wish to be my administrative assistant."

"I should like to discuss the position."

He had been impressed with her confidence ten years ago, but there was a vulnerability about her now that disturbed him.

"I want to move my chauffeur into a supervisory position in the mail room, so I need someone who can drive for me as well as assist me in the office."

"I drove for Judge Sutherland, as you know. My license is current, though I haven't driven in several years."

The sound of her fork on an empty plate prompted him to say, "Please, Miss Seldon, help yourself to more."

Mrs. Swane returned with coffee and a plate of walnut cake with cream frosting. This time she served them both.

"I recall that Judge Sutherland's son is also an attorney. Why didn't he offer you employment?"

"He and his wife were very kind to me, but he has a limited practice with only one secretary, who has been with him for years. I keep in touch with them and also with Mrs. Sutherland, who allowed me to store some personal belongings in her attic after..."

"After what?"

"It was necessary to sell my home about a year before Judge Sutherland died."

"Why?"

He knew she was hesitating and recognized the defense in her tone when she finally answered. "My brother held title to the house for tax purposes. When he died, it had to be sold to settle his estate."

"He died suddenly?"

"In a car accident."

"And your mother?"

"She's dead, too."

"I'm sorry." He sipped his coffee. "My former assistant was never able to master the Braille writer. Do you think you could? I remember you were quite proficient on the typewriter, and the premise is the same."

"I don't know, Mr. Ashley. I've never seen one."

"It's on a table behind my desk. Go and look at it. Examine it thoroughly." When she sat down again, he said, "What is your opinion?"

"Someone would have to show me, but I think I could learn."

"I would instruct you. I'm quite good with it, but obviously I can't transcribe written notes."

The mantel clock chimed the half-hour. "There are more women in business these days, but I've never employed one outside of a secretarial position. I remember offering you that position once."

"Yes, you did."

"I didn't think you'd accept, of course."

She didn't reply.

"My clients are men and prefer to deal with men."

"I understand."

"I make a great many demands on my assistant. I'm a difficult man to work for, as I'm sure you gathered ten years ago."

"Yes, sir."

"You agree with me?"

"Yes, sir."

"Yet you came back."

"I felt I had to try for the position."

"You feel that you can work with me as I am?"

"I'm willing to try."

He remembered her forthrightness, but it was tempered with uncertainty now. She was changed in a way he wasn't sure he liked. Still, a working relationship with her might be interesting.

He compared his first impression ten years ago with the impression she presented now. She'd come into the study out of breath and smelling of...what? Not perfume. Something softer. Something more like a younger Bea when she came fresh from her bath in her pajamas to sit in his lap. Talcum. That was it. Damp talcum.

"How did you come to work at the Children's Home?"

"I...I knew the director, Constance Ervin. I'd been ill and had no place to go, so she offered me a temporary place."

"What was wrong with you?"

"I had pneumonia, but I'm quite recovered now."

"This Miss Ervin was an old friend?"

"No, I...I met her while I was in the hospital."

He knew she wasn't telling him the complete truth, but he decided not to press her.

"I sense that you have a great need for paid employment, Miss Seldon."

"Yes, sir, I do."

"I'd made up my mind to hire one of the men I interviewed earlier, but you seem to have the instincts of a survivor. I, too, am a survivor, you know." He indicated his empty cup. "I'd like more coffee, please."

She poured it.

He sipped as he considered where to go next. He couldn't see her, but he felt her tension tinged with fear. Desperation did that to a person. It had done it to him when he knew his darkness was permanent.

"I'd like for you to live in."

He felt her startle. "I...I'm not sure that would be...entirely proper."

He realized that he had misjudged her. She was needy but not desperate.

"I don't mean to coerce you, but it would make it easier to instruct you on the Braille writer in the evenings. Also, you'd be available to drive for me as needed."

"Did your former assistant live in?"

"He could have, but he preferred a room in a downtown hotel. It suited him." He turned toward her. "Mrs. Swane still lives in and would be a proper chaperone. You'll find her pleasant as always." He didn't add, *Even when I'm not.*

He could tell she was struggling. The decision

was hers to make, but he found himself hoping that she'd make the right one, even though he wasn't sure what that was.

"I'm prepared to offer you thirty-five dollars a week to begin. Medical care is provided to all my employees by a local physician. And though salaries are fixed for the duration of this economic depression, there are bonuses at Christmas, and everyone has a half-day off and Sundays, too. I take Saturday as well, so you would have that also. The last Friday of every month is also a holiday of sorts."

Her sharp intake of breath indicated that his offer impressed her.

"Do you need time to consider my offer?"

Her reply was immediate. "No, sir."

"You'll live in even though you're not sure it's entirely proper?"

He knew he must sound as if he were mocking her, but he didn't really care. If she couldn't deal with him the way he was, she wouldn't be much good as an assistant.

"Yes, sir."

"Do you need some time to get your business in order at Greenfield?"

"I'll need to get my things."

"My present assistant wants to leave as soon as possible, but he's agreed to train someone else. Could you be ready to go to work on Monday?"

"Yes, sir."

"I'll have my chauffeur drive you back to the bus station. Please tell him when you'll be arriving again so that he can meet you. You can't walk with luggage."

He rose and went to the door, opening it for her to precede him. "I look forward to a good working relationship, Miss Seldon."

"Thank you, Mr. Ashley. I'll do my best for you."

He waited until he heard Rod open the car door.

"Miss Seldon?"

"Yes, sir?"

"What happened to Pollyanna?"

Her voice was unsteady. "She...she's gone."

\*\*\*\*

Alan Ashley stood at the door until he could no longer hear the car, then walked to the kitchen. "Mrs. Swane, what's the condition of the south guest suite?"

"Dusty, I imagine. I have the cleaners go over the unused rooms once every three months, but it's been almost that long."

"It will need to be made ready as soon as possible. Miss Seldon is going to live in."

"You hired her?"

He sat down at the table. "Yes, I did. I've met her, you know. She was Judge Sutherland's secretary during that unpleasantness with Sam's father and my cousins."

Mrs. Swane frowned. "I remember her well. Have you thought about this carefully? A woman in your office is one thing, but in your home..."

"People will talk?"

"You know they will."

"Are you concerned about her reputation or mine?"

"She's a young *lady*, Mr. Ashley."

"I need to instruct her on the Braille writer in the evenings. She thinks she can learn how to use it. And I want her available to drive me at a moment's notice."

"You don't go anywhere."

"She's going to live in, Mrs. Swane, so if you'll see to having the rooms cleaned and ready for her, I'll appreciate it."

"I'll call our usual cleaners tomorrow."

"Thank you. Now tell me your impression of Miss Seldon."

"She's changed."

"I thought so, too, but it's been ten years, after all. We're all different in some respects."

"She's very different."

He frowned slightly. "Explain that."

"A good gust of wind would blow her away. She ate enough for two people. There's no color in her cheeks, and her eyes look like they've seen too much of life."

"That's rather dramatic, isn't it? You listen to too many soap operas on the radio."

"You asked me."

"Yes, well, what exactly does she look like? I never knew."

"Tall for a woman. Very black hair that she wears pulled back somewhat severely. Black eyes. And she doesn't paint."

"I believe the term is *use cosmetics.*"

Mrs. Swane sniffed. "In my day it was called *painting.*"

"Attractive?".

"She was ten years ago, and she might be again if she were healthier. Quite a coincidence, isn't it, her turning up here looking for work?"

"She saw my advertisement."

"What has she been doing these last ten years?"

"She worked for Judge Sutherland until he died. She says she took any job she could find after that, but I don't expect there were many. Eventually she became ill, and a friend is allowing her to live at the Greenfield Children's Home and work for room and board."

"Where will she take her meals?"

"I don't care. I know you like your privacy in the kitchen, but I doubt that she'll want to eat with me. Work something out."

"As you like."

"Did she wear a ring? A wedding ring?"

"No. What are you going to do if she doesn't work out?"

"She can always go to the secretarial pool, but somehow I don't think that will be necessary."

"There's a respectable boarding house on Birch Street. It's not so far that she couldn't drive back and forth."

Alan sensed the housekeeper's disapproval. "I'm not going to ravage the woman, Mrs. Swane."

"Mr. Alan!"

"You hinted at it."

Mrs. Swane made a noncommittal sound. "If she was wearing her best, and I expect she was, she's not suitably dressed for an office like Ashley Enterprises."

"She's shabby?"

"Very."

"I'll speak to Ellen. She'll know how to approach her diplomatically. I'll have Jerome give her some money and call it a business expense."

"She'll see through that."

"It doesn't matter what she sees. Ellen can make it clear that she must be decently dressed."

"You could have hired a man."

"I could have, Mrs. Swane, but I didn't. Just have the rooms ready for her on Sunday."

Rod put his head around the back door. "I got her to the station in time to catch the earlier bus."

"What is your opinion of Miss Seldon, Rod?"

"She didn't say anything to me except thank you for driving her to the station."

"Do you think she'll be accepted as my assistant?"

"I think who you hire is your business, Mr. Ashley."

"She's going to live in, so she'll be available to drive me. You can start in the mail room on Monday."

The chauffeur glanced at Mrs. Swane, who shrugged. "Sure, Mr. Ashley."

"As Rod said, Mrs. Swane, it's my business, and I believe I made a good choice."

He rose abruptly and left the room.

## Chapter Five

"You arrived at the worst possible moment," Constance Ervin said, jerking Lenore inside. "That woman is here. Go into my office quickly."

Lenore did as she was told. "Where is she?"

"Talking to Bobbie."

"Why can't she leave her alone?" Lenore sank down in a chair and blotted her damp face with a handkerchief.

"She's one of the worst. And she's angry because Bobbie frustrates her need to be in complete control."

"You said she'd threatened to move her."

"She can't do anything but threaten. I told you I've spoken with the county attorney about the file. It's privileged information that you don't have to release to her." She brought Lenore a glass of water. "How did the interview go?"

"He hired me. I can hardly believe it. Thirty-five dollars a week, with Saturdays and Sundays free to come and visit Bobbie."

"Oh, Lenore, I'm so glad! We'll miss you terribly, but I know you need the money. Wait. I hear Miss Burk in the hall." She opened the door a crack and slipped through.

Lenore hurried to listen at the door.

"She's the most defiant child I've ever worked with."

"We find her quite pleasant, actually."

"She'll tell me what I want to know, or..."

"Again, Miss Burk, I'd suggest that you not threaten her. She's here as you've decreed."

53

"And she'll stay here. Remember, she's not to have any contact with..."

"I believe you made yourself quite clear. Is there anything else?"

The woman stalked through the heavy outer door and slammed it behind her.

Lenore moved away from her listening post as Constance came back. "Constance, I've got to get her away from here."

"You know I'll give you as much of a head start as I can, but running isn't the answer."

"She can't stay here until she's eighteen. Or until that woman breaks her down and..."

"You said that she doesn't know anything."

"She doesn't except for the names of her parents and her grandfather. Neither do I, not really."

"Emalee Burk is being vindictive, Lenore. She grows worse every year. Tell me more about your new position."

Lenore walked to the window and looked out. "I...he asked me to live in so that I could drive for him and learn the Braille writer in the evenings."

"Did you agree?"

"I felt I had no choice. He's quite respectable, and his housekeeper, an older woman, lives in also. And it's a large house. A mansion, actually."

"You said he was quite difficult when you knew him before."

"I don't believe he's changed that much, but for thirty-five dollars a week, as well as room and board, I can work for him. I'll soon have enough money to take Bobbie away."

"You have time to make some decisions. Now go and see Bobbie while I make sure the door locked behind that woman and didn't catch on her fat fanny."

The women looked at each other and laughed.

****

After dinner, Lenore read aloud to Bobbie and two of her friends. Bobbie remained in the library, so called because it boasted a shelf of ragged books, when Lois and Rebekah went off to bed. "I'm glad you got the job, Mum, but I wish you didn't have to go away."

"I'll be back every weekend, Bobbie dear, and it won't be long before I have enough money for us to go away."

"I like it here."

"But you don't want to stay here until you're eighteen, Bobbie, seven more years."

"No, but..."

"We'll have a cozy place again, like the first apartment we took after I sold the house, and you'll go to school as you did before."

"We all like it better having school here. The others at the public school were really mean to us, and they made fun of Rebekah. She's learned a lot since you've been helping us. She's not a dummy like that teacher called her."

"Of course she's not. Some children just need a little extra help, that's all."

"I'm glad her uncle is coming to visit her now. I wish the others could have someone like Rebekah has him, and I have you."

Lenore cuddled the child against her. "I don't know what I'd do without you, Bobbie. I'm so glad Teddy sent you to Mother and me."

"I miss Grandmother."

"I do, too."

"I still miss Papa, too, Mum, but I guess he's forgotten about me."

"I'm sure he hasn't."

"He promised he'd come after me, but he never did."

"Maybe he couldn't come, Bobbie. I'm sure he wanted to."

"Do you think he still might, someday?"

"Maybe he will."

"I don't want to leave you, though."

"Things will work out, Bobbie, you'll see. Now, Matron will be down here wanting to know why you're not in bed, so hurry along."

"When do you have to go?"

"On Sunday."

Bobbie sighed audibly as she kissed Lenore's thin cheek. "Goodnight, Mum."

## Chapter Six

"Alan, I can't offend her, and I will certainly do that if I suggest that her clothing isn't appropriate."

"My dear Ellen, I have no one else to turn to in this matter. I have complete faith in you."

Ellen grimaced at her husband. "What made you hire a woman, Alan?" Sam asked. "It isn't like you to do something so out of character, although as I remember, she was a paragon of efficiency and quite pleasant as well."

"I'll admit it was somewhat impulsive, but I'm convinced it was the right thing. She needed the employment, and she's teachable. She thinks she can learn the Braille writer."

"She might have said that to influence your choice."

"There also was the connection to Judge Sutherland. He thought highly of her. Besides, I owe him for coming to your aid the way he did."

"That was ten years ago, and may I remind you that you paid him well?"

"There's no need to remind me of anything, and I know, of course, that you and Ellen are exchanging meaningful glances as we speak."

Ellen refilled Alan's cup. "I see no way that I can suggest to her that she accept money she hasn't earned to buy clothes that she can't afford."

"She'll be out of place if she comes to the office in her present state," Alan said. "Come, Ellen, you'll think of something. You understand her situation. I remember you telling me several years ago about how you had almost nothing when you came here."

"Give up, Ellen," her husband interrupted. "The thing must be done, and there's no one else."

"All right, but it will cost young Mr. Ashley a dinner for two at Le Monde, and we'll expect him to entertain Bea for the evening."

"You drive a hard bargain, Ellen."

She laughed. "I will deserve everything I get, and don't blame me if she quits before she even begins."

****

Alan delayed going to the office on Monday and eavesdropped from his study door as Ellen re-introduced herself to Lenore in the foyer and explained why she was there. "I'm a coal miner's daughter out of the hills of Kentucky, Miss Seldon. I think if someone had handed me a hundred dollars and offered to drive me into the city to shop, I'd have jumped at the chance. Then again, I might have thrown the money in her face and bolted. So feel free to do whatever you like."

"I'm not offended, Mrs. Bernard, just embarrassed. I know how to dress, but I've had to make do these past few years." Alan strained to discern anger but heard only a weary dignity in his new assistant's voice.

"Please call me Ellen. We'll be seeing a great deal of each other, you know. Now, shall we go and enjoy spending Alan's money?"

When the two women returned at five o'clock, Alan Ashley stood at the study door again and listened to them chattering like schoolgirls as they went upstairs. The shopping trip, it seemed, had been a success. He was waiting at the foot of the stairs when Ellen came down.

"Hello, Alan. Mission accomplished."

"You're a lifesaver, Ellen, my dear. I was in well over my head in this matter."

"She's a lovely person. You did well to hire her."

He lowered his voice. "Did you learn anything about her? She wasn't very forthcoming in our interview except about her employment. She did say that she has no living family. Mrs. Swane says she doesn't wear a wedding ring."

· "That doesn't make her easy prey for you."

"Are you suggesting, as Mrs. Swane did, that I'm going to take advantage of her?"

"Certainly not, but you can be rather intimidating sometimes."

"She knows I won't be easy to work for, but she's desperate for employment."

"All the more reason to be gentle with her, Alan. She's quite...fragile."

"Physically?"

"And emotionally, I think. There's something rather sad about her."

"Women are supposed to ferret out these secrets."

"I did what you asked. I won't spy on her."

"I'm in your debt, my dear."

She laughed. "There's the dinner at Le Monde for Sam and me. Candlelight. Champagne. I'll run around in a day or so and see how things are going. Just be gentle with her, Alan."

"Of course."

"And don't drive her to learn that dreadful Braille writer overnight."

"She says she learns quickly, but I'll be patient."

"I've got to go. Sam will be home in another half-hour bellowing for his dinner."

"I didn't know he bellowed."

"Like a wounded bear when he's hungry."

"Why don't you hire a cook so that meals will always be on time?"

"Because I can't bribe Mrs. Swane to leave you." She tiptoed and kissed his cheek lightly. "Good luck."

He went back to his study but left the door open. When he heard Lenore come down again, he called to her.

She was at the door immediately. "Yes, sir?"

"Ellen says the shopping trip went well."

"Yes, sir, though I didn't need so much money. I have the remainder and all the receipts."

He gestured dismissively. "You can give them to Jerome Vannoy at the office tomorrow. He's head of accounting, and this was a business expense."

"I don't think it was, Mr. Ashley, not exactly, but I'm very grateful. I know that my clothes really were unsuitable for an office such as yours."

"Did you get enough?"

"I believe so. Mrs. Bernard felt I made the right selections."

He opened the glass on his pocket watch. "I believe it's time for dinner. I wonder if you would dine with me this evening. I'd like to tell you more about the position you'll be assuming tomorrow."

` ****

Mrs. Swane placed Lenore at the opposite end of the table. "Bring your plate and move closer," Alan said when the housekeeper was gone. "She thinks I'm going to devour you—or something like that. I'm not, and I'm not going to shout at you across the length of a formal dining table."

Lenore did as he asked.

"That's better. Now, this week, Barrows will be training you to take his place. He's much nicer than I am, so I'm sure you'll do well with him." He waited for her to reply, and when she didn't, he said, "Ten years ago you'd have had an answer to that."

"Perhaps."

"But not now."

"No, sir."

"All right, I'll leave you alone to eat in peace. Mrs. Swane seems to think you need plumping up."

60

"Yes, sir."

"Did you not get enough to eat at the Home?"

"Food isn't always plentiful. The cook does her best."

"Do the children go to bed hungry?"

"No, the adults eat less."

"That's barbaric in this day and age."

"We're in an economic depression, Mr. Ashley. People have to make do."

"The county is responsible to see that the children are cared for."

"If people can't pay their taxes, the county can't pay their bills."

"People should be held accountable to pay."

"What would you have them do? Take food from their own children's mouths?"

"Ah. A flash of the old spirit, Miss Seldon."

"No, sir, just the cold, terrible truth."

****

There was a retirement party for Ernest Barrows on Friday. As Lenore drove them home afterwards, Alan said, "Now you're on your own, Miss Seldon. Does that concern you?"

"A little."

"You're already showing great promise on the Braille writer."

"I'll do my best, Mr. Ashley."

"How old are you, Miss Seldon? Oh, I know that's a question a gentleman never asks a lady, but I can't judge for myself since I can't see you. You were quite young when you worked for Judge Sutherland. You even required a chaperone, as I recall."

"I was very young. Now I'm thirty-two, Mr. Ashley."

"I'm thirty-eight. I view myself as I last saw my face in the shaving mirror hanging from a tree trunk in France, so I don't know how I've aged."

"You look very much the same as you did ten years ago."

"That's a diplomatic answer."

"It's a truthful one."

"Are you comfortable in your apartments?"

"Yes, but I don't really need so much space. A sitting room isn't necessary."

"It's a guest suite. I thought it would afford you the most privacy."

"Yes, of course, it does."

"The house was built only a few years after the Revolutionary War, as you know, but it's been remodeled and enlarged several times. My parents combined some rooms to make suites. They had one for themselves, although I now occupy a single room at the opposite end of the hall from yours. It's sufficient for my needs."

"Has the house always been in your family?"

"Yes, it has. The first Richard Alan Ashley was a Patriot, though it's rumored that his brother was a Loyalist. He was my great-great-grandfather, and he farmed a great deal of land around Rumers Crossing. Over the years, much of the original holdings were sold off, but the house still sits on five acres."

"We had a few old homes in Brookston, but none that dated from the Revolution."

"Brookston was your family's home?"

"For many years. I was born there."

"So your family knew the Sutherlands previous to your employment."

"Judge Sutherland was an elder in the Presbyterian church we attended. He retired the same year I finished business school and offered me a position. My parents felt confident that..." She stopped speaking suddenly.

"That you would be safe with the honorable judge. I remember that he and his wife were very protective of you." He waited for her to defend her former employer as well as herself, but she said nothing.

"I can assure you that you will be safe with me also, Miss Seldon."

"Yes, sir, I'm sure that I will be."

****

He woke in the night and regretted his mocking words. Before he fell asleep again, he considered that a tour of the grounds on Saturday might put her at ease. She'd seen the house, but as she seemed interested in its history, he could tell her much more. The barn-turned-garage reeked of the past, as did the remains of some outbuildings in use when the farm had been a community in itself. He might even take her to lunch after church to show her that he could be considerate. So when he came downstairs for breakfast the next morning and discovered that she was gone, his expansive mood fled.

Mrs. Swane set his plate in front of him. "I don't know where she went, Mr. Alan. When I opened the drapes in the dining room, I saw her walking down the road carrying her suitcase."

"She didn't say anything to you?"

"She was out the door and gone before I came to the front of the house."

"Don't you think that's strange?"

"I think it's strange that you hired her and asked her to live in."

"I explained my reasoning, Mrs. Swane."

"Yes, you did. Eat your breakfast before it gets cold."

****

"Has the social worker been back?" Lenore asked as soon as Constance let her in.

"No."

"I worry about her snatching Bobbie away."

"I wouldn't let that happen. How did things go for you this week?"

"Better than I thought they would. Mr. Ashley's former assistant explained what was expected and showed me around. I'm sure I can do the job. How has Bobbie been this week without me?"

"She's missed you, of course, but she's glad that you have work. Does she know what you're planning to do when you have the money?"

"I don't even know myself, Constance. Canada is so close. It's tempting."

"I don't think the state would pursue you across the border. They haven't the time or the funds these days. My concern is that you might become ill again. You're still not strong, you know."

"I'm all right."

"Bobbie has kitchen duty this weekend, so that's where you'll find her."

"How is the classroom managing?"

"All the children miss you, but Dick has taken over, and everyone is cooperating. Bobbie has made Rebekah her special project."

"Do you really think she can learn?"

"I think Bobbie believes in her, and maybe that will be the key."

"She's such a talented little artist and a wonderful seamstress, but she'll need a basic education to function as an adult."

"That's what we want for all our children, Lenore, and you've been the catalyst for helping them understand that they must be responsible for their own education."

"I just helped them get organized. They couldn't stay in the public school under the circumstances."

"No, of course not. Go and see Bobbie now. She's been hopping around like a bird out of its nest all morning."

\*\*\*\*

On Sunday evening, Alan left the drawing room door open so that he could hear Lenore come in. "Miss Seldon."

She paused at the foot of the stairs. "Yes, sir?"

"I didn't know you were going to be away for the weekend."

"I thought I was free on weekends. I'm sorry if it was an inconvenience."

"You are certainly at liberty, but you might have said something to Mrs. Swane or to me."

"I'll be away every weekend."

"Oh?"

"Yes, sir. Is that all?"

"I wonder if, after you take your suitcase upstairs, you might make some tea and bring it to the drawing room. Mrs. Swane has gone to evening services."

"Yes, sir. I'll only be a moment."

"And see if you can find the butter cookies. Mrs. Swane tends to hide them."

"I'll try, Mr. Ashley."

****

She set his cup on the table beside his chair. "Did you find the cookies?"

"There are three on the saucer."

"You should have put them on a separate plate. I won't be able to get the cup level when I set it down again."

"I'm sorry. I'll go and get another plate."

He felt for the cookies and swept them onto the table. "Never mind. Are you joining me?"

"I...if you like."

She sat down across from him.

"I like this room. My parents always sat here in the evenings when they were home."

"It's a lovely room, particularly the carpet."

"You noticed that, did you? It's Persian and has held up quite well over the years."

"It's beautiful."

"I was never allowed in here."

"Why not?"

"Having produced the requisite heir, my parents seemed to feel they'd done their duty and relegated me to the nursery upstairs. In due course, I went off to Choate, and in the summers I went to camp or accompanied my parents to their vacation home in Maine—under the supervision of a nurse and later a tutor, naturally."

"You had a great many advantages."

"I don't suppose your childhood was anything like mine."

"My brother and I were best friends and close to our parents. We were always together. Our school chums loved to come to our house because Mother and Father made them so welcome."

"An idyllic set of circumstances."

"What happened to your parents?"

"You didn't know that they were on the *Titanic*?"

"No, I didn't. I'm very sorry."

"Don't be. I didn't miss them. I was in my last year at Choate, took a few months to travel and went right to Harvard, where I enjoyed myself a great deal. I was a good student, graduating with honors. Then, of course, there was the war."

"I'm sure you were glad to come home."

"This was never a *home*, but it belongs to me. Everyone must have some place that belongs to him."

"Yes."

"You don't have that anymore, do you?"

"It was painful to let the house go, but it was necessary. I try not to think of it much."

"I was going to give you a tour of the grounds on Saturday. You've seen the house but not the secret room. Would you like to see it now?"

"Yes, of course, Mr. Ashley."

"Don't feel obligated."

"I'd like very much to see it."

"There's a flashlight in the drawer of the table in the foyer. Bring it."

He let her precede him on the winding stairs to the third floor. "The attic is full of closets. They were used for storing seasonal clothes and steamer trunks in the days when people traveled extensively." He took her arm. "It's the second door on the facing wall."

Inside the closet he dropped her arm and ran his fingers along the back wall. "Here it is. You can see the place where I put my penknife when I finally discovered the panel."

"How old were you when you found it?"

"Eleven or twelve, I think. I was home for a few days between the end of the school term and the beginning of camp. I'd been searching for years, but that summer I was determined to find it."

"And you did."

"Yes. The panel slides back...there...and here's the door. It latches automatically, so make sure it doesn't close behind us. We'd be trapped."

Lenore stepped across the raised threshold into a small room that smelled of damp earth. "It's quite terrible to think of people having to stay here for any length of time."

"Only for a few days, I think. If you'll shine the flashlight straight ahead, you can see the tunnel."

"Yes, there it is."

"It comes out against the hill behind the house. Actually, the hill was man-made just for the purpose of concealing the tunnel."

"How was it done?"

He laughed. "Much like the pyramids were built, I expect. A great deal of manpower."

"You followed it?"

"Of course. But it's unsafe now. Actually, it was

probably unsafe even then. I really should see to having it closed up."

"Teddy was adventurous. He would have explored it and teased me for refusing to set foot in it."

"It was full of cobwebs and other things I probably didn't want to know about. But being an adventurous boy like your brother, Miss Seldon, I couldn't resist."

On the second floor landing, Lenore thanked him for the tour and said goodnight. She was opening her door when he called her name.

"I wonder if you'd have dinner with me sometime. There's a little place near the office that I frequent. Giovanni's. Excellent Italian cuisine."

It seemed to him that her answer was a long time coming. "If you like, Mr. Ashley. Goodnight."

Chapter Seven

"And you say she doesn't give any hint about where she goes on weekends?" Alan Ashley reached for the butter cookies as he heard Mrs. Swane set the tin on the table.

"It's her business."

"Yes, of course, Mrs. Swane, but it seems strange that she doesn't say anything."

"Do you want me to ask her?"

"I suppose I do, but perhaps it would be better if you didn't."

"I think so, too."

He laughed. "Mrs. Swane, if it weren't for your butter cookies, you'd be impossible."

She closed the tin firmly as he reached for his fourth cookie. "Mind your manners, Mr. Alan."

"Do you find her, well, rather sad? Ellen described her that way."

"More proud, I think."

"Is that a bad thing?"

"Sometimes. My family was proud, but it wasn't because we were poor."

"What are you saying?"

"Just that she's seen better times and isn't happy that they're gone."

"She's angry about her changed circumstances, you mean. Like I am."

"I don't know, Mr. Alan. You see her more than I do. You'll find out, I guess."

\*\*\*\*

In the following weeks, Alan gave his new assistant every opportunity to confide in him, but he wasn't really surprised when she didn't. Her quiet dignity surrounded her like an impenetrable wall.

She rose to every challenge with which she was presented, learning the Braille writer and the details of Ashley Enterprises so well that she was worth twice her salary. He reflected that she was a comfortable presence, too. He liked listening to her light footsteps moving across the office and the way she always closed one drawer completely before she opened another. Her laughter, though infrequent, warmed him in a way he'd forgotten.

Trent Young, second in command and not easily impressed, stated unequivocally that Lenore Seldon was an asset to the office. Jerome Vannoy in accounting had a difficult time convincing her that her new wardrobe was indeed a business expense and, as such, not her responsibility. He reported that she tried to give him something from every paycheck. Mrs. Fenton found her a pleasant companion in Alan's office, and the two often lunched together in the employee cafeteria downstairs.

"You came, you saw, and you conquered, Miss Seldon," Alan observed one afternoon.

"I beg your pardon?"

"I mean that you've become quite popular at Ashley Enterprises."

"I try to do my work," she said, sounding pleased and embarrassed at the same time.

"You do it very well. Miss Seldon, would you...that is, I'd like to have dinner tonight at that little Italian café I mentioned."

"Certainly, Mr. Ashley. I have work that can be done here while you're dining."

"My dear Miss Seldon, I'm inviting you to have dinner with me." He approached her desk. "Surely it wouldn't give you dyspepsia."

Her moment of hesitation seemed an eternity.

"Whatever you like, Mr. Ashley."

He gritted his teeth. Was it dignity or stubbornness that kept her so removed from him? Finding out what he wanted to know about her wasn't going to be easy, but he wasn't accustomed to being denied.

****

They left the office promptly at five and walked the few blocks to the restaurant. The maitre d' greeted them warmly. "Your usual table, Mr. Ashley?"

"If you please, Tony."

The table for two was in a secluded corner beside a window looking out on an enclosed patio. "I often eat outside in good weather," Alan said. "I'm told that it's quite a pleasant view."

"You never saw it before?"

"No, the café opened after the war."

A smiling waiter approached. "How are you tonight, Mr. Ashley?"

"Quite well, George. My guest may want a menu."

George laid a printed card in front of Lenore. "The chicken fettuccine smells good," he said. "Want to take a chance, Mr. Ashley?"

"I do tend to order the same thing, don't I?"

"Yes, sir, I'd have to say that you do."

"What about it, Miss Seldon? Shall we live dangerously and try the fettuccine?"

Lenore nodded, then found her voice. "That will be fine."

"What will you have to drink, Miss Seldon? I could procure wine under the table, so to speak, but I remember that…"

"Water will be fine, Mr. Ashley."

He frowned. "I wish you'd relax. You're making me quite nervous, and that's not easy to do. I don't often escort a woman to dinner. Actually, I never

71

escort anyone anywhere."

"Never?"

"Not since the war. I was engaged to be married once. Elise's family was very much in favor of merging two distinguished families as well as two very large fortunes. After the war, however, she found my new circumstances distasteful. My social life has been nonexistent except for dinners with Sam and Ellen and a few others who are only slightly uncomfortable with my blindness." He felt carefully for the water goblet that George had placed exactly at one o'clock. "How do *you* feel about it, Miss Seldon?"

He waited, knowing she was forming her words carefully.

"I'm amazed at your ability to do so many things. Sometimes I find myself..."

"Yes?"

"Sometimes I almost forget that you're blind."

"You say the word quite easily."

"Is there a more correct word?"

"Absolutely not. An apple is not an orange. Some people don't like oranges." He was rewarded with subdued laughter. "That amuses you?"

"I find your sense of humor amazing, also. You don't show it often."

"I remember commenting once on your own sense of humor. You don't show that much anymore, either."

"No, sir."

"After the expected initial difficulty, I accepted my blindness as permanent and learned to live with it. That doesn't mean I don't resent it. However, it gratifies me that you seem to accept it, too. In fact, the day that you came to interview, I was testing you when I asked Mrs. Swane to serve our lunch in the drawing room and made you responsible for my plate."

"I considered that, later."

Their dinner came, making conversation unnecessary. Afterwards, they lingered over coffee, speaking of less personal things. "Thank you for dinner, Mr. Ashley," Lenore said as they left the restaurant.

"You'll be going away again on Saturday?"

"Yes, sir, if you don't mind."

"Certainly not." But he did mind. He minded very much, because the house was so empty without her.

\*\*\*\*

"Things are going well with your work?" Constance asked as they drank tea in her small room after the children were in bed.

"The work is challenging, but I find it interesting."

"What about your employer? Do you find him interesting?"

"Why would you ask that?"

"You never mention him."

"He's...well, he's difficult, Constance, but I knew that before I applied for the position. I'm not sure how it happened, but I'm taking meals with him now, and he even took me out to dinner this week."

"Maybe he's interested in you. You're very attractive, you know, and with less worry, better food, and a new wardrobe, you've become even more so."

"Oh, Constance, I can't even think of it. I'm glad he can't see me."

The other woman shrugged. "It was just a thought. He's unmarried, so..." She left the thought unfinished so that Lenore might take it up.

"I don't think any woman could live with him. He's not exactly unfeeling, but he's quite self-centered. Marriage must be a give-and-take situation, don't you think? I saw that with my parents. They were thoughtful of each other and unfailingly courteous, too."

"Well, growing up as I did in an institution much like this one, I didn't have that example, but I would think marriage should be like that."

"Alan Ashley simply isn't cut out to be a husband and father."

"You're sure of that?"

"Not *my* husband, Constance, or the father of *my* children."

"Bobbie seems to talk about her father more since you've been gone."

"For a while I thought perhaps she'd given up on the idea that he was coming back."

"I think she's influenced by the fact that Rebekah's uncle comes regularly now. He's a strange man, in a way, always coming late after study hour."

"Perhaps his employment necessitates that.'

"He gave me to understand that it did. He's quite nice, though, and Rebekah adores him. Avram Rykovsky. He says that the family came from Russia where Jewish people were persecuted. He was concerned that there is no synagogue in Greenfield for Rebekah to attend, no proper religious instruction for her."

"It would be nice if he could take her out of here."

"He told me that he's trying to convince her father to give her up. Her mother, his sister, died in childbirth. He lost track of her for years, but when he found she was dead and that her child was here, he came immediately."

"The father doesn't want her. Why won't he give her up?"

"I have no idea. However, it's given Bobbie food for thought. I think she's secretly hoping that her own father will appear magically just as Mr. Rykovsky did."

"It's selfish of me, Constance, but I hope he doesn't. I don't know how I could give her up."

****

Dinner at Giovanni's became a weekly outing for the two of them. Alan thought perhaps Lenore accepted his invitations only because he was her employer, but that would do for now. Away from the office, it was easier to draw her out. At first, he did most of the talking, but after awhile she began to express her opinions, and he was surprised to find her, like himself, a connoisseur of music and literature.

"Father loved books. Often in the evenings he read aloud to us. Hawthorne, Poe, Jane Austen and Emily Brontë. He read poetry, too, both English and American, and he insisted that I take piano lessons from the time I began school."

"I order the new talking books for the phonograph. Are you familiar with those?"

"I've never heard of them."

"That's what I do in the evenings after dinner, after we work on the Braille writer. I listen to my books or to music. Perhaps you'd care to join me sometime."

He felt a wall go up between them.

"If you like, Mr. Ashley."

But the next evening, when they'd finished in the study, she accepted his invitation into the drawing room to listen to a collection of his favorite Mozart pieces. By the end of the week, she seemed to accept the fact that they would spend every evening together.

****

"I believe she enjoys our evenings," he confided to Mrs. Swane before Lenore came down to breakfast one morning.

"Mr. Alan, are you sure..."

"That I enjoy her company? Yes, I do, very

much."

"That's not what I was going to ask. What if she should get...ideas?"

"What if I get them first?"

"She's not like you, Mr. Alan."

"She's a grown woman. She knows her own mind."

"She's working for you because she needs the money."

"That doesn't help my ego."

"I don't mean for it to. I've tried to talk to her, too, thinking she might confide in another woman, an older woman like her mother."

"But she hasn't."

"Not one word."

"She's rather...companionable in the evenings."

"I hope you aren't taking advantage of her need for this work by forcing her to spend time with you."

"I might be. Does it matter, if it pleases me?"

"You're a grown man. You know what's right."

"And a rather lonely one, Mrs. Swane. You have your activities outside the house. After dinner, I go to my study or into the drawing room alone, or I did until Miss Seldon came."

"I still say good riddance to that other one."

"As do I, but Miss Seldon is not in the least like Elise."

"Have you found out where she goes on weekends?"

Alan's mouth twisted. "Not yet, Mrs. Swane, but perhaps she'll tell me eventually." He unfolded his napkin. "But the house is rather empty without her...isn't it?"

**\*\*\*\***

He wondered if Lenore noticed that he was thinking of more ways for them to spend time together outside of the office. As the August heat gave way to crisp Indian summer evenings, he often invited her for a walk around the grounds of the large house. She appeared genuinely interested in its long history, and he sent her into the library to find the old picture albums showing the house at the various stages of its long life.

He asked Mrs. Swane to rearrange the schedule of meals on Sundays so that she could have a cold supper ready about the time Lenore returned from wherever she went and asked her to place the nested tables in front of the sofa where he and Lenore would have to sit together instead of on opposite sides of the fireplace.

Neglecting to order his talking books meant that he could ask her to read aloud to him. Her quietly expressive diction soothed him after the cares of his business day.

"I'm responsible for a great number of people," he confided one evening. "Most of my employees have families, you see. So far it hasn't been necessary to let anyone go." He reached for his pipe, which he lighted as if he could see it. "And I won't. We'll cut corners somewhere else."

"You live very simply."

"I have an income separate from the business. My grandmother left quite a large trust, and my needs are few."

"But you don't have to worry about...I'm sorry. I shouldn't have said that."

"It was an unfinished thought as so much of your conversation is, Miss Seldon. You're free to express yourself honestly."

"I was almost a member of the family with the Sutherlands, but this is different."

"Are you uncomfortable with our arrangement?"

"A little."

"You've provided me with a great deal of companionship, Miss Seldon. Perhaps you feel I've imposed on your personal time."

"No, sir, I don't feel that way. It's just that in my position..."

"As my employee."

"Yes, sir. You pay me a generous salary, and I have no expenses."

"Are your rooms satisfactory?"

"As I've said before, they're so much more than I need."

"I wanted to afford you as much privacy as possible."

"And taking my meals with you instead of in the kitchen...sitting in here with you after dinner..."

"Mrs. Swane refuses to eat meals with me," he interrupted. "She has her own schedule and quite an active social life with her church meetings and bridge games and dozens of friends."

"I didn't know she was out so much."

"Oh, yes, she's quite the gadabout."

"Perhaps you should get out more."

"I have dinner with Sam and Ellen once a week and I attend church, as well as serve on the vestry, which necessitates regular meetings. All of which is much more than I did ten years ago." He paused. "And now there is you, Miss Seldon. We share a great many interests. I find you a pleasant companion."

"Yes, sir." She returned the recordings to their jackets and put away the album. "Is there anything I can get for you before I go up?"

"No, thank you." He opened the glass on his watch. Only eight-thirty.

"All right. Goodnight, Mr. Ashley."

"Goodnight, Miss Seldon. Sleep well."

When he heard the door close behind her, he slid down in his chair, glowering like a chastened schoolboy. "Eight-thirty. And I had so much more I wanted to say."

\*\*\*\*

"What was it your brother used to call you? Pollyanna?" he asked as they drove to work the next morning.

"Yes."

"Who always saw the positive side of things."

"That's right."

"Frankly, you don't seem like Pollyanna anymore, Miss Seldon. You said that she was gone. What did you mean?"

"I suppose, as I've gotten older, I look at things somewhat differently."

"Why?"

"It gets more difficult to be a perpetual optimist as one grows older and has more experiences, don't you think?"

"I always looked at life quite realistically. I was never under any illusions about what it was."

"That's much better than being Pollyanna and completely unprepared for..."

"For what, Miss Seldon?"

She remained silent.

"I've learned to live with my blindness, but I don't like it any better than I did ten years ago."

"No one would *like* it."

"I always thought nothing could be worse than not being able to see, but being dependent on others is definitely worse."

"You seem very self-sufficient."

"It's hard work."

"I expect it is."

"But you didn't answer my question, Miss Seldon. Why did Pollyanna go away?"

"She never existed, Mr. Ashley, not really. She belongs in the book, not in life."

"Then you're not so different from me, are you?"

"No, sir, I suppose I'm not. Not anymore."

## Chapter Eight

"And so I ended up at the bottom of the slope with my skis crossed, and when I finally got my face out of the snow, my left ski was wearing my knitted cap. Sam was shaking the ski, thinking it was me, and asking if I was all right."

Lenore's laughter, the first real mirth he'd heard from her, gratified him. He liked how it was soft, as he imagined she must be.

"You never skied?" he asked.

"Teddy built a sled from two market boxes once, and we had several years of enjoyment from it on the hill behind our house. I fell off several times, and Mother..."

The study door flew open, and only Mrs. Swane's quick hand kept it from hitting the wall. "You have a guest, Mr. Alan."

"From the sound of your voice, it must be the Grim Reaper."

Lenore laughed again before she glanced at Mrs. Swane's expression and stopped.

"Shall I show her in?"

"Ah, *her*."

Lenore gathered the cups and plates and began putting them back on the tray. "I'll take these out to the kitchen."

Alan's mouth turned down. It had been a cozy afternoon, a little work interspersed with a great deal of conversation and Mrs. Swane's cinnamon tea. Irritation nibbled at his contentment, then swallowed it completely. "I need those notes transcribed, you know." The biting words left his mouth before he considered that Lenore Seldon hadn't been the one to spoil the moment.

"Certainly, Mr. Ashley, as soon as your guest leaves. I'll be in the kitchen with Mrs. Swane." She picked up the tray and followed the housekeeper into the foyer where a foot tapped a rapid staccato on the tile.

"*This* way," Mrs. Swane said to the visitor.

"I know the way, Mrs. Swane."

Lenore lifted her eyes to the amused face. The woman was wrapped in fur too warm for the season. A black dress that missed no opportunity to follow the bone structure over which it draped reminded Lenore of the models she'd seen in magazines.

"Who are *you?*" The voice was no longer amused but frankly curious, even angry.

"This way," Mrs. Swane repeated more like a command than an invitation.

"I'm Lenore Seldon, Mr. Ashley's assistant." The pleasure of the afternoon vanished as Lenore slipped through the door of the breakfast room, feeling suddenly frumpy and out of place.

****

You're looking well, Alan."

"Elise?" Alan rose with a courtesy he didn't feel.

"Very good. You recognize my voice."

Alan didn't say that her affected drawl was easily discernible. "What brings you here?"

"I'm back from Europe and stopping in Rumers Crossing for a few days to sign the final papers settling father's estate, so I thought I'd call in."

"I see."

"You might offer me a drink and ask me to sit down."

"I might, but I won't. Do you have business with me?"

"Business? Of course not. This is purely a social call."

"Why?"

"We were good friends once."

"The past tense is apt."

"Come, Alan, don't sulk." She slid into the place Lenore had just vacated.

"Is that what I'm doing?"

She laughed. "Like a little boy deprived of his favorite plaything." She reached for his hand. "I used to be your favorite toy, although I must say you never took full advantage of the opportunity to play with me."

He removed his hand. "I hear you've just shed husband number two, or is it three?"

"Two. So you keep up with me?"

"Not really, but I hear things."

"I could really use a drink."

"You know where it's kept." He sat down in a chair across from her and listened to her tap confidently across the room to the console where Mrs. Swane usually stocked sherry and some glasses.

"You don't have anything stronger?"

"Do you need something stronger at three o'clock in the afternoon?"

"I suppose this will have to do."

"I suppose it will."

"Which raises the question as to why you're home at three o'clock on a Friday afternoon. I went by your office and found the building locked up."

"Ashley Enterprises takes a holiday on the last Friday of the month. It's good for morale."

"Morale?"

"In these hard times, my employees appreciate an extra day to themselves since salaries must remain fixed for now."

"But your assistant is working. The woman I saw coming out of your study."

"Miss Seldon lives in."

"Oh?"

Alan remembered how Elise's well-shaped brows could almost touch her hairline, an expression calculated to intimidate those afraid of falling out of favor with her.

"She drives for me now that Rod has moved to supervisor in the mail room, and it has provided the opportunity to teach her the Braille writer, something Barrows unfortunately never mastered." He clenched and unclenched his fingers. *Why am I explaining myself?*

"Oh, of course. I see."

"I'm sure you don't see, but it makes no difference." He heard her set her glass on the table with more force than necessary. "Miss Seldon has notes to transcribe, so I'm afraid you can't stay."

"You needn't sound so thrilled that I came."

"You know I'm not."

"I'm giving a party in honor of my return, short though it may be. You'll come, of course."

"No."

"It would be impolite of you not to. Besides, all the old bunch will be there."

"I haven't seen most of them in fifteen years."

"All the more reason to come."

"We're not children at play anymore. We've all moved on."

"I haven't. I shall play forever, and they can bury me with a magnum of champagne and all my jazz recordings."

He made a sound of disgust.

"I want you to come. You can't refuse me."

"I believe I just did."

"Alan, you're making me quite cross."

"Go shopping. That will lighten your mood." He stood up. "Goodbye, Elise."

"If you don't come, everyone will think you're still smarting from being rejected."

Fifteen years ago, he'd have sworn at her, and he considered doing it now. However, he wouldn't give her the satisfaction. "You know the way out."

"Next Friday at seven for cocktails." She brushed by him, lingering just long enough for him to catch the scent of her perfume. The very nearness of the body he once coveted stirred more than a vague desire. As he pictured her smooth, creamy complexion and the red lips he'd kissed often, he felt unwanted longing.

Giving her enough time to get through the front door, he stalked to the foyer. "Mrs. Swane! Miss Seldon!"

"Yes, sir?"

He startled. Lenore Seldon's practical rubber-soled shoes had made no sound as she approached him.

"Miss Seldon, it's time to go back to work."

"Yes, of course." She started for the study.

"Miss Seldon."

"Sir?"

"What kind of perfume do you wear?"

"I don't use perfume, Mr. Ashley."

"No, I thought not." He followed her into the room that had lost its cozy ambiance. The old restlessness seized him. It had faded since Lenore's coming, and he resented its return. "Miss Seldon, do you know if Mrs. Swane has started dinner?"

"She said to tell you that she was going to reheat the roast and vegetables we had on Wednesday, unless you wanted something else."

"Go and tell her that we're dining out."

"What about the notes?"

"They'll wait until Monday."

"Yes, sir."

"Miss Seldon, I'm only a few years older than you are. Must you constantly refer to me as *sir*, as if I'm in my dotage?" His conscience stirred a little as he realized that he was taking a perverse satisfaction in punishing her for his own bad humor.

"You're my employer."

He tried to soften his tone and failed. "But not your grandfather. Go and tell Mrs. Swane, and then go upstairs and change or whatever you must do. I'll telephone Le Monde for a reservation."

Lenore recognized the name. "That's...rather elegant."

"It's very elegant, and it's exactly what I want tonight. Do hurry. It's already late to be starting for the city."

She pressed her lips together nervously and hoped that a reservation wouldn't be available.

****

"I'm taking my bad mood out on you," Alan said grudgingly as they drove toward the city. "I'm sorry."

"It's all right."

"No, it's not. I'm sure Mrs. Swane filled your ear about Elise this afternoon."

"I told her that it didn't concern me."

"She's as protective of me as an old she-bear is of her cub, but she came here when I was only toddling, so I suppose it's natural."

"Yes, s..." Lenore gritted her teeth against the slip.

"I apologize for my sharp words, Miss Seldon. You didn't deserve them. Elise has that effect on me even after all these years."

She didn't reply.

"I haven't seen her since she broke our engagement. She just divorced her second husband."

"I'm sorry."

"Don't be. He's probably poorer but inevitably happier, and she'll find number three before long." *But it won't be me.* He turned slightly in the seat as if he were looking at her. "Did you ever contemplate marriage, Miss Seldon?"

85

For a moment he thought she wasn't going to answer him. "Once. He was killed in France."

"I'm sorry. But you were very young. Surely you might have met someone else."

"I finished business school and went to work for Judge Sutherland. Father became ill and died a few months later."

"Still, you might have met someone."

"I never thought of it. I had my work. Mother and I and...Mother and I were happy together."

"Ah, yes, your family."

"They were very important to me."

"Mine wasn't." He straightened in the seat. "I believe we celebrated at Le Monde when Sam and Judge Sutherland won the case against my cousins."

"Yes, I remember that we did."

"You were uncomfortable."

"A little."

"You don't drink."

"My parents disapproved of spirits."

"I once found that liquor dulled the pain of my circumstances. Does that shock you?"

"It's your business, Mr. Ashley."

"I don't indulge now, as you've seen, except for an occasional glass of wine with a meal."

"No, sir."

He didn't comment on her slip of the tongue. "What did Mrs. Swane tell you about Elise?"

"Mr. Ashley, it's really none of my business."

"I assume she's still very beautiful."

"Yes."

"She invited me to a cocktail party next Friday. I declined, but she said that if I didn't come, everyone would think I was still wounded because she left me. I suppose I'll have to put in an appearance...don't you think? And don't say that it isn't any of your business. I asked your opinion."

"Mother always said that it didn't matter what

other people thought if a person knew the truth himself."

"The truth. So I must decide if, indeed, I'm still smarting. I suppose my pride is wounded. Any man's would be, wouldn't it?" He gave her opportunity to reply, knowing that she wouldn't. "So I suppose I'll go. I'd like for you to come with me."

"I'd rather not, Mr. Ashley."

"Consider it part of your duties as my assistant, Miss Seldon. Ellen can advise you on what to wear. No doubt she and Sam will be there."

"Please, Mr. Ashley, I'd be very uncomfortable."

"I'll need you to drive me, and you can't wait in the car all evening."

"You might go with Mr. and Mrs. Bernard."

"I might, but I choose to do it this way."

*****

They were finishing their dinner when Elise swept in. "Well, Alan, if I'd known you were dining out tonight, I'd have invited you to join us. You remember Freddie Gregg." Her eyes raked Lenore and dismissed her.

Alan stood up and offered his hand. "Gregg."

"You're looking well, old man."

"I wouldn't know." Alan withdrew his hand and made a fist behind his napkin.

"I'm telling everyone that you'll be there on Friday night, Alan. They're all thrilled."

"I'll put in an appearance, Elise. Miss Seldon will accompany me."

For a moment, as Elise turned toward her, Lenore was reminded of a cobra about to strike. Her green eyes, hooded by shadowed lids, blazed like the emeralds that caught the light as they lay on her creamy throat. Then she retreated. "Oh. Well, as you like." Without another word, she was gone.

Lenore pressed her hands together in her lap to still their trembling. "Mr. Ashley, I..."

87

"I said I'd go to protect my image. I didn't say that she'd exact any pleasure from my presence."

"You're using me to strike at her."

"Elise is incapable of being hurt."

"But I'm not, Mr. Ashley."

He ignored her.

The waiter arrived with coffee. "Will there be anything else, Mr. Ashley?"

"I think not, thank you, just the check."

He knew she was watching him as he took out his wallet and extracted two bills from it. "Mrs. Swane arranges the currency in order when she lays out my clothes at night. So I know that I've put a twenty-dollar bill and a ten on the tray."

"That's right."

"Change I can tell by touch, of course, but one doesn't deal with change at Le Monde. Did you enjoy your dinner?"

"The veal was very good."

"I'm fluent enough in French to read the menu if I could see it, but I'm also familiar with the fare here and can order from memory." He rose and came around the table to help her with her chair. "Shall we go now, Miss Seldon?"

****

"Alan, for pity's sake, don't force Miss Seldon to go with you on Friday. It's like sending a lamb to the slaughter." Ellen Bernard's raised voice caused Alan to hold the telephone a short distance from his ear.

"We won't stay long."

"Then why go at all?"

"To prove a point."

"You're acting much as you used to until, well, until Miss Seldon softened you somewhat."

"Yes, of course, a perfect boor. Perhaps you only imagined that she had influenced a change in me."

"She had. Elise Mayhew poisons your spirit."

"Ellen, I need you to advise Miss Seldon about

88

what to wear. Take her shopping if necessary. I'll foot the bill."

"Dressing her, like the ancient Incas prepared their young virgins for the sacrifice."

"That's unworthy of you, Ellen."

"No, it's unworthy of you. I'll do it, but for her sake, not yours."

He held the phone away from his ear again as she slammed down the receiver.

****

Mrs. Swane finished laying out his clothes and went to the door. "You're making a mistake, Mr. Alan."

"All right, it's my mistake, Mrs. Swane."

"She's been upset all week."

"I haven't noticed it."

"You wouldn't. Why are you doing this to her, when you were getting along so well?"

"Thank you for seeing to my needs. Now would you be so kind as to see if Miss Seldon needs any help getting ready?"

****

A uniformed maid took their coats and nodded toward the open double doors on the right. "Please go in."

The noise of conversation dropped several levels as they entered. Lenore's early supper rose in her throat, and her palms grew moist.

"Hello, Lenore." Ellen Bernard took Lenore's arm. "Let me introduce you to some people." She pecked Alan's cheek close to his ear. "I may never forgive you for doing this."

"I'm tending bar," Sam said close to his other ear. "What can I get you?"

"Scotch. Was Ellen watching for us?"

"You know she was. This way." He touched Alan's arm.

Though Ellen tried to camouflage Lenore in a

group of four women well-versed on and sympathetic to the situation, Elise found her. "We haven't been properly introduced," she said, her voice already slurring despite the early hour. "I believe you're Alan's live-in helper. Tell me, how far upstairs do your duties extend?"

The buzz of conversation died. Lenore's face crimsoned, and she drew back as if she'd been struck.

"That's enough, Elise." Jean Young, Trent's wife, took a step toward her hostess.

"I'm just curious." Jade earrings shaped like dragons swung from her ears as Elise leaned into Lenore's flushed face. "You don't seem his type."

Lenore straightened. "I'm his business assistant, Miss Mayhew, and I assure you that I didn't want to come here this evening."

"Well, obviously, you did."

"Only under duress."

"If he wouldn't have me, he most certainly won't have someone like you."

"I thought *you* turned *him* down," Lenore said.

The contents of Elise's glass hit Lenore full in the face. Ellen gasped and pulled a handkerchief from her sleeve.

The liquid stung Lenore's eyes, and the taste, as it dripped onto her lips, heightened her nausea. Without speaking, she turned and hurried across the room and out the door.

Only Elise Mayhew's laughter broke the stunned silence of the gathering.

****

Lenore sat shivering behind the wheel of the car, but not entirely from the chill of the night air. "Miss Seldon."

"Mr. Ashley."

"You may drive us home now." He opened the door and got in. "I heard what you said."

"It was a hateful thing to say. I'm sorry."

"She deserved it."

"Didn't you know that something like this would happen?"

"I suppose I knew it was possible. Probable, even."

"I'm your assistant, Mr. Ashley, not a shield for your ego."

"I take it you don't think very highly of me at the moment."

"I'd begun to change my opinion of you from ten years ago, but now..."

"And what was that opinion ten years ago?"

"I considered you arrogant and inconsiderate of other people's feelings, but I tried to understand what it must be like to be...to lose one's sight suddenly and permanently and be considered less capable because of it."

"What is your opinion of me now?"

"I don't know. You seem to have two faces, the one you've shown me these past three months, and the one you exhibited in this regard. I don't know who you are or what to think."

"If I offered you an apology, would you accept it?"

"Are you offering one?"

"Yes, I am."

"Then I accept."

"But you don't really trust me."

"No."

They rode the rest of the way in silence.

Alan got out of the car under the porte cochere and went inside while Lenore continued to the garage. For a moment he debated whether to wait for her to come in, to take the opportunity to apologize again. Angry at the necessity for the apology—and angry at himself for what he'd done—he hurried upstairs and shut himself in his room.

Chapter Nine

"What possessed you to expose her to that?" Sam leaned against the mantel and tried to control the anger that had been building since he'd taken it upon himself to confront Alan.

"I don't know."

"She's a good businesswoman, but she's been sheltered. You had to know that Elise would attack her."

"She held her own quite well."

"I heard her. But the glass of liquor in her face was the final insult. If it had been my wife…"

"I stand reproved and remind you that Miss Seldon is not my wife."

"She's a woman and deserving of respect."

"I offered her an apology, and she accepted."

"Did she go away this weekend?"

"Yes."

"You'll be lucky if she comes back."

"She'll be back. She needs the money badly, although I haven't determined exactly what she needs it for. There's a hint of desperation about her."

"Is it any of your business?"

"I suppose not."

"Are you going to see Elise again?"

"No."

Sam slid his hands along the smooth mahogany surface above the fireplace. "I hope not. She has a bad effect on you."

"That's been pointed out to me by several people."

"You haven't been like this since Miss Seldon

came. Ellen and I thought her refinement and gentleness might have had some effect on you. But you're still..."

"Arrogant? Inconsiderate? Those are the adjectives that Miss Seldon used last night."

"She was right. Alan, you've always been respected as an astute businessman, but in the last months you've begun to build a reputation as a human being."

"I didn't realize I wasn't considered human before."

"You know what I mean. Why the change?"

"As you and others have pointed out, Elise has a bad effect on me."

"Don't put it off on her. You were well rid of her ten years ago, and you had a choice about what you did last night."

"Did I tell you that she said she could never marry half a man?"

"Too many times. I'm bored with it. You hold on to that like a starving dog guarding his last bone. Is that how you see yourself, Alan, as half a man?"

"I didn't think so...until she came back."

"It's obvious that she thinks you're going to fall at her feet."

"Has she said so?"

"Women talk, and Ellen listens."

"Ah. Well, if it will ease your mind, I have no intention of being husband number three, nor do I wish to be."

"Keep reminding yourself of that." Sam started for the door. "At least I'm speaking to you. Ellen swore that she'd never speak to you again."

"She didn't mean it."

"Oh, she did last night. She paced our bedroom like a caged lion until two o'clock in the morning, berating you all the while."

"She likes Miss Seldon, doesn't she?"

"Very much."

Alan uncrossed his legs and sat forward. "So do I."

"You have an odd way of showing it," Sam said. "I'll let myself out."

****

"It was humiliating, Constance. I almost hated him last night."

"Are you going back?"

"I have to. My savings are accumulating, but I want to have enough to take care of Bobbie until I find work wherever we go."

"I still think going to Canada is unwise."

"There's no other choice."

"You may be right. Somehow I have the feeling that Avram Rykovsky is considering something similar. He was here again last night and told me that his brother-in-law still refuses to relinquish Rebekah to him."

"Does Rebekah understand?"

"Not really. She seems content with his visits and the gifts he brings her. Last night he brought her a china doll much like Bobbie's Alberta."

"Dear old Alberta. She cherishes that doll from her father. She even named her for him."

"Rebekah named her doll Hope."

"Hope?"

"Yes, she seems to have grasped the concept quite well, abstract as it is. She says she hopes that Uncle Avram will take her to live with him someday and that you and Bobbie will have a lovely home of your own where she can come and visit."

"I suppose hope really does spring eternal. It's why I can't leave Alan Ashley's employ for awhile yet. But someday, Constance...someday..."

****

Alan was waiting at the foot of the stairs when Lenore came in on Sunday evening. "Sam seemed to think you wouldn't be back."

"I have to work," she said more sharply than she intended. The more she thought of Friday night's humiliation, the angrier she had become at the person she considered responsible for it.

"That's what I told him. May I take your bag upstairs?"

She crossed the foyer and put the handle against his hand. "Thank you."

Alan let her precede him on the stairs. "Mrs. Swane has gone to church, but she left our supper in the kitchen as usual."

"I'm not hungry."

"I haven't eaten since breakfast, and I'd enjoy the company." He knew she was trying to find an excuse. "I'm unaccustomed to being humble, Miss Seldon, and I've apologized for Friday night." Apologies had always come hard for him, but he hoped that now he sounded contrite.

"All right," she said as they reached the landing. "Where would you like for me to serve it?"

"I have a fire in the study."

She reached for her suitcase, acutely aware that he must know it was cheap cardboard. "I'll only be a moment, Mr. Ashley." She stepped into her room and closed the door in his face.

****

"I like this room even more than the drawing room," he said as he heard her rolling the teacart through the door. "It was my father's, but I made some changes to suit myself."

"It's very nice."

"I'm more fortunate than someone who was born without sight. I remember colors and patterns, so I was able to choose the drapes and furniture myself. Ellen chose the painting over the fireplace, the seascape by Monet. It's an excellent copy of an original I remember from a museum in Europe."

95

"Do you like the sea?" She began to set out their supper on the long table in front of the sofa, making sure that her place was at the far end.

"Very much. I've mentioned that my parents took a house in Maine every summer when I was small. It wasn't a cozy family vacation. My nurse always came along to make sure I stayed out of their way. But I enjoyed playing in the sand and swimming."

Lenore finished serving their plates. "Cold chicken slices at nine o'clock and pea salad at four, an open, buttered biscuit on a separate plate at one, and your coffee at two."

"Thank you, Miss Seldon." Alan moved around the sofa and sat down. "Please join me." He picked up his knife and fork and sliced the chicken neatly. "It took me six months to do this without having the meat slide off the plate into my lap."

"You do it very well."

"I hold my own, as you did on Friday. Sam came on Saturday to give me his opinion of my actions, and Ellen has sworn off speaking to me. Mrs. Swane has been quite cool the entire weekend."

"I'd rather not talk about it."

"I think we must. Ellen pointed out that Elise poisons my spirit, and it's true. I wasn't really in love with her, but her rejection, coming on the heels of my struggle to regain my independence, was a blow to my pride."

"I understand."

"Do you? I'd managed to put her out of my mind until she appeared that day, but I wasn't ready to face her." He brought a forkful of pea salad to his mouth with the precision that never failed to amaze Lenore. She closed her eyes and tried to do as he'd done. She failed.

"What are you thinking?"

"I was trying to eat the pea salad with my eyes

closed," she said. "I couldn't do it."

He laughed. "It takes practice. What made you even try?"

"I was thinking how easy you make it seem."

He reached for his coffee. "The young man you told me about...were you formally engaged?"

"We had an understanding. He lived next door from the time we were children."

"Were you in love with him?"

He waited for her answer, needing to hear that she hadn't been.

"I'm not sure I understood what love means. We were good friends. We shared many interests and came from the same background. My mother said love develops as two people share their lives."

"Your parents had a good marriage, I assume."

"They were devoted to each other."

"So they were in love."

"I suppose they were. I never thought of it, really."

"And you would have had a similar marriage with..."

"David. His name was David Broome. Yes, I think we would have."

He thought her voice caressed the name and wondered if she still grieved his loss. "I wouldn't have had a good marriage with Elise. She was very desirable, of course. We were alike in many ways. Perhaps we still are. The crowd we ran with was composed of the socially elite, but I suppose we behaved in a rather more common way. We drank, stayed out most of the night, and...other things I don't like to remember."

"Please, Mr. Ashley, it's done."

"I wasn't a pleasant person when I returned after the war, but the years have mellowed me slightly, or so I believe. I've become more accepting of my circumstances. I've been successful in business and maintain good relationships with my employees. Sam says that, since you came, I'm almost human."

"I hardly think I'm responsible for..."

"A business is its employees," he interrupted. "You've been quite a satisfactory employee, Miss Seldon. I shouldn't like to lose you."

"As I told you, Mr. Ashley, I must work to support myself. I'm grateful for this position."

He nodded. "Then we understand each other."

"Yes, sir, we do."

\*\*\*\*

Just before noon on Monday, Elise swept into Alan's private office with Mrs. Fenton at her heels. "Hello, Alan. I got past the dragon at the entrance to your cave."

"Mr. Ashley, I told her..." The secretary's distress was evident.

He looked up from the Braille notes he was reading. "Never mind, Mrs. Fenton."

Lenore, who had gone into the small kitchen for a glass of water, pressed herself against the single cabinet, hoping that Elise wouldn't come far enough into the room to see her.

Elise ignored that Alan didn't stand as a courtesy. "It's your lucky day, Alan. I'm free for lunch, so you may take me somewhere. I'm ravenous."

"I'm afraid not, Elise. I'm not free, as you can see."

"Oh, come Alan, put aside these dreary papers." She advanced to his desk and picked up one of his notes. "Good heavens, what's this?"

"Put it down exactly where you found it, if you please."

"But what is it?"

"It's Braille. It's how I read."

She let the paper fall back to the desk as if it burned her fingers.

"And now be on your way."

"You're being very stuffy."

"As you like."

"I didn't intend to skewer your little lamb on Friday night. If you hadn't left in such a snit, I'd have explained..."

"Elise, I shouldn't have been there at all, and it was unspeakable of me to subject Miss Seldon to your venom." He raised his voice slightly, knowing that Lenore could hear him.

"So she *is* someone significant."

"She replaced Barrows as my personal assistant. I need her services and don't intend to offend her further."

"Oh, of course, but Barrows didn't have a room upstairs just down the hall from yours. Well, I suppose it was inevitable that you had to satisfy yourself eventually. I could have made it so much more fun for you."

"Goodbye, Elise." He ran his fingers over the page of raised dots without comprehending what he read.

He waited until the door closed, then buzzed Mrs. Fenton. "Please send word to James at the door that Miss Mayhew is not to be admitted to the building again." He rose and walked to the kitchen. "Miss Seldon, you can come out now. I'm sorry you had to hear all that. It won't happen again." He listened for her light footsteps as she emerged from her refuge. "Are you all right?"

"Mr. Ashley..."

"She's a nasty piece of work, as Mrs. Swane would say. I might use another term, but it would offend you."

"I think I should make other living arrangements."

"Because of what Elise said?"

"Other people must be saying the same thing."

"What was it your mother said? That if a person knew the truth, nothing else mattered?"

"She wasn't speaking of this kind of situation, and I'm certain she wouldn't approve of it. I needed the employment, but I shouldn't have compromised my standards."

"Miss Seldon, I can assure you that your honor is safe with me. I'm quite certain that if some dark night I took a single step in the direction of your door, Mrs. Swane would be there before me."

"Please don't say anymore, Mr. Ashley."

"I was trying to make light of the situation." Now, I'd like to go over those notes you transcribed, and Mrs. Fenton tells me that I have two appointments this afternoon. I want to finish on time. It's Monday, you remember. I look forward to dinner at Giovanni's on Mondays."

"Mr. Ashley, perhaps that's not a good idea, at least while..."

"While Elise Mayhew is lurking about? You've seen her for what she is. Despise her, pity her, laugh at her, but don't give credibility to anything she says or does. Now, about those notes, Miss Seldon."

****

Lenore found it difficult to concentrate for the rest of the day, and she was sure Alan Ashley recognized her distraction. As they walked to Giovanni's, their shoes kicking up the light powdering of snow that had fallen during the afternoon, he said, "The business world takes stamina, Miss Seldon. You must have the flexibility to adapt to many kinds of people."

"I don't think I have that."

"You were quite sheltered in Judge Sutherland's office."

"We had some difficult clients from time to time, but I rarely had to deal with them directly."

"You seemed to manage me quite well."

"I didn't manage you. I simply tried to put myself in your place and do what I could to make things more pleasant."

"But you didn't want to work for me, even at double your salary."

"I would never have left Judge Sutherland—or my mother."

"An admirable loyalty."

"And money wasn't as important then. I had a home."

"Where did you go when you sold your home?"

"We...I went to an apartment." She hoped he hadn't noticed the slip. "It was very nice, but when Judge Sutherland died, I had to give it up."

Alan didn't miss that it was the second time she'd said *we* before she caught herself. "And where did you go then?"

"To a smaller place, a room in a rather disreputable part of town."

"Where?"

"Poole Street."

"The devil you did!"

"You know it, then."

"Oh, yes. My father owned some tenements there. I got rid of them immediately. They were mostly empty, and I was able to relocate the remaining occupants to more suitable lodgings."

"When I became ill, I lost that, too."

"But you had your friend, Miss Ervin, at Greenfield."

"Yes."

They had reached the café. "Here we are, Miss Seldon. Let's live dangerously tonight, shall we? Let's try the lasagna."

****

Alan thought she seemed less tense the rest of the week and considered that she might have forgiven him, finally, for the cocktail party. On

Thursday night, she read aloud from the newspaper before he suggested listening to the radio. He twirled the dial until he caught the strains of Guy Lombardo's orchestra.

"That was one of my favorites," Alan said, leaning forward in his chair, his feet moving in time to the music. "Do you dance, Miss Seldon?"

"Oh, yes, all my friends danced at school parties."

"I haven't danced in years. I don't suppose you'd indulge me?"

"There's hardly room in here, Mr. Ashley."

"We could turn up the radio and go into the foyer."

"I'm not sure I remember how."

"Neither am I, but I'd like to try, wouldn't you?"

"Perhaps."

He stood for a moment in the middle of the foyer to orient himself, then held out his arms and was rewarded with the feel of Lenore Seldon stepping into them. Careful not to hold her too closely, he said, "All right, on the next beat." They moved off not quite in time to the music.

"Is it coming back to you?" he asked.

"I think so."

"The tempo is nice, but I believe we're a bit behind. Shall we pick it up?" He quickened his steps as he spoke. "Are you keeping watch for obstacles?"

"Yes...oh, Mr. Ashley, the stairs." She finished her warning as his heel met the bottom step, and he toppled, pulling her down with him into his lap. For a long shocked moment they sat still, breathing harder than the exercise warranted. She was lighter than he'd supposed, but her hair, when he reached to touch it, was as silky as he'd imagined. Sliding his hands to her cheeks, he brought her face forward until their lips touched.

He thought that she responded briefly, but,

before he could speak, she jumped from his arms and ran up the stairs.

\*\*\*\*

She didn't appear for breakfast, but she was waiting by the door at the appointed time for leaving. "You've had no breakfast," he said.

"I wasn't hungry."

"I see." He opened the door and let her precede him to the car under the porte cochere.

They'd driven several blocks in silence when she said, "Mr. Ashley, I really should make other living arrangements."

He knew why, but he asked anyway, adding, "I thought we'd settled all that. I find it convenient for you to live in and don't wish to make a change."

"Mr. Ashley, it's not..."

"We're both adults, Miss Seldon. I am a man, and you are a woman. We shared a brief kiss in the spirit of the moment."

"It shouldn't have happened."

"Was it so repulsive to you?"

"No, but it shouldn't have happened."

"Actually, it was quite nice," he interrupted. "It might even happen again."

"It can't."

"Why not?"

"I'm not Elise Mayhew."

"No, thank God. Can't we put that behind us? She's gone off again to heaven knows where, according to Sam. I won't mention where he said he hoped she'd gone to."

"I mean that you can't play with me as you might have played with her."

"Played with her? If you mean were we intimate, no, we weren't, though I'm sure she considered it more than once. I might have considered it, too."

"Mr. Ashley, please."

"I keep forgetting that you don't think in those

terms, Miss Seldon."

"The arrangement was questionable from the beginning."

"Miss Seldon, please pull over for a moment."

She stopped at the curb beside the park.

"I don't want you to leave. The house is empty enough without you on weekends. I've come to care for you as a good friend."

"Please don't."

"Is there someone else?"

"No."

"Then I will be bold enough to admit to courting you—or trying to. I suppose my skills are clumsy, unused as they have been for so long, and perhaps you don't consider me a good candidate for..."

"Stop it. Please, Mr. Ashley, don't say anymore. I should have ended it long ago. It's my fault for encouraging you."

"You haven't encouraged me at all. Quite the opposite. What are you afraid of, Miss Seldon?"

"I can't become...involved."

"Why not?"

"I have responsibilities."

"I see. Can you tell me about them?"

"No."

He shook his head. "All right, Miss Seldon. You may drive on to the office."

****

He followed Mrs. Swane into the kitchen when Lenore disappeared upstairs immediately after dinner. "Miss Seldon is thinking of making other living arrangements."

"What did you do to her now?"

"I didn't do anything." He sat down at the table and ran his hands through his hair. "All right, I kissed her. Some familiar music was on the radio, and I asked her if she danced. So we went into the foyer for a quick turn, but I backed up too far and fell on the stairs. She ended up in my lap, and...it just happened."

"You haven't been in so much trouble since you were a little boy." He thought she sounded amused.

"I'm not in trouble. I'm...in love."

"So that's how it is."

"That's how it is."

"She's a fine young woman, not..."

"I know. Not like the *other one*."

"I don't have to tell you that you come from different backgrounds."

"Come, Mrs. Swane, you of all people aren't going to say she's of a different social class. You grew up in near poverty, but you consider yourself as good as anyone, as well you should. You are a culinary genius, and you manage this house as well as I manage Ashley Enterprises."

"It's my gift, that's all."

"You know all about my parents. Despite their so-called social class, they were as morally decadent as..."

"Don't speak ill of the dead."

"You know what they were."

"It had nothing to do with me." She poured coffee for both of them and sat down. "I never felt poor. I just didn't have any money, that's all, and my formal education ended when I was fourteen. Still, I consider myself as much of a professional as anyone in your office."

"I couldn't manage without you."

"No, you couldn't."

"And I don't see how I can get along without Miss Seldon. I never realized just how lonely I was until she came."

"It's up to you to keep her here if that's the way you feel."

"She seems to have made up her mind otherwise."

"You run one of the largest businesses in this country. How many employees do you have? Almost a hundred? Surely you can deal with one young woman who, it appears to me, also cares for you, even if she doesn't want to."

"Why do you think so?"

"Women know these things about other women. She spends a great deal of time with you that she doesn't have to."

"She's not spending any time with me tonight."

"Did you ask her to?"

"I usually don't have to ask."

"Go sulk somewhere else, Mr. Alan. I'm done cleaning the kitchen, and this is my bridge night."

He pushed back from the kitchen table. "You're deserting me, too."

"I'm going to play bridge, as I do every Friday night."

He paused in the swinging door to the dining room. "You're the only real mother I ever had, you know."

"Go pick up your toys, Mr. Alan, before someone makes off with them."

****

Alan went up early and, after some hesitation, knocked on Lenore's door. "Miss Seldon."

When she didn't answer, he decided that she was asleep and turned away. Then her muffled voice came through the door. "Yes, sir?"

"I...are you all right?"

"Yes, sir."

"I telephoned Rod and asked him to drive you to the station tomorrow. More snow is forecast, and the temperature is dropping. You shouldn't walk."

"Thank you."

"Miss Seldon."

"Yes, sir?"

"Nothing. Goodnight."

"Goodnight, Mr. Ashley."

****

Closeted in his study with Sam, who had brought some papers to sign, Alan missed Lenore's return on Sunday afternoon. Later he wandered into the kitchen, wondering what Mrs. Swane had left for supper and whether Lenore would appear to serve it. Finally he went into the drawing room and built up the fire before settling down to listen to some music on the radio. When he heard someone in the foyer, he called out, "Mrs. Swane? Are you back from church?"

"Would you like for me to go and see if she's returned?"

"Ah, Miss Seldon. I wondered if you were coming down."

"I just came down for some tea."

"I'm sure Mrs. Swane left supper for us. I was waiting on you to serve."

"I'm sorry. I didn't think about that. I'll only be a moment."

"And could you possibly find some of those butter cookies that Mrs. Swane hides so skillfully?"

"I'll try, Mr. Ashley."

He returned to the drawing room and sat down again. Was it time, as Mrs. Swane suggested, to pick up his toys? The sound of Lenore's footsteps heightened his anticipation.

"Did you find the cookies?"

"No. They weren't where I saw her put them on Thursday."

"She moves them around with regularity, it seems. Perhaps you'll keep a sharp eye out next week."

"I'll try." She set his plate on the table beside his chair and described the arrangement of the food on it.

He heard a rustling sound as she moved across

107

the carpet to her own chair and decided that she must have on her dressing gown. For a moment he felt pleased at the intimacy, though he realized that she would have dressed if he could see. The thought made him scowl as he added another log to the fire and returned the poker to its holder with more force than necessary.

"I've told you that I was very young when Mrs. Swane came here. Her father had died, and she was the oldest of nine, so it was necessary for her to help out. Later, when I was in school, she married and moved away. Unfortunately, her husband died in the flu epidemic after the war. The very day I returned home from the rehabilitation center, she arrived and announced she'd come to take care of things. I was, as you might imagine, both gratified and relieved."

"She's been very kind to me."

"You're not unhappy here?"

"I'm not unhappy, Mr. Ashley, but you've put me in an uncomfortable situation."

He ignored her. "It occurs to me that we still know very little about each other, yet we've gotten along from the beginning. Don't you think we've...gotten along?"

"We've worked well together."

"I agree. You've made a number of changes in the organization of my office that are most beneficial. The straight-edge, for example, that allows me to sign my name without having to work around someone's pointing finger."

"It was a simple thing to have the metal shop construct."

"But it was your idea. You saw my need and stepped up to meet it. I'm appreciative of that."

"I try to do what I can."

"You do a great deal, Miss Seldon."

"I think it's very easy to blur the lines of a professional relationship when we live in such...close proximity."

"So you're still on that, are you?"

"I just feel strongly that I should make a change in my living arrangements."

"That doesn't suit me at all."

"I shouldn't like to lose my position."

"I'm not threatening to let you go, Miss Seldon. Shall we talk about something else?"

"What would you like to talk about?"

"Do you have any family at all left in Brookston?"

"No."

"I hope you won't mind my asking why you found it necessary to sell your home."

"I thought I explained that after Father died, Teddy put it in his name and paid the taxes. The house had to be sold to pay off the indebtedness of Teddy's estate when he was killed so unexpectedly. I had some savings, but not enough to pay what he owed."

"What kind of work did you do after Judge Sutherland died? You only said that you took what you could get."

"Day work mostly, addressing envelopes, filling temporary positions at various offices. I was more fortunate than some. I thought the position keeping accounts at a grocery market would be more or less permanent, but when it seemed I was being asked to receive illegal shipments of alcohol after hours, I gave my notice and left as soon as I could."

"Many honest businesses have been used as fronts by bootleggers since Prohibition, Miss Seldon. The wine at Le Monde, the alcohol served in private homes—it's all illegal, but people get around the Volstead Act one way or another. Under the circumstances, you couldn't stay and do what they asked, but you have nothing for which to reproach yourself."

He hesitated. "You'll pardon my forthrightness, but Mrs. Swane said you looked as though a good gust of wind might blow you away the day you appeared on my doorstep."

"I told you that I'd been ill."

"Yes, with pneumonia. That can be deadly."

"I was in the hospital for quite some time, and then Constance...Miss Ervin...invited me to stay at the Home in Greenfield."

"You knew her before?" He waited to see if she'd be consistent in the lie he knew she'd told him earlier.

"I...met her while I was ill."

"I see. You didn't know her before."

"No."

He waited for her to go on, but she didn't.

"Would you like more tea, Mr. Ashley?"

"I would indeed, Miss Seldon, if you'd be so kind."

As she rustled past him, he berated himself again, this time for his uncharacteristic timidity. Though he'd acquired some information, he was no closer to the mystery of her weekend disappearances than before. She'd assured him that there wasn't another suitor, but somehow that didn't ease his mind. So what was it that took her away? Surely not a second job. Why would she need more money?

As she came back and set down his cup, he caught the scent of lilacs. This was a new dimension, and it was one of those times he wished for his eyes. What did she look like? Did her face match her soft, cultured voice? Was she beautiful? Was she old beyond her years, as her voice indicated tonight?

He waited until she was seated again. "Miss Seldon, perhaps you'd indulge me a moment more. What do you look like?"

"Look like?"

"Yes. Mrs. Swane only described you as rather

thin with dark hair and eyes. I didn't press her for more information." That wasn't entirely true, but it would do.

"I'm quite ordinary," she said after a moment. "My height is from my father."

"Go on, please."

"My hair and eyes are black, also like my father. Mother and Teddy were blonde."

"How do you wear your hair?" He could have bitten his tongue. "I apologize if I'm being too personal." He heard her move in her chair.

"I wear it pulled back and coiled at the base of my neck."

"So it's quite long?"

"It falls well below my shoulders."

"Ah. Is it down tonight?"

"Yes."

"Miss Seldon, I really wish that you'd reconsider making other living arrangements. It's quite convenient for me to have you here."

"It's too...personal."

"Are you opposed to personal relationships?"

"Not at all."

"I'm surprised that you never married. Is there any reason other than the fact that you were with your mother?"

"I never met anyone else. Brookston is a small town. Most people who marry there meet in school or their neighborhood, as I met David."

"Was he in college before the war?"

"He'd completed one year."

"What was he studying?"

"Architecture."

"What a coincidence! I wanted to be an architect, but I always knew that I'd have the responsibility for Ashley Enterprises someday. I still draw plans—in my head, of course."

"You might work with a draftsman to get those

plans onto paper."

"I suppose so. I've always said that I was going to remodel this place. I'm sure it needs work."

"A little paint here and there, perhaps. The lighting is..." She stopped.

"Yes, the lighting. Well, as I don't need it, I suppose I never thought of it. Don't be embarrassed, Miss Seldon. You bring up a valid point. No one else has ever mentioned it."

They sat in silence for a few minutes.

"What would make your living arrangements here more comfortable? Taking meals in the kitchen with Mrs. Swane? Going upstairs immediately after dinner?"

"I just feel I shouldn't be here."

"But I want you here." He despised the petulance that crept into his voice. "And I'm accustomed to getting what I want."

"I'm sure you are."

"Is that an indictment, Miss Seldon? I'm a wealthy man. I work very hard to keep my business profitable in these difficult economic times. Don't you think I deserve to have what I want?"

"I'm not sure we always deserve or need what we want."

"What do you want? I'm curious."

"The security of employment."

"That's all?"

"That's enough."

"You never thought of having a home of your own? What about children?"

"I've learned not to desire what I can't have, Mr. Ashley. I'm content."

"You don't give that impression."

"I..."

He heard her rise and knew he'd cornered her. "I've offended you on two occasions. I'll try not to let it happen again."

"I should go up now."

He rose, too. "If you must. Thank you for bringing supper."

"You're quite welcome."

Alan waited until her footsteps faded before he sat down again. *That didn't go very well, now did it? You learned very little that you didn't know already. And you were too much of a coward to come right out and ask her where she goes on weekends.*

\*\*\*\*

On Monday they ate dinner at Giovanni's, as usual. Afterwards, Alan asked her to drive to the city park. "It's too cold to get out of the car," he said, "but I thought you might like to see the statue of my great-grandfather. He was instrumental in getting Rumers Crossing on the map. It was a farming community before he brought in the first bank and other businesses."

"It's really too dark to see much."

"When one lives in a dark world twenty-four hours a day, sunrise and sunset don't mean much."

"Sighted people take a great deal for granted, don't we?"

"Why should they do anything else? If you'll drive through town, you can see the original bank building on the corner of Elm and Main Street."

"You showed that to me from the courthouse before."

"I remember now. You asked about it."

He directed her to several more places, almost impossible to see at night, but the tour served the purpose of prolonging their time together. He wondered if she suspected his strategy.

"The town is growing, but the proximity of Canon City only thirty miles away is a deterrent. I suppose we'll never have amenities such as a live theatre or a symphony or the ballet. Still, I'm not inclined to leave here or move my offices."

"Ashley Enterprises is the mainstay of this community, isn't it?"

"Since the crash in twenty-nine, yes, it is, but I have hopes that some of the failed businesses will regenerate themselves eventually. You have a head for business, Miss Seldon. Perhaps you might find yourself in charge of one someday."

"Oh, no, I think not."

"Why? Because you're a woman?"

"I don't like being in charge. I'm best at following orders."

"What if I ordered you to stop the car?"

"Now? Here?"

"Yes. Do it, Miss Seldon." When the noise of the engine died, he turned to her. "Are you afraid of me, Miss Seldon?"

"A little."

"Why?"

"I don't know."

"I think you do. I think you're attracted to me as I'm attracted to you, and you feel that it's not proper."

She didn't reply.

"You can't hide behind your silence anymore than I can hide behind my sightlessness, though God knows I've tried." He pulled her into his arms and managed to find her lips. For a moment she struggled against him before giving herself up to the pleasant but frightening feelings he engendered in her.

"You are attracted to me, aren't you?"

"It's wrong." She extricated herself from the embrace.

"I won't argue with what you're convinced of. Did David Broome ever kiss you like that?"

"He...no. He never kissed me at all, not on the lips."

"You were children then. You're not a child any

longer."

"But I have..."

"You have what?"

"Nothing. We should go home, Mr. Ashley."

"Then drive home and run and hide away from me in your room. But you can't hide from yourself, no matter where you are. I know that better than you." He sat back in the seat. "However, if it helps your feelings, I won't touch you again."

****

Lenore spent a sleepless night, unable to rid herself of the memory of Alan Ashley's arms around her and his lips caressing hers. A restless longing engulfed her normally quiet body. What it longed for, she didn't even want to consider.

He was everything she believed him to be, arrogant, selfish, cynical...all that, and yet there was more. Somewhere inside of him there was something else struggling to get out, something finer and kinder than what she saw most of the time.

She knew too much about his business dealings to perceive him as anything but honest and ethical. He kept his employees at arm's length, but he knew about them and even cared about their lives.

What he said was true. She was attracted to him, and she knew it was wrong. Perhaps moving out of this house would be sufficient. What if it was a mistake, though? What if he terminated her employment? What then? She couldn't go back to Greenfield and tell Bobbie that there would be no more money coming in to assure their future.

****

Somehow she got through the rest of the week. She ate dinner with him at night but went upstairs immediately afterwards. There were no more evenings before the fire listening to music or reading aloud or just talking.

She missed all of it, especially being near him in

a setting that wasn't about business, but it was the only way.

****

The next weekend stretched out interminably, and Alan's mood was dark by Sunday evening. He stepped out of the drawing room as soon as he heard the front door open. "Miss Seldon."

She whirled around. "Oh, Mr. Ashley. You startled me."

"When you've settled yourself again, would you step into the study, please?"

"Yes, sir. I'll only be a moment."

When she couldn't put it off any longer, she joined him downstairs. "What may I do for you, Mr. Ashley?"

"You might serve supper."

"Yes, sir."

"Miss Seldon."

She paused at the door.

"Did you have a good trip?"

"Yes, sir."

"I see."

Lenore had made up her mind to be congenial but to avoid letting herself be drawn into any personal conversation. She broke her own rule immediately without realizing that she'd done it or why.

"Our parlor was much smaller than this," Lenore said as they settled into the drawing room after supper. "It had Mother's piano, and later Teddy bought us a radio from his first paycheck."

"Good memories are important. When I came back after the war, I thought about selling the house and moving into an apartment nearer the office, but I kept putting it off. There's an attachment here, you see. I was always fascinated with the history of the house."

"It must have been lonely for you, growing up

116

alone."

"In a way, but I was an imaginative child and had many playmates that only I could see. Then I was sent away to school when I was eight and never really lived here again."

"Not even in the summer?"

"Camp."

"Oh."

"My parents, as I mentioned, were on the *Titanic*. While they were traveling on the continent, they decided to cut short their trip. Though they always traveled first class, only second class accommodations were available to them at the last moment. Otherwise, they might have been saved. Or perhaps not."

"It's too bad."

"I didn't grieve for them."

"I can't imagine that. I still miss my parents. I still find myself wanting to tell Mother something, and when I remember that I can't, it makes me very sad."

"You confide in your friend Constance Ervin, I suppose."

"Yes."

"I have no one to talk to about my deepest feelings."

"I thought you were close to Mr. Bernard."

"Perhaps it's different with men. I have so much pent up inside me..." He stopped. The last thing he wanted from her was pity.

"As I was saying, I hardly knew my parents, so I didn't miss them. School and college kept me busy, and then I enlisted and went to France. I was injured in the fall of 1918, spent the next two years learning to live without my sight, came back to take over Ashley Enterprises, and encountered the opposition of my cousins and Sam's father. You know the rest."

117

"Do you have any contact with them...with your cousins?"

"None, but I'm sure they're out there waiting."

"Waiting? For what?"

"For me to die, I suppose, or drive the business to ruin."

"That's...despicable."

He turned his face away so she couldn't see his satisfied smile. "Well, I don't intend to do either, not right away. "Did your brother have children?"

Was she hesitating again?

"He married rather late. I never met Roberta. It wasn't a happy marriage from the very beginning, and they were divorced at the time of his death."

"A failed marriage is always sad, don't you think? I'm thankful I didn't have the experience. I was well rid of Elise, despite the damage to my pride. I plunged into business and put aside all thoughts of anything else until..." He stopped and finished his sentence silently. *Until the day you turned up on my doorstep, out of breath and smelling of damp talcum.*

"I see people better than most sighted men. I see through them. I haven't gotten where I am now by being a poor judge of character." He suddenly wished for his sight, if only for a moment. How was she receiving his words?

Only the ticking of the clock above the fireplace broke the silence that followed. Finally Lenore rose. "I should go up now."

"Of course. I've kept you. Goodnight, Miss Seldon."

"Goodnight, Mr. Ashley."

He slumped down in his chair. The woman was infuriatingly proper. She was an iceberg, larger than the one responsible for the *Titanic's* sinking. *Yes, Mr. Ashley. Of course, Mr. Ashley. Yes sir. No, sir. Goodnight, Mr. Ashley.* In spite of that, he loved her.

There was no other word for it. His waking thoughts were of her, and he fell asleep with the scent of her in his nostrils. How could she not know?

\*\*\*\*

The next evening, as they drove home from the office, he said, "There's a performance of the symphony next Friday night. Sam and Ellen always come for me. I'd like it if you'd join us."

"I'd rather not, Mr. Ashley."

"But you love music."

"Yes, but I..."

"You'd be doing me a great favor, Miss Seldon. I rarely go out socially because I make the odd man. It won't be like the cocktail party."

He thought he heard her sigh. "All right, if you like, Mr. Ashley."

"The dress is always formal. Ellen can advise you."

"All right."

"Take your half-day on Wednesday and go into the city with her."

"All right."

"Miss Seldon, it is becoming most difficult to carry on a conversation with you when you have one stock reply...*all right*."

"I'm sorry."

"Yes, well, stop at the newsstand and get a paper. There's a business article I'd like you to read to me tonight before you go upstairs."

\*\*\*\*

They ate dinner mostly in silence. Before she finished reading the newspaper article aloud, he searched his mind for some way to detain her.

"Tell me more about growing up in Brookston. Your brother went to college—why didn't you?"

"It didn't seem as important for me to go as for Teddy."

"Was your brother drafted?"

"Not until near the end of the war. He never went to France."

"What about David Broome?"

"He enlisted."

"What was his unit?"

"I don't remember. It's been so long ago."

"How long was he there before..."

"Three months, I think."

"I was there only eight months before a shell exploded in our trench. All the men with me were killed." He listened for any sign of interest from her. "Sometimes I wondered why I lived. I was, as I've told you, very angry, and—I'll say it before you do—I'm still angry when I let myself dwell on it."

"I think I was a little angry about David, too," she said after a moment. "It changed my entire life, especially the way I looked at life."

"But you were still Pollyanna for a time."

"I had to try harder to be her after that."

"Was there anything else you wanted to do? Besides become a businesswoman, I mean."

"I didn't really want to do that, but I had to earn a living."

"No secret ambitions?"

"I thought of being a missionary."

"A missionary."

"Father forbade it, of course."

"Did you feel a *calling?*"

"I thought I did, but I suppose not, since I didn't pursue it."

"You were what? Nineteen?"

"Eighteen. There was a Bible college in the next town, but Father enrolled me at Lane-Thompson."

"I've told you that I wanted to be an architect, but there was Ashley Enterprises to run. Now it's out of the question. We're filled with ambition when we're very young, I suppose. Our lives are before us, and we never think of how the course we've set might change, how our lives could become something very different from what we imagined. But they do, don't they? Yours changed as well as mine."

"But you've been very successful."

"The business has been very successful. I have good people. Trent Young. Jerome Vannoy. Sam. Together we've been able to stay afloat through these depressed economic times. But personally..."

She stood up quickly. "Goodnight, Mr. Ashley."

"I wasn't finished speaking."

"I really should go up."

He was aware that she was already moving toward the door. "All right. Goodnight, Miss Seldon."

He realized that the conversation had become too personal for her comfort. What was she afraid of? Afraid. That was it. She wasn't afraid of him so much as she was afraid of sharing herself with him. She didn't want to know him because she was afraid of what she might feel. Perhaps she already felt something for him. The thought pleased him.

He had told her that he was accustomed to having his own way, and it was true. It had also been easier before, but she was making it difficult now. She wasn't toying with him, he was sure of that. She was transparently honest. But there was something...

Upstairs he paused outside her door and whispered, "Goodnight, Lenore. Goodnight, my love."

****

The next night, when Sam Bernard dropped by with information on a new acquisition, Alan Ashley stretched his long legs toward the fire and drew on his pipe. "Sam, I believe I've fallen in love with Miss Seldon."

The attorney chose his words carefully, wiping the smile from his voice. "And does she return your affections despite everything you've done to disprove them?"

121

Alan grimaced. "She ignores them, but I think...I rather think there's some attraction on her part."

"Are you going to press your case?"

"And frighten her off? She's skittish enough."

"What do you mean?"

"It's just a feeling I have. She doesn't speak about herself. Oh, it was obvious she was down on her luck when she came to me three months ago. But there's something about her that doesn't lend itself to inquiry, though I'll admit I've tried to draw her out. Mrs. Swane is no help. The thing that worries me most is that she disappears every weekend. She leaves on Saturday morning and doesn't come back until Sunday night."

"She's off the clock, of course."

"Well, yes, but the house is so empty without her."

Sam lost the battle to conceal his pleasure. "Well, that's telling. You haven't asked where she goes?"

"To tell you the truth, I'm afraid to, though it's crossed my mind to have Rod find out where she gets off the bus. It's none of my business, and she might tell me so."

"I'd ask, if I were you. That is, if you want this to go farther."

"What's your opinion about it?"

"About it going farther? You encouraged me to follow my heart with Ellen. I can't do less for you."

"Ellen is a lovely woman, even if she does get into my business more than is warranted."

"She's the love of my life. I couldn't wish any less for you, Alan. As for Miss Seldon, I'm impressed with her business ability, though I'll admit to questioning the wisdom of your decision at the time. You hired her rather precipitously, you know."

"Something told me I couldn't let her get away."

"Yes, I'm glad for your sake, and the business's,

that you didn't. Everyone I hear speak of her seems to think she's quite a wonder."

"She mastered the Braille writer in record time. Just having a list of my appointments on my desk every morning—and the transcribed notes in the afternoon—I tell you, Sam, I've never felt so in control of my own business."

"You've always been in control, Alan. It's not so different with her, is it? She's your eyes the same way that Barrows was."

"Yes, but it *is* different. I don't have to memorize everything. That was a strain, I can tell you. No, having it in front of me in black and white—or rather, in raised dots—has been a particular encouragement." He laughed, startled at his own joke. He turned toward his friend. "What do you really think of her, Sam? You know I value your opinion."

"I've hardly seen her outside of the office, but Ellen is quite impressed with her—says she's a *thrifty shopper*, which is her highest praise."

"I gave Ellen express instructions to take her to all the shops, and those two went to the department store, more specifically, the bargain basement."

"Ellen said that Miss Seldon wouldn't hear of anything else. She insisted she'd never shopped anywhere but a department store. According to my wife, who is a discerning consumer, she made some excellent purchases for a fraction of the cost."

"Mrs. Swane said that also, after she helped her put away her new wardrobe. Well, she had to have it, Sam. Mrs. Swane said she was almost beyond shabby. Neat and clean but mended."

"Yes."

"I've considered that there might be someone else in the picture, though she denies it."

"A man? She *is* extremely attractive, though unusually quiet."

"Yes, and the whole idea terrifies me. If she marries and leaves..." He relit the pipe that had been allowed to go out during the conversation. "Ah, well, I've been rejected before and lived through it."

"Elise wasn't good enough for you."

"She seemed to see it the opposite way."

"I have to get home, Alan. I hope things work out for you."

Alan put aside his pipe and rose, too. "I'll see you out. You didn't give me your advice yet."

"Was this a professional visit?"

"No, no, I don't need legal advice when it comes to Miss Seldon, though perhaps a lifetime contract might give me more protection."

"Then, as a friend of long standing, I'll give you the only advice I know. Keep talking to her. If she refuses to confide in you after awhile, perhaps it's best for the relationship to remain purely professional."

"You're right, of course. I'll consider it carefully. Meanwhile, perhaps Ellen might ask a few pertinent questions when she takes Miss Seldon to shop for a dress to wear to the symphony."

"Well, I'll admit that women can often ferret out secrets better than men—and Ellen is particularly sensitive to people's feelings."

"She always has been, especially since hers have been so thoroughly trampled."

Sam shook his head. "My family will never change, but Ellen's grown accustomed to their condescension. We've gone on with our lives."

"I've gone on with mine, too, Sam, but I realize suddenly that it's a rather empty existence."

Sam Bernard rested a hand on his friend's shoulder. "Then do something about it."

"I intend to. Goodnight, Sam, and thank you."

****

On Friday evening, Alan rose from his chair

beside the fire as he heard Lenore enter the drawing room. They both stood uncertainly, waiting for the other to speak. Finally, he said, "I believe at this point I should be gallant and say that you look lovely, and I will if you'll describe yourself to me."

"The dress is dark green satin with a high neck and long sleeves, and the black velvet cummerbund matches the evening wrap. I'm wearing Mother's pearl earrings." She stopped short of saying that she had pawned the matching pearl necklace for rent and grocery money.

"My dear Miss Seldon, you look lovely."

****

The hall clock was chiming midnight as Alan unlocked the front door and held it for her. "I hope you enjoyed the evening, Miss Seldon."

"Very much, Mr. Ashley."

"Even the dinner at Le Monde?"

"It was very good."

"Even if I told you that I ordered *escargot*?"

"*Escargot*?"

"Snails. The very large ones are considered a delicacy."

"Oh, I hope not! You didn't...did you?"

"No, I was teasing you. I told Ellen that I was ordering them for her the first time she and Sam went to dinner there with me. Sam said she examined every bite before she put it into her mouth."

Lenore laughed. "And so I should have if I'd known about *escargot*."

"Rod will be here tomorrow morning at nine to take you to the station."

"Thank you."

He hung his overcoat in the closet beside the stairs.

"What are you thinking, Miss Seldon?"

"I'm thinking of how much we take for granted,

those of us who have our sight, and how much I..."

"Your thoughts are always unfinished."

She shook her head. "It's not important."

"Did you really enjoy this evening?" He took her arm and started up the stairs.

"Very much."

"Perhaps you'll accompany me another time also."

"If you like."

On the landing he said goodnight and walked away smiling.

## Chapter Ten

Lenore paced Constance Ervin's small office. "I keep telling myself that I won't get into a personal conversation with him again, but it happens before I realize it. I should have refused to go to the symphony with him last night, too."

"It's obvious that he's interested in you."

"He mustn't be. He hinted once that he was courting me, but I didn't think he was serious."

"Why not? And do you want him to be?"

"I'm not the sort of person he would choose as a wife. And, no, I don't want him to be serious. Even if I didn't have Bobbie, it wouldn't work."

"Why not?"

"I'm not in his social class."

"It doesn't sound like he socializes much."

"I wouldn't be accepted in his world, and I don't want to be."

"If he were poor..."

"If he were poor, he wouldn't be who he is. There's something fine about him, Constance, but that doesn't negate his arrogance." Lenore stopped pacing and sat down. "I should have enough money by next summer. Living in as I do, and which I shouldn't, I have no expenses."

"You don't have to give me money every month for Bobbie."

"It's only fair. You took me in when I had nothing and fed me when I might have starved. I know how difficult it is for you to manage on the uncertain county funds. I know how much of your own pitiful salary you spend on these children and that sometimes you don't get paid at all."

"I manage."

"At least you'll have one less mouth to feed, as well as mine on weekends, when I leave with Bobbie. I just hope I don't put you in an unfavorable light because of her sudden disappearance."

"When you're ready, just take her and go. Don't even say goodbye, and I can tell the Burk woman that I didn't know."

\*\*\*\*

"What does Mr. Ashley look like, Mum?" Bobbie curled at the foot of Lenore's iron bed in the unused matron's room she'd occupied when she first came and that she now used as a guest.

"Oh, he's tall and has auburn hair that's rather wavy."

"Not white?"

"Why, no, Bobbie, he's only a few years older than I am."

"He's not old like Judge Sutherland?"

"Not at all."

"Oh. Is he handsome?"

"I suppose he is."

"Do you like him?"

"I get along with him. He's a very powerful man in the business world, Bobbie. He's not grandfatherly like Judge Sutherland."

"But you mostly like him?"

"It doesn't matter whether or not I like him. He pays me a salary."

"What do his eyes look like?"

"They're blue, rather cloudy and unfocused sometimes, and there are tiny little scars around them like starbursts. He wears dark glasses most of the time, so you can't see them."

"I saw a blind man sitting on a corner once. He was holding a cup, and people were putting money in it."

"Mr. Ashley doesn't have to beg. He's very wealthy."

"Does he have any children?"

"He isn't married."

"Do you think he likes children?"

"Well, he's very fond of Bea Bernard. I've told you about her."

"Bea is a lovely name. Beatrice. I'd rather be Beatrice than Bobbie."

"Would you rather be called Roberta? That's a rather elegant name."

"No." Bobbie jumped off the bed. "That was my mother's name, and I hate her."

"You mustn't hate her, dear." Lenore reached for the child, who eluded her arms.

"I do, and I think...I think I hate Papa, too. He promised to come for me, and he didn't do it, and now..." She ran out of the room but returned in a few minutes. "I'm sorry, Mum."

"It's all right. Come back and sit with me. Why all these questions about Mr. Ashley? You were never curious before."

Bobbie crawled up onto the bed and settled into Lenore's arms. "If Mr. Ashley likes Bea, he might like me, too, and if you married him, we could live in his beautiful house and be a real family."

"Oh, my, your imagination is working hard."

"It would be nice, wouldn't it?"

"Bobbie, I'm not going to marry Mr. Ashley. I'm not..." She caught herself before she said that she wasn't in love with him. It wasn't true. She *was* in love with Alan Ashley, and the thought terrified her.

"Oh, well, it's nice to think about."

"We'll have our own home again someday, Bobbie. I promise you that we will. Maybe even by next summer."

"Rebekah's uncle asked her if she'd like to live with him."

"Did he? Is that what made you start thinking about all this?"

"Sometimes I think about how it was when I lived with Papa. I had a big room and a dollhouse and pretty clothes. I had all that when we lived in the house in Brookston, too. Remember how Grandmother made clothes for Alberta when she sewed for me? Alberta and I were twins."

"I remember, Bobbie dear."

"Maybe Papa will come back, and you'll fall in love with him and get married, and we'll all live happily ever after."

"Life isn't like a fairytale, Bobbie."

"I know, but it's nice to think about sometimes."

Lenore pressed her cheek against Bobbie's hair and tried to think of something more to say, but there were no words that would make the present go away—or the past come back.

****

Alan spent another solitary weekend wandering the house and feeling oddly disconnected from the familiar surroundings. Somehow the rooms seemed cold and uninviting without Lenore Seldon's presence. Mrs. Swane noticed his mood at breakfast on Sunday. "When you were a little boy, I used to tell you to find something else to think about other than what was troubling you."

"Is that your suggestion now?" .

"No. My suggestion is that you marry Miss Seldon as soon as possible."

"Marry her?"

"That's what you want to do, isn't it?"

"I suppose so. Yes, I do."

"Then do it."

"I thought she was slightly suspect as far as you were concerned."

"No more than the strange dogs you used to encounter when I'd take you out walking. I didn't want anything to hurt you."

"I'm not sure that's very flattering to her."

"Well, as I said, she's not the other one."

"I suppose I'm something of a coward. I wouldn't want to be rejected a second time."

"You were well rid of Miss Elise Mayhew."

"Yes, well, it still injured my pride. And Miss Seldon is still talking about making other living arrangements because she finds this too...personal. She gave the impression of being subjected to the Spanish Inquisition because I almost insisted that she accompany me to the symphony Friday night."

"She looked beautiful."

"So Ellen told me more than once."

"You used to put off picking up your toys, too."

"Mrs. Swane..." he began, but she was gone.

****

A swirling snow began at noon. At five, Rod telephoned that he was leaving to meet Lenore's bus. He called again from the station. "There's a drift this side of Greenfield. The stationmaster says he doesn't know when it will be cleared."

"You mustn't stay indefinitely. Leave word for her to call you when the bus arrives."

It was after eleven o'clock when Rod delivered Lenore to the house. Alan met her in the foyer. "Lenore... Miss Seldon. You're home."

"I'm so sorry for disturbing you this late," she began.

"I was frantic when you didn't come. I've known those drifts to be unmovable."

"They sent crews out from all the surrounding towns," Rod said.

"Rod, I can't thank you enough for what you've done," Alan said quickly. "Please take tomorrow off for your trouble."

"That's not necessary, Mr. Ashley, but I think you'd better let me drive you and Miss Seldon

131

tomorrow. It's pretty bad out and bound to get worse before morning. I'll be here as soon as the roads are clear enough to be safe. Goodnight."

Lenore locked the door after him. "I'm really very sorry," she apologized again.

Alan cut her off. "Yes, you said that. Come in by the fire. And you've missed dinner, too."

"I had some crackers with me."

"Mrs. Swane has already retired, but I'm sure she left something for you. And you might make some tea."

"It's very late, Mr. Ashley."

"I know that, but you must have something to eat." Her sigh of resignation irritated him. "And I'd like some tea, also." He had an urgent need to be near her, to sense her presence, smell her, think of how it would be to unpin her hair and bury his face in it.

She returned in a few minutes, pushing the teacart ahead of her.

"Did you..."

"Yes, sir, I found the butter cookies."

"Mrs. Swane says I've turned you to a life of crime already."

She poured their tea and retired to her usual chair.

"You had a pleasant visit?"

"Oh, yes."

"You went to Greenfield." He heard Lenore's teacup rattle in the saucer as his words sank in.

"How did you know?"

"Rod reported to me that the bus leaving at nine-fifteen stops first in Greenfield. The bus driver confirmed that you get off there."

"You asked him to spy on me?"

"Is that where you go every weekend?"

"You asked Rod to spy on me!"

"No, I...yes, I suppose I did." He heard her get

up. "Sit down, Miss Seldon. You have an annoying habit of running away from any conversation that doesn't suit you."

"It doesn't suit me to think that you had Rod ask the bus driver about me. It's none of your business."

"Oh, do sit down and don't be dramatic, Miss Seldon. It doesn't flatter you. Naturally, I was curious because you were so secretive."

He heard her sit down. "What I do with my free time doesn't concern you, Mr. Ashley."

"Is there a particular reason why you visit Greenfield every weekend? Is it to see your friend there—or to get away from me?"

"We spend too much time together during the week. I need..."

"I'm a proud man, Miss Seldon. I won't beg, but I would very much like to know why you spend every weekend in Greenfield. Perhaps you have a lover after all."

He heard her gasp. "That's a vile thing to say!"

"Do you have a better explanation for your shadowy comings and goings?"

"I leave, and I come back. If you're dissatisfied with that, I'll give my notice now."

"You're being dramatic again. Come, Miss Seldon, if you go to Greenfield to visit your friend, why don't you say so? If you have a..."

"Don't say that again!" Her words forced themselves from between gritted teeth.

"Then be honest with me—for a change."

For a long moment he thought she wasn't going to answer his question. At the same time, he knew that she had no choice if she wanted to maintain her image and reputation.

"I have a niece living there."

"In the Home?"

"Yes."

"I see. Why did you never mention her before?

Never mind, you'll say it was your business. But now that you've told me, I'd like to know how she came to be there."

His hands gripped the arms of his chair in anticipation, and perhaps in dread, of what he might hear. He could tell, as she finally began to speak, that she was choosing her words carefully and that there were gaps in her story, but at least she was giving him some information.

"My brother and his wife didn't have children, but she had a child by a previous marriage, a little girl. There were circumstances that made Teddy feel that she shouldn't be with them, so he asked Mother and me to take her."

"How old was she?"

"She was just six then."

"How old is she now?"

"Eleven."

"So you've had her with you for several years."

"Judge Sutherland tried to get the mother to sign papers giving me guardianship, but she wouldn't do it. She didn't want Bobbie and never contacted her, but she wouldn't let her go, either."

"Do you know why?"

"Teddy felt that she was being pressured by her own father, Bobbie's grandfather, but I don't really know."

"So you kept her with you until..."

"Until I became ill. While I was in the hospital, a social worker took her to Greenfield, and when I couldn't produce anything showing that I had the legal right to have her with me, she said that Bobbie would become a ward of the state."

"Did they contact the mother?"

"I didn't know where she was, and Bobbie didn't want to go back to her anyway. We're very close. She even looks enough like me that people often think we're related, and she calls me *Mum*. She read that in a book somewhere."

The unusual warmth of her words chilled him. "Mum. Well, you'll forgive me, Miss Seldon, if I ask the obvious. Is she, in fact, your child?"

He heard the breath explode out of her body like air out of a punctured balloon, and the chair moved as if she'd risen hastily.

"I told you the truth, Mr. Ashley. She was my brother's stepdaughter, but if loving her and taking care of her makes her my child, then that's what she is." He sensed her movement past him toward the door and realized that he'd committed the worst judgment error of his life. It was the third strike against him.

"Miss Seldon, I apologize. Please don't go."

The door opened.

"I said I apologize."

"Mr. Ashley, my moral character is my own affair, but I want you to know that there's never been a day of my life when I couldn't look at myself in the mirror." Her anger and outrage added a new, oddly-compelling dimension to her personality.

While he was sorry he'd insulted her, he enjoyed seeing her display some spirit. "Again, I apologize for the question."

"It wasn't the question. It was the fact that it would even cross your mind." Her voice trembled.

"Please sit down, Miss Seldon."

She took another step, then stopped, but he knew she was still poised for flight.

"What I failed to discern, as I sought to know more about you, was that you've been very sheltered. I, on the other hand, was not. Therefore, the question came from my own experience, my own knowledge of the world." He put the tips of his fingers together as he pondered his next words.

"Belonging to a prominent family, I moved in the highest social strata. Elise offered herself to me

135

more than once. I told you that I didn't accept her offer, but I would be less than honest if I didn't admit wanting to, from a strictly physical standpoint."

"Mr. Ashley, this isn't a proper conversation for us to be having."

"I believe it is necessary. Please hear me out." He heard her take yet another step and stop again. "Later, when I was at Harvard, it was expected that a boy would pass through certain...*rites*, shall we say...into manhood. It was expected of me, but when the time came, I became convinced that I was not making a decision for myself, and I valued my independence. So, though it was not on moral grounds, I let my fellow students believe that I was far ahead of them, and that was the end of it. To be quite blunt, I lied."

He rose and went to the fireplace, found the poker and stirred up the fire. "Later, when I was in uniform, similar situations arose. Again, I declined all invitations and for the same reasons. But I am, at least mentally, Miss Seldon, no saint."

"No, you're not, Mr. Ashley."

He turned around. "Ah, Miss Seldon, your anger is almost refreshing."

"Is that all?"

"Not quite. When I came home after the war, an old friend came to see me, and in the course of conversation, he mentioned...how do I put this delicately...my mother's numerous indiscretions and those of my father. To be fair, he thought I already knew, and I managed to pretend that I did. It never occurred to me that my parents strayed outside of their marriage. They shared a room upstairs. Now I understand that it was for appearances...the servants, you know.

"When he left, I was as outraged as you are now. I felt betrayed, soiled somehow, to have been the product of a dishonored union. The knowledge made me somewhat cynical, I suppose. Now do you understand why I asked the question?"

"That doesn't excuse your behavior tonight."

"Miss Seldon, what I am so clumsily trying to tell you yet again is that your honor and your reputation are quite safe with me. Mrs. Swane is, after all, a proper chaperone. Now I have one more question. Would you consider bringing your niece here to live? There's more than enough room in this house, and she could attend school with Bea at Arlington Hall. I'd take care of her tuition, and..."

"I've protected her as much as I could for five long, difficult years, and now Constance cares for her as she does all the others. It's a struggle, but money doesn't guarantee goodness. Bringing her here would be like...like throwing her into the lion's den! I'd never expose her to..."

"To me?"

The door closed, leaving him speaking to an empty room.

## Chapter Eleven

It snowed through the night, and by morning it was obvious that all commerce was halted for the duration. Lenore was nowhere to be seen when Alan came downstairs.

"What time did Miss Lenore finally get home last night?" Mrs. Swane asked as she brought in the coffee.

"After eleven."

"From the reports on the radio, I don't imagine you'll be going to the office this morning."

"No."

"Would you like for me to go up and tell Miss Lenore that she needn't hurry?"

"She's probably packing."

"Packing? Why? She just got back."

"I wounded her feelings again last night," he confessed.

"I'm not sure I want to know about it. You seem intent on driving her away."

Alan leaned on his elbows, almost upsetting his coffee. "She finally told me that she goes to Greenfield every weekend because she has a step-niece living in the Home there, an eleven-year-old for whom she became responsible when her brother's wife left him. He died after that. I made the mistake of asking her if the child was actually hers."

"Mr. Alan! You didn't!"

He sat back, ready to defend himself. "As I recall, you weren't altogether certain that she should even be here."

"I never set out to find fault with her, and I

surely wouldn't have accused her of anything like that."

His remorse returned. "It was clumsy of me."

"It was unspeakable of you."

"It's done now."

"You'll be lucky if she doesn't come downstairs packed to leave despite the weather. Did you apologize?"

"I tried."

"She's usually down before this. Maybe she's already gone. She moves around like a shadow."

Thinking of Lenore struggling through the snow with her suitcase sent a chill of fear through Alan. "You don't think..."

"I'll go up and check on her."

Alan leaned on his elbows again and reflected that Mrs. Swane's succulent waffles were growing cold in front of him and that he didn't care.

"She's coming," Mrs. Swane reported a few minutes later. "It's obvious that she didn't sleep much last night. I can't believe you would say such a thing to her. If she wants to leave, I'll call Rod myself."

"You said that the radio reports that the roads are drifted. She can't go anywhere today."

"I might even help her pack."

"Mrs. Swane, I apologized."

"What possessed you to ask her such a thing?"

"She mentioned that the two of them look very much alike. It was a natural assumption."

"I wouldn't have assumed it." She turned toward the sound of the door opening. "Good morning, Miss Seldon. What would you like for breakfast?"

"Whatever you've prepared will be fine, thank you, Mrs. Swane." She went to the sideboard and poured a cup of coffee before taking her place at the table.

"We won't be going to the office this morning,

Miss Seldon," Alan said. "The roads are drifted. However, I have some letters to dictate. We'll work in the study for awhile."

"Certainly, Mr. Ashley."

"I apologize again for what I said last night."

"It's done."

"But not forgotten or forgiven."

She didn't reply.

****

When Lenore joined him in the study later, a fire blazed in the stone fireplace that covered most of one wall, and he'd opened the drapes to reveal the back lawn blanketed in white. "I enjoy the warmth of the sun through the glass even though I can't see it," he commented. She didn't reply.

After dictating half a dozen letters, he sat in front of the fire while Lenore typed them for his signature. She'd just finished when Mrs. Swane brought in a late lunch.

Lenore put away her dictation pad and covered the typewriter. "Please join me for lunch, Miss Seldon."

"Thank you, but I'm not hungry." He heard her start toward the door.

"I've behaved abominably, Miss Seldon. There's no other word for it. Mrs. Swane has raked me over the proverbial coals and says she'll call Rod if you want to leave."

"I have to work, Mr. Ashley."

"Even for someone like me?"

"Even for you."

"I've been sitting here reflecting on how I've treated you. Ten years ago I resented Pollyanna, and now I think I resent that she's gone."

"Why would it make any difference to you?"

"I'm not sure. Perhaps I'm looking for reasons to explain my behavior."

"I don't suppose you need to explain it. You can

140

do as you please."

"It doesn't please me. I've bullied you—and I've always hated bullies."

"Mr. Ashley, I overreacted last night. I suppose it *was* a natural assumption, given the moral climate of the day, so I should apologize also for my outburst."

"Not in the least. You had every right to defend yourself."

"No, knowing the truth about myself should have made whatever you thought unimportant."

"Could we start over? Last night's offer stands. You did understand my offer to bring your niece here?"

"Yes."

"There is no need for you to be separated from her. Obviously you care a great deal about her. She can share your room or have one to herself, whatever you like. And if she prefers public school to Arlington Hall, she has that option also."

He heard the sound of her sinking down in the leather chair across from him. "I can't bring her here, Mr. Ashley."

"Because she's a ward of the state? That's easily remedied. Orphanages are overcrowded these days, and funding is in short supply. Sam should have no problem arranging for her to come here in your custody."

"What about her mother?"

"I suppose there would have to be a perfunctory search for her."

"Bobbie always believed that her father would come for her as he promised before her mother took her away."

"That was a long time ago, and you said the two of you are very close."

"I couldn't keep her away from her father, though it would break my heart to give her up. She says he always called her *his best little girl...his shining star.* When she first came to Mother and me, she spent all her waking hours sitting by the front door waiting for him."

"Does she still speak of him?"

"More now, Constance says, since I've been living away from her. The social worker was so angry with me because I wouldn't give her any information that she said that I wasn't even to see Bobbie. Constance made sure I was hidden whenever the woman came."

"The mother as much as abandoned the child, and the social worker exceeded her rights."

"I don't know, Mr. Ashley, but I can't leave her there until she's eighteen. She's lost enough of her childhood as it is."

"Please accept my question as just that, a question and not a judgment, Miss Seldon, but if the two of you were together, why did you seek employment out of the Home?"

"I needed the money. Enough to take her away."

"Take her where?"

"To Canada. I don't think the state would even look for us there, and..."

He shook his head. "That's a very bad choice."

"It's all I could think of."

"You could be charged with kidnapping, and then you'd certainly never see her again."

"They wouldn't bother with one child."

"Perhaps not, but there's a better way. I'll telephone Sam and explain the situation to him. He'll give you sound legal advice."

"It's not your responsibility."

"I think perhaps it is," he said. "I only wish you'd told me sooner."

When Lenore went upstairs immediately after lunch and didn't come down again, Alan went back to his desk and called Sam.

"I'll have to have more information than you're giving me," the attorney said. "I should speak with Miss Seldon myself."

"She's quite upset."

"Why is she upset? This has been going on for some time, hasn't it?"

"Last night when I finally managed to ferret out the story, I...um... asked her if the child was hers."

"Ah, Alan, you didn't!"

"Well, what was I to think, Sam? She said they even look alike."

"Would it make a difference if the child was hers?"

"I don't know. I suppose there might have been circumstances..."

"Alan, you told me that you were in love with her. I wonder if you're just in love with the idea of not being alone anymore?"

"You know me better than that. It doesn't matter, because the child isn't hers."

"Before you go any farther with this, you should consider whether or not you could accept the child if she did belong to Miss Seldon."

"You're not my moral conscience, Sam."

"No, I'm your friend, and I don't want to see you hurt. I don't want to see Miss Seldon hurt, either, nor, most especially, the little girl. I have a daughter of my own, and I know how vulnerable children are. Think about what I've said, and call me back tomorrow."

Alan hadn't been really angry in a long time, but he was angry now. Making his way to the cabinet, he took out a bottle of wine and filled a glass. He could remember nights when he'd drunk enough to dull his misery, but that had been years ago, and he was a different man now. Or was he?

He set the full glass aside and began to pace the clear path he always kept between the sofa and his desk. What he felt for Lenore Seldon, he had never felt for Elise. He once considered her beautiful and charming, but in truth she'd been a vain, silly little piece, a product of her environment, as he had been until the war. No, he was well rid of her, as Mrs. Swane repeatedly stated. He had no regrets that she was gone, but he would very much regret letting Lenore Seldon slip though his fingers. Yet he knew he'd moved too quickly and frightened her, and now he'd insulted her. He deserved to lose her, but he wasn't accustomed to losing, at least not often. There had to be a way.

He sat down and reached for the cushion leaning against the arm of the sofa. For the first time in years, he let his mind wander into forbidden territory. What would it be like to hold a woman in his arms, to make love to her? What would it be like to make love to Lenore Seldon?

****

"I telephoned Sam Bernard last night," Alan said as they drove to the office the next morning over the cleared but snow-lined roads. "He's willing to look into the situation, but he wants to talk to you first."

"You're very kind, Mr. Ashley, but she's my responsibility."

"I'm not being kind, and you're not being very responsible. How long can you run?"

"As long as I have to."

"That's insane!" He hit the door with the flat of his hand, startling her so that the car swerved slightly. "Think, Miss Seldon! Think of what it would mean to live in a country where you don't have a citizen's rights. Think what it would mean to be always looking over your shoulder. What if you became ill again?" He closed his eyes against the desperate fury of his own words. What was happening to him?

"Please, Mr. Ashley, I..."

"No, never mind, Miss Seldon. I'm completely out of line here. If you change your mind, you can let me know. Otherwise, we'll say no more about it." He took a deep breath to calm himself. He hadn't realized that the old fury was still there, only hiding beneath years of carefully cultivated control. He considered Lenore Seldon a light in his darkness, but her very brightness had exposed the dimness of his soul. He felt the pain of that exposure more than he'd felt the pain of his injury.

****

"There was a file," Lenore said, breaking the silence on the drive home that evening. "Dan Sutherland gave it to me when I left Brookston."

"What was in it?"

"I don't know. I never opened it."

"But it has information about Bobbie?"

"Judge Sutherland tried to find out something about her. He told me a little of it, about her father. His parents were immigrants, I think. Bobbie's mother disappeared, and Teddy went to look for her in the town where Bobbie was born, to try to get her to give me custody, at least temporarily. He died there, or rather on his way back from there to Dallas."

"And you never looked at the file?"

"There was no need. If Judge Sutherland wasn't successful in finding out more, how could I possibly be?" She hesitated. "Maybe I didn't want to know."

"But you still have it?"

"Yes. The social worker took it, which is how she knew I didn't have custody of Bobbie. She didn't read all of it, however, before giving it to Constance. When she couldn't get any information from Bobbie, she wanted it back. Constance spoke with the county attorney, who said it was privileged information between a lawyer and his client. That's when Miss

Burk said I wasn't to see Bobbie again."

"So you have it with you?"

"In my room."

"What about your other things?"

"I went back to the boarding house where Bobbie and I lived before I became ill. The owner had let the room, of course, but she'd stored our things. There wasn't much, but I especially wanted to get the Pink Lady."

"The Pink Lady?"

"A picture I bought for Bobbie that last Christmas. She saw it in a secondhand store and fell in love with it. When I told her I'd gotten it back, she was overjoyed." Lenore's voice broke. "I left some of Mother's things with Mrs. Sutherland, and someday I want to get them, too."

"All this time I might have helped you."

"It wasn't your responsibility."

"Please don't keep saying that. It makes me ashamed of my affluence and my selfish, insulated life."

"Why? You were born into the life you live, and you didn't cause the Depression."

"I've never been homeless, either. Even when I was recovering in several hospitals, I always knew the house was here waiting."

"I'm glad. It's a beautiful house."

"And very empty, though not so much since you came. There's more than enough room for one little girl."

He felt Lenore turn the car onto the winding drive that led to the house. When she stopped under the porte cochere and switched off the motor, she said, "All right, but I can't afford Mr. Bernard's legal fees for too long."

"Don't think of that, Miss Seldon. Think of Bobbie."

****

"She's had this file for several years, but she doesn't know what's in it." Alan held out a thick manila envelope. "However, she agreed that you could look at it."

Sam opened his briefcase and put the envelope inside "Why wouldn't she read it, if it's so important?"

"She's afraid, I suppose. What she doesn't know can't hurt her. I don't know, Sam. Just look at it and tell me what you think."

\*\*\*\*

Sam telephoned Alan's office the next day. "I stayed up half the night reading that file twice. I read parts of it three times. Alan, if Amos Sutherland hadn't put these things down, I wouldn't believe them, even with the newspaper clippings he found to back them up."

"What do you think her chances are of getting the child?"

"About as definite as having snow for Christmas. If all this is true, her mother is dead, and her grandfather may well be in prison by now. I'd suggest that you let me turn this over to Emory Roth. He did a good job investigating the people at Ashley Enterprises ten years ago when my father was trying to help your cousins take over. He's the one to sort through this tangle."

"Then do it, Sam. If Miss Seldon thinks that there's no chance of getting Bobbie out of Greenfield through legal channels, she'll take her across the border into Canada. She's already told me so."

"I'll call him and make an appointment today if possible. Meanwhile..."

"Miss Seldon needn't know."

"I don't like to go behind her back but, no, she doesn't, not if she has in mind to take the child out of the country."

"Sam said the file was quite detailed," Alan said

when Lenore asked him about it that evening. "I expect we'll have a definite report in a day or two. Meanwhile, are you planning to go to Greenfield on Saturday as usual?"

"Bobbie would be disappointed if I didn't come. It's difficult for her to be away from me."

"It's just as difficult for you to be away from her, isn't it?"

"Yes, it is."

"You've made the right decision to let Sam handle this, Miss Seldon. Now we must just be patient and wait for his analysis of the situation." His hand moved toward her, but he caught himself. *At least you won't run this weekend...but when you find out that I haven't told you the complete truth, there's always the next.*

\*\*\*\*

Emory Roth telephoned after dinner to say that he would be there within the hour. "A private investigator? Is anything wrong?" Lenore asked when Alan told her.

"I would think his urgency means that everything is right."

\*\*\*\*

"It was good of you to come after hours, Roth." Alan extended his hand. "Miss Seldon, this is Emory Roth, a private investigator who worked for me ten years ago during the unpleasantness with my cousins. He's read the file and wants to discuss it with you."

"I thought Mr. Bernard had it."

"He felt that it required Mr. Roth's attention also."

"Why didn't you tell me that?"

"I trusted Mr. Roth to come back with a clear picture of the situation. Until then, needless speculation could only upset you."

"Don't you think I should have made that

decision?" Her voice was cool.

"Perhaps so, Miss Seldon. Shall we sit down and hear what Mr. Roth has found out?"

The investigator opened his briefcase and removed two file folders. "First of all, Miss Seldon, if you had read the information that Judge Sutherland compiled, you would have learned that, when your brother was killed, the state police investigated and found a gun in his car—the same gun used to kill Bobbie's mother just a few hours earlier."

"Her mother is dead?"

"She was shot in her bedroom the same night that your brother died, and as I said, the gun was found in his possession."

"He didn't own a gun."

"You're right. It wasn't registered to him. It wasn't registered at all, but he had possession of a murder weapon, and he was dead and couldn't defend himself."

"Teddy couldn't...you didn't know him."

"Miss Seldon, I'm not making any accusations. He went to Barnwell looking for his ex-wife and apparently found her. Both of them ended up dead."

She covered her face with her hands and slumped against the sofa. "Teddy was a kind, gentle man. He wasn't a murderer."

"Did the state police believe they'd found their killer?" Alan asked.

"I was able to learn that the case is still open but not active. That means that they had doubts about the evidence pointing to him."

"That's positive, Miss Seldon," Alan said, wishing he dared take her hand.

Roth opened the second folder. "Furthermore, soon after the mother took her away, the child's father disappeared from Barnwell under a cloud of suspicion about a robbery at the store he managed. He didn't contest the divorce or the fact that his ex-wife was awarded sole custody of Bobbie, but nothing was proved against him, either."

"I can't believe anything bad of Bobbie's father. She adores him," Lenore said.

"Children usually love their parents," Alan said, realizing the fallacy of his words even as they left his mouth.

"The grandfather, Robert Harcourt, is a very powerful man in the county. The state police have been investigating him for years, but they've never been able to get enough evidence to indict him for anything. Several grand juries have been convened without results. He rules the town of Barnwell like a small fiefdom. No one says anything that he doesn't tell them to say. In the mid-twenties, he brought in the Klan and cleaned out an entire Negro community in one night. He's a dangerous man, and it appears that he is also interested in finding Albert Rycroft."

"Albert Rycroft!" Alan's head snapped back.

"Bobbie's father. She was born Roberta Annette Rycroft." The investigator noted the shock on his client's face. "Mr. Ashley, is there something..."

Alan walked to his desk and sat down. "Roth, a young corporal named Albert Rycroft saved my life in France."

"I might be able to find out if it's the same man."

"Do that, please. If Bobbie is his daughter, I owe her anything I can do to make her life better."

"I'll see what I can find out." Roth turned to Lenore.

"Roberta Seldon left a will naming her father as Bobbie's guardian."

"Oh, no! She's terrified of him."

"That's a strong word, Miss Seldon."

"She saw him strike her mother several times, and he...on several occasions he struck her and threatened to leave her in an empty grave in the cemetery behind his house."

"The child couldn't have been very old the last time she saw her grandfather," Roth suggested. "Children often imagine things."

Lenore laced her trembling fingers together. "She didn't imagine it. She told her father about what the man had done, and it precipitated an enormous quarrel between her parents. She was afraid..."

"Afraid of what, Miss Seldon?" She turned at the sound of Alan's voice closer to her than she wanted.

She shook her head.

"You have to speak to me, Miss Seldon. I can't see your face or read your expression."

"I never meant for it to go this far. Please, just leave things alone."

"What is Bobbie afraid of?" Alan sat down beside her on the sofa and took her hand. "We have to know."

She wrenched her hand free. "She heard her father tell her mother that he'd kill Robert Harcourt if he hurt their child."

"Is that all?" Alan sat back, relieved.

"Isn't that enough?"

"People often make threats in the heat of anger," Alan said. "I'm sure it frightened the child."

"So much that she never told him that the situation continued, and that her grandfather even...behaved...inappropriately." The last words were choked almost beyond understanding.

"Behaved inappropriately?" Emory Roth asked. "What does that mean?"

"Bobbie said that he'd been drinking and made her sit on his lap and..." Her voice dropped to a whisper. "Please don't ask me."

"We're all adults here, Miss Seldon," Roth said. "I have to know the entire story if I'm going to help you."

"He touched her." The words were like an explosion. "He put his hands under her dress and touched her. She bit him, and then her mother slapped her and locked her in her room for three days."

"That's a lot of detail for a five-year-old to remember."

"She was almost six then, living in Dallas with Teddy, but he was out of town on business when the grandfather came. She's very bright, Mr. Roth. She knows what happened."

"How did she come to tell you all this?"

"Mother had just died, so Teddy was there for the services. She overheard Teddy telling me that he was going to look for Roberta and try to get custody for me. Bobbie became hysterical and begged him not to go. She said that her grandfather would know where she was and would come and get her and that she'd rather die...like Mother...than go back."

Lenore swayed dizzily and leaned back again. "Teddy tried to comfort her, but it was no use, and that night she woke screaming, and it all came out. She was eight then. She knew exactly what she was telling us. She didn't make it up."

Roth grimaced. "Sam will have to depose her in front of witnesses so he'll have evidence against Robert Harcourt. I don't mean to minimize the child's trauma, but in order for you to gain custody, a judge will have to know everything."

"Is there more?" Alan asked, hoping there wasn't.

"Unfortunately, yes. Robert Harcourt runs the county with his own handpicked people and a small but effective quasi-militia. Everyone is afraid of him. His right-hand man is Floyd Avenall, a smalltime crook who's spent time in the penitentiary at Huntsville. He's not very smart, but he's almost as dangerous as his boss."

He paused, searching Lenore's face for another possible emotional storm. "As I said, I've cultivated a source there. Just the mention of Robert Harcourt was enough to give me credibility with them. They want him badly and are willing to cooperate with anyone who might help them. I have the impression that they don't care what they get him for as long as they take him out of circulation."

"And they think you might?" Alan asked.

"They were interested in the fact that I know where the granddaughter is, because Robert Harcourt has been trying to find her. They believe he needs her in order to get to her father."

Alan heard a sound of strangled panic from the woman beside him. "Does he have any idea where she is?"

"I'm afraid so. At least, he knows where Miss Seldon is."

Lenore sprang from the sofa. "I've got to take her now. I'll go to Greenfield tonight."

"He only knows where you are, Miss Seldon. If you stay away from Greenfield for the time being, the child is safer there than anywhere else." Emory Roth had dealt with hysterical women, and this was a woman who would quell her emotions enough to act on her fears.

"But he'll find out."

"Yes, he will, eventually, but there are measures we can take."

Alan found Lenore's wrist, pulling her down onto the sofa again. "What do you suggest, Roth?"

"First of all, have your attorney file for custody for Miss Seldon. He'll probably only be able to get temporary custody, say thirty to ninety days, but that buys us some time. I suspect that the will making Harcourt Bobbie's guardian may not exist, but since he controls the county records through his handpicked clerk, I can't prove that right now."

"I'll telephone Sam immediately."

"If you can get custody and bring the child here, Harcourt will know where she is, but that will force him to produce the documents giving him guardianship—if they exist. The information I've uncovered, and what Miss Seldon has just told me, will help Mr. Bernard build a case against him and, hopefully, make the temporary guardianship a permanent one."

"If he knows where the child is and knows that he can't win in court, he might try to take her by force," Alan said.

"When Miss Seldon has physical possession of the child in this house, I'll arrange for security measures."

"Guards, you mean?"

"Exactly." Emory Roth returned the folders to his briefcase. "Don't go to Greenfield this weekend, Miss Seldon. With your permission, I'll telephone someone there and alert them to the situation."

Lenore appeared dazed. "I...she'll be afraid without me..."

The investigator leaned toward her. "Understand me, Miss Seldon, the situation is critical. The child's safety must come first before your own emotions. Now, to whom do I speak at Greenfield?"

**** 

Alan caught Lenore on the stairs as he came back from seeing Emory Roth to the door. "Miss Seldon." He could sense that her whole body was shaking, and she seemed spent, almost in a trance.

"I believe we must talk, Miss Seldon."

Lenore followed him into the study. "I'm very sorry for the trouble I've caused you, Mr. Ashley. I never intended to let my personal life interfere with my employment."

"You haven't caused me any trouble, Miss

Seldon. It's you I'm concerned about."

"You needn't be."

"No?" He sat down beside her. "As I've mentioned, I've learned to see people, to see through them, and I sense your fear and understand it. It's fortunate that I learned about Bobbie now rather than later, or else her grandfather might have appeared on the scene with no warning. He can take her, you know, either with the will, if it exists, or by force."

Lenore shuddered. "I know."

"Possession is nine-tenths of the law, as they say. If we can establish Harcourt's unfitness as a guardian, which is possible because of the ongoing investigation, a court might be persuaded to grant you complete custody at some point."

"But it's a tremendous risk."

"Life is a risk, Miss Seldon, but the alternative isn't very appealing."

"She's not your responsibility. Bringing her here wouldn't be the thing to do."

"You don't think she'd be happy here?"

Bobbie's words and earnest expression...*living in Mr. Ashley's beautiful house like a real family*...filled Lenore's ears. "I didn't mean that. She'd settle in. Bobbie finds her niche anywhere. Even in that terrible room on Poole Street."

"It must have been very difficult for you."

"We were together. That's all that mattered. That's why I can't risk losing her now. I'm grateful for what you and Mr. Bernard are trying to do for me, but I'm afraid."

"Of losing Bobbie, or of losing control of your life?"

"Both. It doesn't matter, don't you see? I can't take a chance on failing again in my responsibility to her. I promised her we'd have a home together again."

"You promised her that you'd take her out of Greenfield to Canada. Come, Miss Seldon, it isn't like you not to have thought things through."

"I've thought the best that I can."

"I've said this before. You never had a legal right to Bobbie, and you have none now. If the grandfather does indeed have custody of her, any decision you make on her behalf is against the law."

"What else can I do?" The panic in her voice stirred Alan's resolve.

"You've been given several viable options. You can run, Miss Seldon, but if you're caught, you may never see Bobbie again."

She moved to get up, but he caught her arm.

"And I'll never see *you* again." He took her face in his hands.

"Oh, please...please..." She tried to pull away from him, but he grasped her shoulders.

"Don't you know that I'm in love with you, Lenore? I think I've loved you since that first day you appeared on my doorstep, out of breath and smelling of damp talcum. I've admitted to courting you these past few months, but you've ignored all that. Not that I blame you; I've been a boor."

He heard her sharp intake of breath.

"You've seemed willing enough to spend time with me. Why? Because you felt that your employment depended on catering to my whims at home?"

Still she didn't speak.

"Say something, Lenore. Tell me that you have no feelings for me and never can, and that's the end of it."

She shuddered. "I don't know what I feel. I've wanted to be with you and known it was wrong. I've thought of you when I shouldn't, felt horribly wicked when you touched my hand at the Braille writer or took my arm..."

He took her face in his hands again and traced her brow, eyes, nose, and cheekbones, then let the tips of his thumbs rest beside her mouth. "You are beautiful," he whispered, drawing her mouth to his.

He kissed her lightly at first, then more urgently, but he didn't hold her, as if giving her permission to leave. She didn't.

"This is wrong," she whispered.

"Why?"

"I don't know, but it is."

He kissed her again and thought that this time she responded. "Marry me, Lenore, and let me take care of you and of Bobbie."

"Marry you!" She jerked away from him.

"Is the idea so shocking?" He pulled her close again and put his lips against her throat. "She'll have every advantage here. *You'll* have everything."

"Don't...don't...please..." The warmth of her slender body remained close despite her words.

"I love you, Lenore, and more than that, I want you. My body aches for yours."

He felt for the pins in her hair and removed them one by one until it cascaded down her back. "I've wanted to do that for such a long time."

"Please...Mr. Ashley..."

"Surely this intimate setting calls for the use of my given name. Tell me what you're thinking...what you're feeling."

"I don't know... I'm so confused and afraid."

He caught one hand and lifted it to his lips. "Do you feel anything for me, Lenore?"

She tried without much effort, to pull away again. "I...yes...yes..."

"Do you love me, Lenore? Do you want me as I want you?"

"I don't know what it means to love, to be in love...to want in that way. David and I were children together."

"But you didn't feel for him what you feel for me."

"No, and what I feel now frightens me."

"Why?"

"I've been alone for so long."

"As have I."

"And I'm not...you're above me."

"Do you mean because I'm wealthy?"

"It would be so much simpler if you were poor." She gasped, shocked by her admission.

His laughter filled the room. "Oh, Lenore, only you would say something like that."

"I only meant..."

"I know what you meant, my darling. You've earned your way in the world, but so have I. Oh, I know the business was left to me, but I've made it work, don't you see? We're not so different."

He kissed her again, this time with more passion, and her sudden response after a moment fueled his ardor. "I think you do feel something for me," he whispered.

"I can't help myself."

"Then stay with me, and we'll bring Bobbie here. After we're married, we'll adopt her. She'll have my name and all the advantages that go with it." He stood up, lifting her with him. "I'm almost afraid to let you be alone tonight. I don't want you to think too much." He stroked her hair. "I want to make love to you, Lenore, to hold you all night and wake in the morning with your hair in my face and know that you're no longer just a dream."

He kissed her again before stepping back, not wanting to frighten her further with his desperate need. "But I won't. Go upstairs now, and if you must think, consider everything I've told you. Consider your options for having Bobbie with you and the fact that you can't run forever." He touched her face again. "And that I love you as I've never loved anyone before."

****

He was waiting for her on the stairs when she came out of her room the next morning. "Did you sleep well?"

"I hardly slept at all."

He sat on the top step and drew her down with him. "I didn't, either." He kissed her, gratified that she didn't resist.

"I know you're right about Bobbie. I can't be certain that we won't be found, but you can't be certain that Mr. Bernard can get custody for me, either."

"I believe that he can."

"I'd like to believe it, but I'm so frightened."

"You've said that." He kissed her again. "Let's go down to breakfast now, and after we check in at the office, we'll go for a drive. I don't think either of us is fit to concentrate on business today."

He took her arm as they walked downstairs but dropped it just outside the dining room. "We won't say anything to Mrs. Swane just yet. She knows my feelings for you, however. We'll make our announcement tonight at dinner, after we've had time to settle a few things."

"I'm sure she doesn't approve..."

"On the contrary, she's your staunchest defender." He opened the door and waited for her to precede him.

****

As they drove to the office, Alan told her more about Albert Rycroft. "The Germans overran our position only minutes after he carried me to safety. He saved my life."

"You're sure it was Bobbie's father?"

"Somehow I think so. Roth may be able to confirm it, but even so, because of you I have a personal interest in her safety and well-being."

159

"I tried so hard to take care of her, and we were all right until I took pneumonia."

"You couldn't help becoming ill."

"But if I hadn't been taken to the hospital, Bobbie would never have gone to Greenfield. No one would have known that she wasn't mine."

"You said it wasn't a bad place."

"She's sheltered and fed."

"That's more than many children are these days. Lenore, stop the car here."

"We're still a block from the office."

"I judged as much." He waited for her to pull over before reaching across the seat to embrace her. "I just need to hold you a moment."

"There are people passing."

"I can't see them. If you close your eyes, you won't see them, either."

She couldn't help laughing. "Your logic is questionable."

"But not the fact that I'm very, very much in love with you." He felt for her face and brought it close to his.

****

They left the office just before noon and stopped for lunch at a small tearoom. Alan caressed her fingers across the table as they waited to be served.

"Thomas Greer, my pastor, speaks of having faith in a larger plan in place for all of us. I'll admit to paying only lip service to that premise, but now I find myself thinking that he may be right. Perhaps now I'm reaching for the lost faith of my childhood."

She savored his touch. "I used to have faith when I was a child. I believed that if I were good, as I was taught to be, everything would work out for the best."

"Perhaps it has."

"I seem to have lost everything."

"I thought I'd lost my life. Oh, I was still

breathing and walking around, but the prospect of living the rest of my life in darkness was overwhelming. All my plans for the future, all my dreams were gone in an instant, and I had to accept that I could never recover them."

She looked away from him. "And you still feel that things work out for the best?"

He lifted her hand to his lips. "I didn't until now. Until you came into my life."

"I don't really understand."

"I'm not sure I can explain it to you, Lenore, but perhaps all we have left to us is faith—and love."

Chapter Twelve

Sam telephoned Alan after dinner. "Emory Roth contacted me when he couldn't reach you this afternoon. A state police officer called him with some disturbing information. Robert Harcourt has employed someone to look for Bobbie."

"How did the man know?"

"He said they don't ask each other too many questions. Emory understands that the man is passing along information that he doesn't have to share."

"Go on."

"He believes that the grandfather brought about the separation between his daughter and Albert Rycroft and that he insisted on Roberta keeping the girl even though she had no affection for her."

"Bobbie was a hostage of sorts?"

"A pawn, at least. Harcourt seems to be a dangerous man, Alan. Don't underestimate what he's capable of doing. Albert Rycroft has something that Harcourt wants, and the man can use Bobbie to get it."

"What made him try to find her now, after all these years?

"Emory's not sure. Before, as long as he knew where Bobbie was, he could bide his time. It's possible that Roberta led him to think that she could produce the child. Now she's dead, and something must have happened recently to make him feel that he needs Bobbie."

"Do you think he's responsible for his daughter's death? For Teddy Seldon's death?"

"Emory gets the feeling that the state police do, but like everything else Harcourt has done, they can't prove it. However, Harcourt has hired a private investigator who works for him from time to time, and the man left Dallas yesterday headed for New York—specifically, for Brookston."

"Do you think he knows that Bobbie is at Greenfield?"

"There's no way of knowing. I gather that Miss Seldon has kept in touch with Dan Sutherland and his mother. Emory is going to contact them tonight to warn them and to find out if there's anyone else who might know about Bobbie. Meanwhile, see if you can impress upon Miss Seldon that she's going to have to cooperate fully if we're to be successful."

"I think she will. Now."

Sam laughed. "Did you lock her in the secret room?"

"No. I asked her to marry me."

"The devil you did!"

"She didn't say yes, but she didn't say no, either. And she admitted to returning my affections."

"I congratulate you."

"Yes, I'm rather congratulating myself. She's just coming into the study now, so I'll tell her what you've said."

"All right. Get in touch with Emory after you speak with her. I'll call you tomorrow."

****

After dinner, Alan persuaded Lenore to sit with him in front of the fire. "We really shouldn't," she said after they'd shared several lingering kisses. "What if Mrs. Swane..."

"The good lady has retired. Would you like for me to lock the door?"

"No."

He laughed. "You're perfectly safe, darling Lenore."

163

"You know that's not what I meant."

He began to take down her hair. "It's just that I need to press my advantage fully."

She snatched her hairpins out of his hands. "I can't think when you do that."

"I don't mean for you to think, only to sit here and let me love you."

"I've never...I mean...I'm so ignorant about..."

"Lovemaking?"

"Mother never spoke of such things."

"That might well work to my advantage also."

"Please, Mr. Ashley..."

He sighed. "You've yet to call me by my name." He tipped her head back and put his lips against her throat. "Don't," she said, "please...Alan."

"That's better. Do you really want me to stop?"

"Mrs. Swane said you were a perfect gentleman."

"I'm a man, Lenore, and you, I firmly believe, are very much a woman." His fingers toyed with the top button of her blouse, but he thought the better of continuing.

"I don't think I ever really understood that before," she said, her voice so soft that it was almost lost in the sound of a log falling. "Being around you has made me feel very much unlike myself."

He wrapped her hair around his hand and felt her trembling. "Am I frightening you?"

"Quite a bit."

He sat back. "Perhaps it's time for some tea before bed."

"Yes, I'll get it."

He laughed as he listened to her racing for the door—and hoped that she'd remember to pin her hair again in case she ran into Mrs. Swane. "Bring the butter cookies," he called after her.

\*\*\*\*

Lenore sat at the dressing table to brush her

hair. She could still feel Alan's hands in it. What she'd said to him was true. She was ignorant of all but the basic information about her body. As a young woman, she'd asked for none, and her mother hadn't offered it.

She leaned close to the mirror and studied her face. She was no longer nineteen, but neither was she an old woman. There was still time for love and marriage...and children. Did Alan want his own children? How would Bobbie fit into that kind of plan? Would she feel different? Or worse, rejected?

Replacing the brush on the dressing table, Lenore went to her bed and slipped beneath the covers. Was Alan thinking of her at this moment, wishing that she were beside him? What would it be like to share his bed and the physical intimacies of marriage? She shivered and closed her eyes. Even as a girl, she hadn't imagined more than simply walking down the aisle in her mother's wedding dress to meet David at the altar. Her fantasies had ended there, perhaps because she had no knowledge of more.

Bobbie had spoken of their being a real family. Would it be so? Would Alan accept her and love her for herself and not because he felt obligated? It had to be that way. Bobbie deserved the security of a loving home. She had been rootless too long.

Worry nibbled Lenore's consciousness, then turned to fear. Alan seemed to believe in happy endings, but she wasn't sure. What was the right thing to do? To whom did she owe her first consideration? The mantel clock in the sitting room chimed midnight before she finally fell asleep.

****

They had been at the office only a few minutes the next morning when Sam called. Finally Alan hung up the telephone and turned to Lenore, who was filing some papers. "Emory Roth has spoken with Miss Ervin at the Greenfield Home. She suggests that you telephone Bobbie yourself and explain the situation and why you won't be coming this weekend."

Lenore grasped the open drawer to steady herself. "She'll be very unhappy."

"Miss Ervin said she'd stay with Bobbie while she took the call. You might also tell her that Sam feels he can get the temporary custody order by Christmas. That will give her something to look forward to." He pushed the telephone toward her. "There's nothing to be gained by delay. Would you like for me to step out?"

"No, please...stay."

"Please stay, *Alan*." He reached for her hand and brought it to his lips.

"Please stay...Alan."

"That's better."

She was crying when she hung up. "Constance will help her understand, but she's very frightened."

"Only temporarily."

"What if her grandfather breaks in and takes her?"

Alan stroked her fingers. "I wasn't going to tell you this for fear it would make you more anxious, but Emory has placed two security people at Greenfield. No one except Miss Ervin will know that they are there."

"It's like something out of a cheap novel."

"Sometimes life is more like a story than a story."

She pulled her hand away. "I have to take these files downstairs to Mr. Young."

"Everything will be all right, Lenore. You'll see." But as he listened to her hurry away, he wasn't as sure as he'd been last night.

\*\*\*\*

Alan insisted that Lenore telephone Bobbie

every evening after dinner. Finally, just a week before Christmas, at his urging, she told Bobbie about his proposal. She held the phone where he could hear the child's response.

"Really, Mum? Really and truly? You're going to marry Mr. Ashley, and we're all going to live in his big house and be a real family after all?"

"It seems so, Bobbie dear, just as you envisioned it."

"Oh, Mum, it's wonderful. I can't wait to tell everyone. When are you coming for me?"

"Soon, I hope. Mr. Bernard is working very hard."

"I miss you, Mum. I wish you'd come soon."

"As soon as I can, Bobbie, I promise."

"She sounds pleased enough," Alan said when the conversation ended.

"She had it all planned weeks ago."

"Did she really?"

"Oh, yes, but I told her that it was just a fairytale."

Alan touched her hair. "Children's dreams do come true sometimes, though mine never did until now."

"Alan, are you sure you can accept Bobbie? How will you feel when you have children of your own?" She felt him stiffen.

"We'll cross that bridge when we come to it," he said. "What we must think of now is getting Bobbie here and settled in."

"She settles in wherever she goes and makes friends easily."

"An excellent trait."

"I know she sounds very young, but you must understand that she's older inside."

"She appears resilient."

"Children survive what we would find crushing, but I want to protect her from having to survive more."

"Next year we'll decorate for Christmas, Lenore. There was always a huge tree in the corner of the drawing room and piles of gifts—which I opened alone, I might add. Bobbie won't have to do that."

"I don't want her spoiled."

"Slightly indulged, perhaps?"

"Not even that."

"Can you spoil a child with love?"

"No, only with things."

"Doesn't she deserve..."

"I want her to have what she needs, but she's become accustomed to doing without luxuries, as have I, and it would overwhelm her."

"Surely there are things she needs that we might shop for."

"I'll make a list of those when she's here."

"You're going to thwart me at every turn."

"I'm going to try." She moved away from him slightly. "It's not a good idea for us to sit like this every evening."

"Why not? There's a great deal to talk about."

"We don't talk, Alan."

He put his lips against her temple and moved down her jawline, finally finding her lips. Unable to resist, he unpinned her hair at the same time.

"I wish you wouldn't do that," she began. "I've told you I can't think when you do."

"I don't want you to think." His lips moved to her throat. "I love you so," he murmured. "Wanting you the way I do is painful."

She pushed herself away from him. "I know."

"You know?"

"My emotions are in such a jumble, and when I'm with you, close to you like this, I'm not sure I'm strong enough to deny you anything you want."

"Then you're not as ignorant in these matters as you thought."

"If I knew more, I might be able to deal with my feelings."

"Perhaps we should consider letting Thomas Greer marry us quietly this week."

"Isn't that rushing things?"

"Does it seem so to you?"

"A little."

"We spoke of remodeling, and I want to have my parents' suite done over for us. I was thinking that my childhood room would be perfect for Bobbie. It has windows overlooking the front, and a window seat could be built in, giving her a perfect place to read."

"All she wants is the Pink Lady over her bed."

He pulled her closer. "All I want is you in mine."

****

As he opened the door to his room that night, he was aware that someone was inside, near the window he judged, but he felt an odd lack of fear. "Who's there?" he called out.

"Rycroft, sir."

"Ah. I won't ask why you're here."

"Where is Bobbie?"

"Why do you want to know?"

"She's my daughter."

"Your daughter."

"That's right. I've been looking for her for a long time."

"And now what?"

"I'm going to keep the promise I made to her years ago, that I'd come for her someday."

"How long has it been?"

"Too long. A lifetime, it seems."

"You realize that she's very attached to Lenore Seldon?"

"That's how I tracked her here."

"How did you get in here?"

"That isn't important. I didn't enter your home

to take anything or do you harm."

"No, of course you didn't." Alan closed the door. I'm assuming that you couldn't come for Bobbie before now."

"I didn't want to. It was better that she was hidden."

"Lenore didn't hide her."

"No, sir, I realize that, but she did me a favor. I've known for some time that her home was in Brookston, so I spoke with Daniel Sutherland..."

"When?" asked Alan sharply.

"Two weeks ago. He told me that she was working for you."

Alan felt his way toward the chair near the unlit fireplace and sat down. "If you'd spoken to him a few days later, he wouldn't have told you."

"I know that."

"Do you know about Robert Harcourt?"

There was a long silence. Finally, the other man spoke. "I know about him."

"So you feel you have to take Bobbie now in order to protect her."

"Yes."

"Why is Bobbie a pawn?"

"I can't tell you. I wouldn't want to involve you."

"I owe you a great debt."

"You owe me nothing. We were soldiers."

"As I said, Bobbie is much attached to Miss Seldon. I've asked Lenore to marry me, you see. My attorney is trying to get custody for her, and when we're married, I'd like to adopt Bobbie and give her my name and all the advantages that go with it. She'll have the best of everything. Education, travel, the opportunity to live in a home with two people who love her..."

"I love her, too," Albert Rycroft said softly. "She's my daughter."

"I'm going to tell you where she is, Albert. Not

telling you would be morally wrong. But consider what she could have here and what you can offer her. I have the feeling that you live a hidden life."

"But not a dishonorable one."

"I didn't mean to imply that. Forgive me. But you're a man, and she's a child. Lenore worries that she's had to grow up too fast. We want to give her childhood back to her."

"Can you guarantee that Robert Harcourt won't get her by fair means or foul? I know about Roberta. I know about Lenore Seldon's brother."

"Did he kill them?"

"I can't prove it. No one can."

"Does he hold something over you?"

"No, he wants something from me."

"Why can't you give it to him in exchange for Bobbie's safety?"

"It's not mine to give."

"I see. To answer your question, I can't guarantee anything, but I have faith that she will be safe here with Lenore and me."

"Faith? Faith in what?" For the first time, Albert Rycroft sounded unsure of himself.

"I'm not certain, Albert. I've spent these past years raging against God because I'm blind, but lately I've begun to realize that I can't discount Him entirely."

"I live by my wits, Captain Ashley. I can't afford to deal in faith."

"I understand."

"Where is Bobbie?"

Alan took a deep breath. "At the Greenfield Children's Home."

"At...good God! She's been within reach all the time."

"I don't understand."

"My sister's daughter is there, placed by her stepmother because she's slow. I've been going to see her regularly for months."

"And you never saw Bobbie?"

"I always go at night after the children have gone upstairs. Miss Ervin lets Rebekah stay down to spend time with me."

"A tangled web."

"Are you going to warn them about me?"

"No, but I'd ask this much of you. Don't simply take her and run. Talk to her. Make sure that she wants to go with you. I believe you love your daughter and want the best for her. Perhaps neither of us has considered what's really best. Perhaps Bobbie is the only one who can tell us."

He was aware of movement and heard the soft sound of the door opening and closing. Realizing what he had done, he wondered if he had closed the door to his future with Lenore. Yet he knew he'd had no choice. Albert Rycroft deserved an end to his quest, and Bobbie...Bobbie deserved the opportunity to choose. He hoped her father would give it to her.

Chapter Thirteen

"You told him? You told him where to find Bobbie? How could you do it?" Lenore rose so hastily from the breakfast table that her napkin spilled from her lap. "I've got to get to her before he does. We have to get away before he takes her."

"Lenore, please, darling."

"Please? You betrayed me, Alan. I trusted you with Bobbie's life, and now...how could you do it?"

He followed her upstairs to her room and walked in without knocking. "He had a right to know, Lenore. I owed him something."

"Owed him something? And do you owe me nothing? You said you loved me. Are you hoping he'll take her? Hoping she'll be conveniently out of the way, and this legal nightmare will end?"

"No, of course not." He reached for her, but she stepped away.

"You've always been accustomed to having your own way, haven't you? You do what's best for Alan Ashley and don't worry about anyone else. You've seemed different these past few weeks, but you aren't. You're still the same arrogant, self-centered man you always were."

"Lenore, please listen to me."

"I've listened too much already. I've wasted time in which I could have been getting Bobbie to safety."

"You understand that you're breaking the law by taking her across the border. And you said once that you couldn't in good conscience keep her away from her father."

"I don't care. She's mine, Alan, mine. I've had

173

her for almost six years. I've been the only real mother she ever had. Her own didn't want her, and her father...her father took his time coming for her. It's too late now. He can't have her. She's mine."

"He had his reasons. I have the feeling that he felt she was safer with you for the time being."

"She's going to be safe with me forever."

"Mr. Alan." Mrs. Swane stood in the doorway.

"What is it, Mrs. Swane?"

"Leave her alone."

"What?"

The housekeeper advanced into the room. "Go downstairs, Mr. Alan."

The authority in her voice that he remembered from childhood moved him to obey. Standing at the top of the stairs, he heard Mrs. Swane speaking in measured, even tones.

"This isn't best for either of you, Miss Seldon, but I understand how you feel. She's your child, and you must do what you consider is best for her."

He turned to confront the woman, then paused to gather his scattered thoughts. He was convinced that he'd done the right thing concerning Albert Rycroft, but he was counting on the man to consider the best choice for Bobbie, which was leaving her here. He'd been naive, and now the impact of what the other choice might mean hit him full force.

"Miss Seldon, if you'll sit down and calm yourself, I'll pack for you. You need to think things through before you leave the house."

Alan listened for Lenore's reply, but there was none. In the silence, he assumed Mrs. Swane was making good her offer to pack. For the first time in months, he cursed his blindness. If he had his sight, if he could see what was happening... if, if, if. He struck the banister a stinging blow with his open palm.

"It's very cold this morning, Miss Seldon.

Walking to the bus station isn't a good idea. You must keep well. I'll telephone for a taxi."

Alan thought he heard Lenore say something, but the words were muffled.

"I'll pack the rest of your things, what you can't take with you, and see that they're sent to you when you're settled."

"Thank you, Mrs. Swane." Lenore sounded slightly calmer. "It's for the best."

"I don't think it's in your best interest or the child's and certainly not Mr. Alan's. He loves you. If he acted on his conscience, it doesn't mean he doesn't care about your feelings."

Lenore didn't reply.

"I think that's everything, Miss Seldon. Put on this sweater under your coat in case the bus is chilly."

Hearing their footsteps, Alan hurried downstairs and sequestered himself in his study. In a few minutes, he heard the door. "Has she gone?"

"Yes."

"Mrs. Swane, I had to tell the man about his daughter. If he takes her—and I tried to convince him that she would be better off here—it's better than having her grandfather win in court."

"You said he wouldn't."

"A case is never decided until it's decided. Roth seemed to feel that she was in danger of being taken by the grandfather before we could even get into court."

"I've never had a child, Mr. Alan. You know my baby was stillborn soon after my husband died. But I can feel Miss Seldon's fear."

"I feel it, too, Mrs. Swane. She feels helpless, and God knows I've lived with being helpless and hopeless for years. It's galling for a man to be dependent on others to lay out his clothes and lead him around..."

"We all need help, Mr. Alan. That doesn't mean we're helpless. No one sees you that way."

"I see myself that way."

"That's still the problem, isn't it?" She closed the door softly behind her.

\*\*\*\*

Alan telephoned Mrs. Fenton and asked her to send Rod to drive him to the office. He was putting his day's schedule, neatly transcribed into Braille, into his briefcase when the phone rang. "Harcourt's man has arrived in Rumers Crossing. It's imperative for Miss Seldon to be careful," Emory Roth said.

"She's gone."

"Gone?"

Alan told him what had happened.

"You know what this means, Mr. Ashley. She's walking into a dangerous situation for herself and the child."

"Unless Albert Rycroft gets to the child first, and he's certainly had a head start." He explained the previous night's encounter.

"Is that what you want?"

"You know it's not, but it might be the best for the child if the only alternative is having her grandfather snatch her and wreak havoc with her little soul and body."

Roth blew out his breath tiredly. "I'll go up to Greenfield myself and see if I can sort things out."

"I'd be grateful."

"Call your attorney and see if he can expedite the custody decision. Today, if possible."

"I'm sure he'll try."

Alan pushed the button to end the call and dialed Sam's number.

\*\*\*\*

"I have sixty days for her," Sam said when he telephoned Alan just before noon. "I'm leaving now to drive to Greenfield. Miss Seldon hasn't had time to do anything yet. She'll have to sneak away tonight after dark. The director, Miss Ervin, is entirely in sympathy with her, but she's bound by the law."

"I'd like to go with you, Sam."

"Is that a good idea?"

"I can't sit here and let her slip away from me without trying one more time to convince her to stay."

"Alan, I understand what you did and why you did it, but Miss Seldon isn't going to forgive you so easily."

"I know that. I just need to see her."

"All right, I'll be there in half an hour."

\*\*\*\*

Emory Roth flagged them down half a block from the Home. "The social worker with the vendetta against Miss Seldon and the little girl is raising Cain in there. Apparently she saw Miss Seldon arriving. She's threatening to take the child to a new placement."

"She can't do that," Sam said. "Judge Morrill just granted Lenore Seldon temporary custody for sixty days pending a permanency hearing."

"Has there been any sign of Albert Rycroft?" Alan asked.

"He may be here, but he hasn't made his presence known," the investigator replied. "I'm trying to get a photograph of him so that we know who we're looking for."

"What about Harcourt?"

"His picture I have, and the security men have a copy. I'd suggest you take those papers in, Bernard, and run off that shrew."

"With pleasure. Alan, I think you should wait in the car. I'll try to persuade Miss Seldon to speak with you. She may see things in a more positive light with these papers in hand."

"No, I'm going in with you, Sam. She has to

understand that I'm not apologizing for doing the morally correct thing."

"Suit yourself."

They could hear the shouting as soon as they entered the building. "I can certainly take her under the circumstances. Her custody order forbade any contact with Lenore Seldon."

"On the contrary, Miss Burk, the forbidding was a mean, unnecessary act, motivated totally by your petty prejudices."

Sam and Alan followed the voices to a small office just past the stairs. There, three women faced each other defiantly. Lenore Seldon stood with her arms crossed around Bobbie as if shielding her. The girl's face was a study in pure terror.

"Excuse me," Sam said. "I brought the custody papers, Miss Seldon."

A middle-aged woman in an ill-fitting suit whirled around. "Who are you?"

Sam dropped Alan's arm and stepped into the office. "I'm Samuel Bernard, Miss Seldon's attorney. Judge Merrill signed papers this morning granting her temporary custody of Bobbie for sixty days."

The woman's hard face mirrored shock. "I don't believe that."

Sam extracted the sheaf of papers from his briefcase and held them out. "The only stipulation is that she not be removed from the state of New York until a final determination is made."

"How did you get him to sign these papers?" the social worker demanded.

"I simply presented the facts, Miss Burk, and he agreed that it wasn't necessary for the child to remain at Greenfield."

"But he didn't have my report."

"On the contrary, the state furnished him a copy."

"Why wasn't I notified?"

"That was out of my hands. I only requested the report for him." He handed the papers to Lenore. "We'll move ahead with the petition for permanent custody now."

Constance Ervin sank into the chair behind her desk. "Thank God," she murmured.

"Does this mean I can go with you, Mum?" A small, soft voice pierced Alan's consciousness.

"Yes, Bobbie dear, yes, you can."

"Are we going back to Mr. Ashley's beautiful house?"

"I..." Lenore began, but Alan stepped through the door and interrupted her.

"My housekeeper, Mrs. Swane, and I are looking forward to having you with us, Bobbie."

Lenore didn't loosen her protective clutch. "It's almost Christmas, Mr. Ashley. Bobbie and I will spend the holidays here."

"Don't you have to work, Mum?"

"Suppose we discuss all this?" Alan said smoothly.

"There's nothing to discuss." Lenore's voice sounded sharp and accusing.

"I think there is," Alan said almost as sharply. "Forgive me, Miss Ervin, I'm Alan Ashley, Miss Seldon's employer. I wonder if there's somewhere Miss Seldon and I might talk privately."

"There's the library," Bobbie said. "It's my favorite place. Lois and Rebekah and I made a reading corner, and we go there every night after supper."

"That sounds like the very place." Alan turned slightly, gesturing in the direction of the door. "Shall we, Miss Seldon?"

He sensed her as she came nearer and reached to take her arm. She stiffened. "I don't know this place," he reminded her.

In the room that Bobbie had called the library,

179

Lenore showed him to one of three worn chairs. "There's nothing to discuss."

"I don't believe you thanked Sam for his efforts on your behalf."

"I'll do that before he leaves."

"I'll be glad for you to remain here for the week, but I'll expect you back in Rumers Crossing on the twenty-sixth. The week between Christmas and New Year's is quite full with end-of-the-year inventories and such."

"I no longer work for you, Mr. Ashley."

"Last night you were planning to marry me."

"That was before..." She burst into tears and covered her face with her hands.

Alan had her in his arms immediately. "Lenore, my darling, everything will be all right. I love you. Bobbie will have every advantage, everything you want for her."

"I want her safe."

"She'll be safe."

"You can't be sure of that."

"I can have faith."

"I can't, and your sudden claim to it is a little late."

"For whom, Lenore? You or myself?"

"I have to take Bobbie away where she'll be safe."

"Sam knows what you're thinking of doing. He could report it to Judge Merrill, who would rescind his order and might even issue a warrant for your arrest if you try to take her."

She moved away from him. "I'm sure Mr. Bernard will do whatever you tell him to do."

"That wasn't a threat, Lenore. I'm sorry you took it that way." He reached to find her, but she backed further away. "All right, stay here and consider your options. If Albert Rycroft wants his daughter, he'll find a way to take her, and there's nothing you can do about it. Perhaps he'll give her a choice."

"A choice?"

"I suggested it. I didn't just throw her away, Lenore. I discussed with him in detail about the advantages of leaving her with you...and with me. It's been six years. She's firmly bonded with you now."

"She still believes he'll come for her someday."

"And so he has, but there are always ways to work things out. He doesn't have to take her to be part of her life."

"Do you honestly think he'd let you adopt her?"

"I don't know. That seems to be irrelevant right now, as our marriage isn't definite anymore."

"I can't marry you. Not now."

The old chill settled around his heart. "Did you stop loving me this morning, or did you ever really love me at all?"

"I..."

"Love is very new to me, Lenore. I didn't have it from my parents, nor did I feel anything for them except a rather wistful desire to be part of their lives. I wasn't in love with Elise."

"You asked her to marry you."

"You had what you term an understanding with David Broome, and yet you said that you didn't understand what being in love really meant."

"We've both been impulsive," she said, retreating slightly from her anger. "I filled a void in your life just because I was there. Marriage is more than that."

"You filled an emptiness in my soul, Lenore."

"I can't marry you. I have a responsibility to Bobbie."

"Which I have offered to help you meet."

"No...no, it's wrong. I've known it from the beginning, and now...please leave me alone. Please."

She ran from the room. A few minutes later,

Sam Bernard came in. "Are you ready to go?"

"Yes."

"I take it that you and Miss Seldon didn't reach an understanding."

"She has rejected me quite thoroughly."

"She's frightened, Alan."

Alan took Sam's arm. "It's done."

The bitterness in his friend's voice chilled Sam Bernard's heart.

Chapter Fourteen

On Christmas Eve, when Rod brought him home, Alan handed the man an envelope. "I'm sorry I've had to ask you to take on the added responsibility of driving me again."

"I don't mind, Mr. Ashley, and that's not necessary."

"Please."

Rod took the envelope. "Thanks, Mr. Ashley. I'll put it to good use."

"With two growing children, I'm sure there's always good use for extra funds."

"Yes, sir, you're right about that."

"We'll remain closed through the twenty-sixth, as usual."

"Shall I come for you the next day?"

Alan hesitated with his hand on the door. "I hope Miss Seldon will have returned by then." *But I'm not counting on it.*

"Yes, sir, I hope so, too, but you can give me a call if you need me."

"I'll do that. Enjoy your holiday, Rod, and give my regards to your wife."

"Merry Christmas, Mr. Ashley."

Alan listened as the sounds of the car faded. *Merry Christmas. Tonight I might have had a family. Tonight I might have made love to the only woman I ever truly cared for. The problem is, she didn't love me enough.*

The telephone was ringing in his study as he entered the house. "Merry Christmas, Uncle Alan. Daddy will be over to get you around seven."

"You'll have to excuse me tonight, Bea."

"But Uncle Alan, we always spend Christmas Eve and Christmas Day together."

"I'm sorry, but you'll have to do without me. Goodnight." He hung up, berating himself for hurting Bea. She loved him, had loved him since she could crawl into his lap and read the bumpty book. *But she's fourteen now, old enough to accept that things change, and they have. I dared to hope, but I was a fool.*

Now he was crushed, ground down as he had been when he woke in darkness and heard the doctor say that it would be forever. He went into the empty kitchen. Mrs. Swane had gone to visit her sister, as she did every Christmas. Expecting him to be well fed by the Bernards, she had not left any meals prepared, but he felt around in the refrigerator to see what was there. Some bananas, a plate of cold chicken from the night before. Well, that would do.

He was eating his solitary dinner in the kitchen when the front door chimed, but he ignored it. Probably Sam. He would give up and go away. Alan put his elbows on the table and leaned his head into his hands.

*I'm sulking like a child, and I hate myself for it. But I brought it on myself. I trusted her, let myself love her, allowed myself to hope that I might be a normal man in spite of everything. But it's over. Over.*

He spent Christmas Day in his study, where he lighted the fire Mrs. Swane had laid before leaving. Attempting to make notes on the Braille writer, he found he had no concentration and spent the rest of the day sitting in front of the fire and consuming a bottle of brandy. The raised dots on his watch told him it was almost midnight when he woke in a stupor.

In the kitchen he finished the cold chicken and went up to bed, thinking grudgingly of Lenore. Where was she? Waiting to sneak away over the border? Already there? Had she thought of him at all or regretted their parting?

He tried to put the memory of her warm softness out of his mind and found it impossible.

****

"You're too late for breakfast and too early for lunch," Mrs. Swane told him when he came downstairs at midmorning. "But I made cinnamon rolls, and there's coffee."

"Did you have a pleasant visit?" he asked.

"Oh, yes. Nola's son and his family spent the day with us."

"I'm glad."

"Is there any news of..."

"No."

"I'm sorry."

"Perhaps it's for the best after all."

She watched him consume three cinnamon rolls in short order. "Didn't the Bernards feed you yesterday?"

"I didn't go."

"Why?"

"I wasn't in the mood to socialize, Mrs. Swane," he snapped.

"Your mood isn't particularly sociable this morning, either."

"I apologize for lashing out at you."

"A child in the house might have been nice," she said after a few minutes.

"It didn't happen. Besides, I'm too old to take on the responsibilities of a family."

"Are you?"

"I want things my own way. I wouldn't be able to accommodate anyone else in my life."

"Maybe not." She picked up his cup and saucer

185

and took it to the sink. "I'll serve lunch at one."

Alan had just stepped into the foyer when he heard a key in the front door. His heart lurched. "Lenore?"

"Yes."

"You came back."

"Bobbie refused to go with me Christmas night."

"Refused?"

"She said she didn't want me to get into trouble and that perhaps Mr. Bernard could get permanent custody for me after all. I didn't tell her about her father."

"You didn't bring her with you?"

"She asked to stay a few more days. Rebekah's birthday is tomorrow, and the children are planning a party for her."

"I remember you mentioned her when we spoke of the Home. She's the child with some learning difficulties but very talented artistically."

"That's right. Since the children left public school because of repeated bullying, they've taught themselves, and Bobbie has made Rebekah her special project."

"What will happen to her when Bobbie leaves?"

"Someone else will pick up with her. Lois, probably, although she's not as patient as Bobbie."

"Perhaps the child needs a special school..."

"No. Not an institution."

"I didn't mean that."

"Her stepmother convinced her father to send her to Greenfield because she was slow. At least there she's loved for herself. And her uncle visits her regularly."

"Her uncle?"

"Someone named Avram Rykovsky."

Alan tried to sort out what she was telling him. "Lenore, in the confusion, I'm not sure I told you everything. When I told Rycroft that Bobbie was at

Greenfield, he was clearly shocked. He said that he'd been visiting a niece there for several months."

"Albert Rycroft is Rebekah's uncle? He's Avram Rykovsky?"

"It would seem so. Was he there during Christmas?"

"I don't think so."

"Perhaps he's changed his mind."

"Or he's biding his time. Constance said he was trying to get Rebekah's father to let him have Rebekah. Maybe he'll take both of them. I shouldn't have left her."

"We'll drive to Greenfield for her tomorrow evening after she's been part of the festivities. Then Emory Roth can shift the guards from there to here."

"You understand that I'm only continuing to work for you in order to pay the expenses of the legal proceedings."

"Whatever you want, Lenore. I won't press you." Hope died in him a second time. "You might let Mrs. Swane know you're here. Luncheon will be at one, and I'd like to do some work before then, if you don't mind."

"Yes, sir, I'll only be a few minutes. I..."

The tears in her voice broke his resolve, and he had her in his arms before she finished speaking. "Lenore, I thought I'd lost you. I was afraid that I'd never see you again."

Lenore struggled only briefly before she collapsed against him. "I should have taken her. We could be in Canada where no one would ever find us."

"What kind of a life would that be for either of you—always on the run, always looking over your shoulder?"

"Her father will take her sooner or later."

"Things can be worked out. He doesn't have to lose her completely. She hardly remembers him."

"She remembers enough."

"But you didn't tell her that he was here."

"No. but I can't stop thinking that if he doesn't take her, it's possible that her grandfather might gain custody or even take her by force."

He held her away from him. "Stop it, Lenore. You're letting fear control you."

She was silent for a moment, and he sensed that she was studying him.

"Do you think I wasn't afraid when I woke in the darkness that would become my world for the rest of my life? Don't you think I'm afraid now? I stepped outside the protective wall I'd built around my life and allowed myself to love you, and a short while later, you rejected me."

"I felt betrayed."

"I understand all that, but can you understand what I feel?"

"I'm sorry."

"That I love you?"

"We're so different."

"Are we? You're everything that I thought had passed me by forever. I'm no longer a brash youth, Lenore. I need you. You anticipate my needs almost before I'm aware of them myself."

"I did the same for Judge Sutherland," she said.

"I'm quite sure you did, but I like to think that you extend yourself a little more for me."

"If I can be your..." She stopped.

"Be what, Lenore? My eyes? In a way, you are, but more than that, you're my heart."

"You hardly know me. I came off the streets practically penniless, and I have a responsibility to Bobbie..."

"Which I want to share with you, if you'll let me." He drew her back into his arms, and this time she came more willingly. "There's a strength in you that you don't even recognize." He took her face in his hands. "And you see me, I believe, as a man, just a man, not a blind man."

He found her lips and kissed her. "You don't have to be afraid of loving me, Lenore."

"Your friends will say..."

"My true friends will rejoice with me."

"But if marrying me hurts you...if it hurts Bobbie..."

"Only losing you would hurt me, and as for Bobbie, you said she wants to come here." He took her face in his hands. "I love you so very much. Now go and tell Mrs. Swane you're back, and we'll talk about the arrangements for bringing Bobbie here tomorrow after the birthday party."

****

They lingered over a late supper and, after Lenore had returned the dishes to the kitchen, they sat together in front of the fire sharing soft kisses. It was midnight before he saw her to her room. "Sleep well, my love."

"I'm not sure that I can sleep at all," she whispered.

****

Lenore's body jerked upright as she heard Bobbie calling her.

*Mum! Mum! Help me, Mum!*

She threw back the covers. "I'm coming, Bobbie! I'm coming."

*Mum, I can't see you. I can't find you. I'm scared, Mum. I'm so scared.*

"Bobbie! Bobbie!" She found herself standing in the hall wearing only her nightgown. Her fear crept back like the cold seeping into her bones. Groping her way through the darkness to her room, she promised herself that she would have Bobbie with her before tomorrow night and that no one, not even Alan Ashley, would keep her from doing what had to be done.

Chapter Fifteen

They were about to leave for the office the next morning when Sam Bernard arrived. He didn't return Lenore's greeting. "I need to speak with you, Alan. Privately."

"We'll step into the study."

"It's about Bobbie, isn't it?" Lenore clutched the banister for support.

Alan slipped his arm around her. "*Is* it about Bobbie, Sam?"

"I'd prefer to speak with you privately," the attorney hedged.

"If it concerns Bobbie, Lenore must know."

"Alan..."

"Let's have it, Sam."

The attorney stepped closer. "Last night there was a fire at the Home. No one got out."

Lenore crumpled to the floor.

\*\*\*\*

Mrs. Swane knocked on the study door. "She's awake. I think you should go up."

"All right. Has she said anything?"

"She blames herself, of course. Have you found out any more?"

"I spoke with the fire marshal. He said it was the furnace. Lenore had mentioned that it frequently gave trouble. I'd planned to speak with Miss Ervin about it today, when we went to get Bobbie, and offer to replace it."

"The county was responsible."

"The county has no money."

"You did all you could, Mr. Alan."

"Did I? I've been sitting here wondering about that."

"Go up to Miss Lenore. She needs you."

*****

He found Lenore curled on the loveseat before the fire, clutching a china doll in her arms. "This is all I have left," she murmured, breaking into tears as Alan joined her. "Bobbie asked me to bring her doll home to wait for her here. It's her most precious possession, the last thing her father ever gave her. She named it for him...Alberta." Lenore buried her face against the doll. "I left her to die. I left my little girl to die."

Alan gathered her in his arms. "You couldn't know. I'm so sorry, my darling Lenore. She was the daughter I never thought to have."

"All those children...Constance...she was my friend, the first I'd had in such a long time."

"I told the fire marshal that I'd see to the burial. They deserve more than a pauper's grave."

"Do you think she knew, Alan?"

"It all happened very fast."

"She was so brave. She never complained about anything. That awful little room where we lived, cardboard in her shoes, being taken to the Home. She never complained about any of it."

Alan winced at the pictures her words painted in his mind. "She learned that from you, I'm sure."

"Sometimes it was as if she were taking care of me."

"You took care of each other."

Lenore shook her head. "No, I didn't take care of her. Oh, Alan, I left her to die."

****

Mrs. Swane brought a light lunch to Lenore's sitting room. "Mr. Roth is on the telephone. He says it's urgent."

Alan was gone only a few minutes. "Lenore,

Emory Roth will be here shortly, and Sam Bernard, as well. You'll want to hear what Roth has to say."

"What can he say? Bobbie's dead. I wish her father had taken her after all. I'd have given her to him rather than let her die that way."

He sat beside her again and took her hands. "That's what Roth is going to discuss, Lenore. From what his men reported, Albert Rycroft *did* take Bobbie."

\*\*\*\*

"I've told her what your men observed," Alan said, resting his hands on Lenore's shoulders as she sat on the sofa in the study. "Now we'd both like to hear the full report."

"There were two security men, one in front and one in the alley beside the kitchen."

"Obviously Albert Rycroft found his way in, just like he did here," Alan interrupted.

"Just before the explosion, the man stationed in the alley saw something moving and went to investigate. He saw two people, an adult and a child, hurrying away, and he ran after them. Then he heard the explosion, which made him turn around. My men responded to the explosion first, trying to help those inside, but it was no use. When they tried to follow the man and the child again, it was too late. We have to assume, based on what you told us, that Albert Rycroft took his daughter."

"Or her grandfather took her," Lenore said.

"I think not, Miss Seldon. The child was going willingly. She was holding the hand of the adult and walking along with him. He wasn't dragging her. Nothing suggested fear or coercion, and my men are well-trained to observe things like that."

There was a long silence. "If I could only be sure that her father has her."

"I think you can, Miss Seldon. We know that Robert Harcourt is well under six feet, and the man seen leaving the vicinity was much taller."

"I'm three inches over six feet," Alan said. "I remember Albert Rycroft as being almost as tall as I am."

"Do you have any idea where he took her?" Lenore asked.

Emory Roth nodded. "I was able to learn that he has a British passport."

"So it's really over," Lenore murmured. "I'll never see her again." She closed her eyes. "Oh, Bobbie, you were *my* best little girl, *my* shining star, too."

Alan circled the sofa and took her in his arms.

****

Alan was surprised when Lenore appeared at breakfast the next morning. "Surely you aren't thinking of going to the office."

"I need to work," she replied. "Thankfully no one at Ashley Enterprises knows about Bobbie. I couldn't bear their sympathy."

"Lenore, are you still angry with me for telling Albert Rycroft where to find Bobbie?"

"In a way, but in the end it saved her life."

"If there'd been no fire..."

"She was mine, but she was his, too, and I...I'd have been selfish to deny them the chance to be together." She brought her plate to the table and sat down. "I realize there was nothing else you could do."

"I considered that telling him might cost me everything."

"Yet you told him. It's what I'd expect of you, Alan."

"Sometimes we don't have choices in life."

****

Emory Roth telephoned just before noon. "I have more information, Mr. Ashley. Albert Rycroft used his passport to board a freighter bound for

Palestine."

"I see. Well, he's beyond our reach, isn't he?"

"And there's something else. No one remembers seeing a child with him."

"He'd have had to smuggle her aboard, wouldn't he? She had no passport."

"That's true, but there's always the possibility that he left her here with someone. I can look into it."

"I can't believe that he'd take her and then leave her behind."

"I'll admit that's not probable. What more do you want me to do in the matter?"

"For now, nothing. She's with her father, the person who has more right to her than anyone else. At least she's not in danger of being taken by Robert Harcourt."

"Shall I keep an eye on him?"

"Harcourt? No, if he traced her to Greenfield, he assumes that she died in the fire."

"Then I suppose, our business is concluded."

"You've done exceptional work, Roth. I'll expect your charges."

Alan hung up and leaned his head in his hands. The cat-and-mouse game had ended. Bobbie was gone. At least she hadn't met the horrible fate of the other children in the Home, and yet the question nagged him—had he left anything undone? Any possibility overlooked? Anything unsaid to Albert Rycroft? If he had, he couldn't put his finger on it. Now, somehow, he and Lenore would have to move on, hopefully together.

****

That evening, Alan caught Lenore on her way upstairs after dinner. "Don't shut me out," he said. "I've lost her, too. Somehow I already thought of her as mine."

"I don't mean to shut you out. It still seems so

unreal."

"And I don't mean to press you, Lenore, but I think we need each other more than ever." He took her arm and started for the drawing room. "Would you like some music tonight?"

"Whatever you'd like."

"See if you can find some Mozart."

She went to the music cabinet. "Were you always so knowledgeable about music?" He recognized her valiant effort at a normal conversation.

"I always liked it. After I lost my sight, it was one of the few pleasures I could still enjoy until I learned Braille."

For awhile, they listened in silence, but when Lenore rose to change the record, Alan said, "Don't put on another. I'd like to talk."

She sat down again.

"I still want to marry you, Lenore."

"You're all I have left."

"Don't marry me for that."

"No, I'm not, Alan. I...love you. I'll always grieve for Bobbie, but I hope I can give you a child, a son of your own."

Abruptly, Alan rose and strode to the fireplace. "Lenore, I must tell you something. I should have told you sooner, but..."

She looked up. "What is it?"

"I will accept your decision not to marry me based on what I'm going to tell you. I'll help you find other living arrangements so that our association will be strictly professional. I'll even find you a position with one of my subsidiaries if you feel that you must disassociate yourself from me entirely."

"Alan what are you talking about? I don't understand."

"You will. When I was fourteen and in boarding school, I was quite ill. Mumps, scarlet fever, pneumonia. I was so ill that the doctor sent for my parents, but they were busy elsewhere and didn't come for a long time. Eventually, my father came, but he left after speaking with the doctor and without seeing me."

"Oh, Alan."

"Before I left Choate for Harvard, the doctor asked me to come to his office. He was very kind, but very blunt, when he told me what the combined illnesses, especially the mumps, had probably done to my developing body." He turned around. "And so, my dear Lenore, though I assure you that I can fulfill my husbandly duties, I can never father a child."

The long, punishing silence refueled the frustration of his darkness.

If only he could see her, read the emotions in her eyes and expression.

As the silence continued, he supposed that she must be shocked beyond words. After all, she was still a young woman.

He had justified saying nothing to her earlier because of Bobbie, but now circumstances had changed. Having lost Bobbie, she would naturally want a child of her own.

He heard her rise and start toward him, stopping just short of his reach. "You've lost so much," she said. "We both have."

"I no longer wallow in self-pity, though it's not entirely foreign to my mind."

"We're both learning that self-pity is a selfish thing."

"It's unproductive, certainly."

"I felt that we were worlds apart because of your wealth and position."

"And do you still feel the same?"

"In a way, I do, but...I think for the first time I see us as two people whose souls have been wounded repeatedly and yet somehow survived."

"I like the sentiment. I agree with it."

"I grew up with David Broome. We were comfortable together, and I've tried to remember what I felt for him. That's why my feelings for you frightened me. They're so strong...so..."

"Physical?"

He wondered if he'd really heard her almost inaudible, "Yes."

"Perhaps that's because you were only a girl then, and now you're a woman. Perhaps you were ready for that attraction...for desire." He put his hands on her shoulders. "I love you, Lenore. I love you as I never knew it was possible to love another human being." He felt the tremor that ran through her body. "We can adopt, my darling. There are so many children these days who need good homes."

She leaned her head against his shoulder. "Could we have a very quiet wedding, Alan? Just the Bernards and the Youngs and the Vannoys—and of course, Rod and his family and Mrs. Swane."

"When?"

"Whenever you like."

"Next week. I'll speak with Thomas Greer and arrange for Le Monde to cater a luncheon afterwards at the office. We should share the day with everyone there. Later we'll go away to the Catskills, to a little hotel where I used to stay when I was at Harvard."

She relaxed against him and savored his hands as they stroked her back.

"I mentioned having my parents' suite remodeled to suit us, but you can oversee that after we're married. The bedroom I occupy now has a large bed that will accommodate us for the time being."

"Alan..."

"Are you blushing, my dear Miss Seldon?"

"I'm afraid so. Do you deliberately try to shock

197

me?"

"Sometimes, perhaps." He found her lips and kissed her briefly. "Don't be afraid of me. Inexperienced as we both are, you won't recognize my clumsiness."

"I've always thought of you as graceful. Everything you do is so fluid, so seemingly effortless."

"I've worked hard to make it seem so, but sometimes, at the end of the day, I'm exhausted from trying to impress people as a seeing person."

"I never realized that."

"I didn't mean for you to."

"But now you'll let me help more."

"You do help, Lenore. Just your very presence is soothing."

She removed his glasses and laid them aside. "You don't have to wear these at home."

"I'm told that I'm not a monster, but I know there is visible damage."

"Your eyes are cloudy and somewhat unfocused, and there are small scars under them, like starbursts. That's all."

"That's enough."

Drawing his face down to hers, she put her lips against one eyelid, then the other. "We'll find a baby boy with blue eyes just like yours."

****

The fire sputtered, rousing them from the warmth and security of each other's arms.

"It's late," Alan said, rising and lifting Lenore with him. "Telephone Ellen tomorrow and tell her the news. She'll want to help you with your plans."

"I know she'll be glad. What about Mr. Bernard?"

"Sam has been aware of my feelings for a long time." Alan banked the fire expertly before taking her arm.

At the top of the landing they shared several more long kisses before going to their respective rooms.

"Sleep well, my darling," he whispered. "I love you."

Chapter Sixteen

The next day, Ellen Bernard swept Lenore out of the office before lunch, insisting that the after-Christmas sales couldn't wait, and a few minutes later, Mrs. Fenton came in. "There's a young man on the telephone who insists on speaking with you, Mr. Ashley. He won't give his name, but he says it's urgent."

Alan reached for the telephone. "Thank you, Mrs. Fenton. I'll take it." He lifted the receiver. "Alan Ashley."

"Bobbie Rycroft is inside the first confessional booth at the Catholic church in Greenfield."

"Who is this?"

"Please, Mr. Ashley, go get her now. Please. Before the other man finds her."

"Who..."

There was a soft click as the caller hung up.

For a moment, Alan sat frozen with the telephone still against his ear, trying to make sense of what he'd heard. Had Rycroft not taken Bobbie after all? Was the call a cruel joke? Yet the boy's voice had an urgency that told him the words were true. He buzzed Mrs. Fenton. "Find Rod and send him up here, please. And then dial Emory Roth for me."

\*\*\*\*

Emory Roth was waiting outside the church when Alan arrived. "No one has come in or left since I got here."

"Did you go inside?"

The investigator leaned in through the car

window. "This could be a hoax, but I didn't want to frighten her off if she's really in there."

"Somehow I don't think it's a prank, Roth. I think she's in there. We know at least one child got out." Alan stepped out of the car. "If you'll be so kind as to get me inside, Rod, I'll see if she's really there."

The younger man offered his arm. "Four shallow steps, sir...I'll get the door." He lowered his voice to a whisper which nevertheless echoed in the cavernous building. "The confessional booths are on the right, three of them. There's a font on the left, six steps, maybe. Otherwise, you can walk straight ahead."

Alan nodded and dropped Rod's arm. "Bobbie?" He stepped forward, listening.

When there was no answer, he took another step and called her name again. "Bobbie, it's Alan Ashley."

He waited. "Bobbie, I've come to take you home. Lenore is very sad without you." There was a soft stirring to his left.

"Someone called my office an hour ago and said I'd find you here."

He heard a door opening and then the sound of footsteps. A small bare hand slipped into his gloved one. "Dick called you."

"Who is Dick?"

"He's the oldest. He helped Miss Ervin look after us and took over the schoolroom when Mum left to work for you."

He felt her shivering. "Do you have on a coat, Bobbie?"

"Only the pink sweater that Mum gave me for Christmas. I guess my coat burned up."

"It will be warm in the car."

"Is Mum there?"

"She was out of the office when the call came. I couldn't reach her. But she'll be at home later, and she'll be overjoyed to see you."

201

Rod got a blanket out of the trunk and tucked it around Bobbie after she was in the back seat. "Thank you very much," she said politely. "I was a little cold."

"Are you hungry, Bobbie?" Alan asked as Rod started the car.

"Dick didn't have any more money for food."

"We'll be home in less than an hour, and Mrs. Swane will make you whatever you want."

Bobbie burrowed deeper into the blanket. "I didn't know what to do."

"What do you mean?"

"Rebekah woke me up and said to come outside with her to meet her Uncle Avram. It was Papa."

"You saw him?"

"Not exactly. It was dark, but I know it was Papa. He called me his best little girl and his shining star."

"Did he say anything else?"

"He said he had to go away again but that he knew you and Mum would take good care of me. But I don't know how he knew about you."

"I'm sure that he took care to learn everything he could about your circumstances," Alan parried.

"He took Rebekah instead of me."

Alan recognized the pain in her voice. "Did he explain why he was taking Rebekah?"

"Because she didn't have anyplace else to go."

"I see."

"It's not fair. He could have taken me, too."

"Did he explain why he didn't?"

"He just said that he wanted me to stay with Mum and you."

"What happened then?"

"He started walking away with Rebekah, and I ran after them. I heard a noise, and when I looked back, the Home was on fire. Everything was orange and yellow, and the smoke was black...it made me cough."

"It must have been very frightening."

"So I started running after Papa again, but he was gone. Then someone grabbed me, but I kicked him, and he let me go, so I ran, and then I turned a corner, and there was Dick. He works nights and..." She ran out of breath. Alan waited for her to go on.

"He saw the fire, too, and he said we couldn't do anything, so we just ran and ran."

"Where have you been all this time?"

"Dick knew about an old garage that was all closed up. We stayed there."

"Why didn't he contact me before this?"

"He wanted to, but..."

"Yes?"

"I...I lied. I said that Papa was coming back for me."

"Did you tell him about Rebekah?"

"No."

"About the man who frightened you?"

"No...not until later."

"I see. What led him to call me?"

"The man came back."

"You're sure it was the same one?"

"Dick told me to stay in the garage, and I did, but I looked out the window sometimes...and that's when I saw him."

"Would you recognize him if you saw him again?"

"Maybe."

"Was it your grandfather?"

"No, but..." Her voice trailed off.

"But?"

"But he reminded me of someone."

"Someone you associate with your grandfather?"

"I think so."

"So you told Dick."

"That's when he said he was going to call you to

come after me."

"He did the right thing, Bobbie. Lenore and I thought your father had taken you."

"I didn't mean for Mum to be sad, but I thought...I really wanted Papa to come back. I couldn't believe that he'd just leave me again." She began to cry. "I hate him now. He took Rebekah, but he didn't take me. I hate him."

Alan gathered her in his arms, but he knew that he couldn't comfort her.

****

Mrs. Swane came out of the kitchen when she heard them in the foyer. "This is Bobbie." Alan put his hand on the child's shoulder. "It's a long story, Mrs. Swane, which I'll explain tonight. Lenore is with Ellen Bernard in the city and can't be reached, and I have an appointment in exactly twenty minutes. I'm sure you'll see to Bobbie's needs."

Mrs. Swane took Bobbie's hand. "We'll be just fine, won't we, Bobbie?"

Bobbie replied in a tone that implied she wasn't really sure she believed the strange woman. "Yes, ma'am."

Alan leaned down. "Now, Bobbie, Lenore will be here before I return. If I can locate her some way, she'll be here sooner. Mrs. Swane has been taking care of me since I was just walking, and I have the utmost confidence in her. Actually, she runs the house and all of us in it."

Mrs. Swane made a sound of disgust. "Go back to the office, Mr. Alan. Are you hungry, Bobbie?"

"Yes, ma'am."

"We'll go through to the kitchen first and get you something. Then I'll take you upstairs and let you soak in Miss Lenore's tub."

****

Lenore and Ellen returned to the office just before five o'clock. "She insisted on coming back here to see if there was any work she needed to do," Ellen said. "How are you going to manage without her, Alan?"

"I'll continue to work," Lenore said. "I love what I do."

"There's nothing to be done here," Alan said, "but there is something at home that needs attending to."

"Oh?"

He turned to Ellen. "Have Sam call me tonight at his convenience."

"All right." She hugged Lenore. "I'll talk to you again on Saturday."

Lenore glanced through some papers on her desk. "I'll take these home and transcribe them for you tonight. I'm sorry we were so long. I told Ellen I couldn't take more than two hours, but she was so insistent."

"Ellen can be that way, but no matter. I went out myself this afternoon."

"I didn't know you had an appointment elsewhere."

"It was unexpected. Rod drove me. I think he misses getting out now that he spends all day supervising the mail room."

Lenore organized the papers into a folder. "I'm ready if you are."

"You sound much brighter than you did this morning."

"I told Ellen about everything. It helped."

"It usually does."

"She pointed out that Bobbie's father will likely get in touch with me sometime and let me know about her. If he cares so much, and I believe he does, he won't separate us entirely."

"I shouldn't think so."

"And it's best for Bobbie to be with him..." She began to cry. "Oh, Alan, she was my little girl. I'll miss her so."

Alan folded her in his arms. "No, Lenore, you won't. You have her still."

"What?"

"She's waiting for you at home, darling Lenore. I'll tell you the story on the way."

When he reached for his briefcase and turned back, he realized that she was already out the door.

Chapter Seventeen

Bobbie wore one of Lenore's blouses and a skirt, pinned up to fit, when they joined Alan in the dining room that evening. No mention was made of her recent experience as she ate two helpings of everything and drank two full glasses of milk.

"You'll have to buy a cow, at this rate," Mrs. Swane said, setting a third glass in front of Bobbie.

"Who would milk it?" Bobbie asked.

"Why, you would, of course," Alan replied. "After all, you're the one who drinks all the milk."

Bobbie giggled. "Cook had to put water in the milk..." Her smile faded.

"I have apple cake for dessert," Mrs. Swane said smoothly. "Will you have it in here or with coffee in the drawing room?"

"In the drawing room, I believe, thank you. Bobbie, suppose you help Mrs. Swane prepare the teacart." Rising, Alan made his way around the table and held Lenore's chair. "We'll be waiting for you."

"Has she told you her story?" he asked as soon as the dining room door swung shut behind them.

"Some of it. But I don't understand why her father went to so much trouble to find her and then left her behind."

"Perhaps he knew she'd be better off with us. Or perhaps he could only take one child and felt that Rebekah needed him more. A man has to be made of something fine to make such a sacrifice."

"What if he comes back and wants Bobbie, too?"

"We'll deal with that if it happens, Lenore. I'll speak with Sam about filing the custody suit or wait until we're married and petition the court to grant an adoption."

"Either way, her grandfather will know that she didn't die in the fire. The other man must have been someone he employed to look for her."

"Roth says so, but I'll take certain precautions...security measures."

"Guards like you sent to the Home? It's a terrible way to live...being watched...being afraid."

"Only temporarily."

"Oh, Alan, I..." She broke off as Bobbie came in pushing the teacart ahead of her.

"I asked Mrs. Swane why it was called a teacart when it was used for coffee, and she said that's just the way it is."

Alan laughed. "And if Mrs. Swane says it, then it's so. Now, Bobbie, will you serve?"

****

After Bobbie returned the teacart to the kitchen and came back, Alan steered the conversation to more serious topics. "You say that you came outside that night because Rebekah woke you and told you that her uncle was waiting to meet you."

Bobbie nodded, then remembered that he couldn't see her. "Yes, sir."

Lenore stroked Bobbie's head as it rested against her knee. "When we first heard the news, I felt I'd left you to die. Then when Mr. Roth said he was sure you were with your father, I was glad for you."

Bobbie pressed closer to Lenore. "He left me and took Rebekah. I hate him."

"Hate shrivels the soul, Bobbie," Alan interrupted. "I understand that you're angry with him, but consider two things. Number one, he saved your life. If he hadn't come for Rebekah and asked her to bring you outside, you would have been asleep like the others in the building, with no hope of escape when the furnace exploded. And number two, think of what giving you up must have cost him. I would imagine it broke his heart."

"You don't know."

"Yes, I do, Bobbie, but that's another story."

Bobbie stretched her hands toward the fire. "It was so cold in that garage," she murmured.

"Emory Roth is trying to find Dick," Alan went on. "I'll offer him anything he needs—a home, employment, the opportunity to complete his education. Do you have any idea where he might be, Bobbie?"

"He took me to the church and put me in that little booth and said for me to stay there until you came."

"What was he planning for himself?"

"He wasn't going to stay in Greenfield. He didn't want to get picked up and put in another home. He said he could take care of himself."

"He's seventeen," Lenore said. "He'd have been released from custody in another year, though I think Constance would have found a way to give him a home at Greenfield as long as he needed it."

"Well, if he can be found, Roth will do it, and he won't be returned to an institution."

"Are you and Mum going to get married now?" Bobbie asked.

"How do you feel about that, Bobbie?"

"I want you to."

"You won't be losing her, you know."

"It won't be the same as when it was just the two of us, but it will be very nice."

"Now there will be three."

"Like a real family."

"That's right. I've spoken to Lenore about adopting you once we're married."

"Why?"

"Well, to give you my name so that you'd be an

Ashley too."

Bobbie sat up. "Mrs. Swane and I talked about things. She says I'm a princess now."

"A what?" Alan laughed at the earnestness of her statement.

"A princess, and I live in a castle, and..."

"You're just Bobbie," Lenore said firmly.

"But Mrs. Swane said I was a princess, and Mr. Ashley said that if she says something it must be so, because she runs everything."

Alan laughed. "You can't refute her logic, Lenore."

"I can keep her from being overindulged." Lenore took the child's face between her hands. "You'll have everything you need now, Bobbie dear, but no more."

Bobbie laughed. "I know, but it's fun to talk about."

Alan tried not to smile. "In a sense you will be a princess, Bobbie. You'll have many advantages here. But if you were to make a list of things you want, what would be on it?"

"Alan..."

He waved his hand. "I'm just curious."

"I'd like to have *The Pink Lady* hanging over my bed again and my pink sweater back, but Mrs. Swane said she'd wash it tonight. And I'd like cinnamon toast for breakfast tomorrow. Grandmother used to make it for me, and I haven't had it in such a long time."

Alan laughed. "I think those things can be arranged, don't you, Lenore?"

Lenore smiled. "Of course."

"No requests for diamond tiaras and a coach and four?"

"What is that?" Bobbie asked.

"Something you don't need," Lenore said firmly. "Now I'm going to take you upstairs to bed."

"Will you be back?" Alan asked.

"If you like."

"I think we have more to discuss."

"All right."

Bobbie stood in front of Alan. "Goodnight, Mr. Ashley. Thank you very much for coming after me today and bringing me to this beautiful house."

He reached for her hands and folded them between his. "Goodnight, Bobbie. Sleep well."

\*\*\*\*

"Lenore, we can postpone the wedding until Bobbie settles in," Alan said as soon as she came back. "It might be the best for her."

"There's still the question of permanent custody."

"I realize it's like a cloud hanging over us, but it will pass."

"I want to believe that."

"Bobbie is an interesting child. She reminds me of Bea in a way, very open and friendly. We'll have to introduce them soon."

"She's struggling with what happened to her friends at Greenfield."

"That's to be expected."

"I don't think she quite realizes the horror she escaped."

"Perhaps she won't."

"I realize it, though. Oh, Alan, I got to know all of the children and the matrons in the six months I lived there, and Constance Ervin was a wonderful friend."

He held out his hands and waited until she took them. "It's very painful even for me, and I didn't know them at all."

"I suddenly realize how alone I am except for Bobbie."

"You have me."

"I suppose I can't quite grasp that you're part of

211

my life. I keep expecting to realize that I just imagined all this."

"You didn't." He kissed her.

"Alan, you must be very sure that this isn't an impulsive move on your part. We're both lonely, but that isn't a reason to do something that we'll spend a lifetime regretting."

"Do you love me, Lenore?"

"With all my heart," she said without hesitation.

"Then only a lifetime commitment will do."

Chapter Eighteen

Bobbie was waiting on the second from the bottom stair when Alan and Lenore returned home the next evening. "You can't ever guess what's happened." Without waiting, she plunged on. "Mrs. Bernard and Bea came today and brought two enormous boxes of the most beautiful clothes. Bea got out of school just to come and visit, and she says she grows so fast that I'll have more new things before I can wear all of these. And she says we're going to be practically sisters and that we'll go to school together and..."

"I can't wait to see them." Lenore interrupted the torrent of words. "We'll have a fashion show after dinner."

"They're so wonderful. I can't wait for you to see them." The words died on her lips as she realized that Alan couldn't see them. "I'm...sorry," she said.

"I can't wait to see them, either," Alan said. "Perhaps you might use the library as your dressing room and make the drawing room your stage. And, of course, there must be a running commentary on each garment."

Bobbie stared at him. "I..." Then she looked at Lenore who smiled and nodded. "All right," she said, the joy back in her voice. "Right after dinner."

During dinner she watched Alan's every motion. "How do you do that?" she blurted.

"Avoid wearing my dinner? I didn't always."

"I didn't mean to be nosy, sir."

"You must ask all the questions you like, Bobbie, and never be uncomfortable with my circumstances.

213

I am blind, but I see through the words of others."

"Yes, sir."

"What else did you do today besides fall heir to a vast new wardrobe?"

Bobbie took another swallow of milk, draining her glass. "Well, I helped Mrs. Swane in the kitchen, and then she told me it would be all right if I looked at the books in your library, and I found ever so many I want to read."

"I should have suggested it myself. Please help yourself to anything you want, though the books in the locked glass case are very rare and quite expensive. My father collected them."

"And then I went outside and walked all around the house, and it's the biggest house I've ever seen. It's bigger than the Home."

"I'll take you on a tour of the inside on Saturday. Did you know there's a secret room?"

Bobbie's eyes widened. "A real secret room?"

"Do you know your history?"

"I think so."

"During the Civil War, this was a safe house on the Underground Railroad, one of the last stops for slaves escaping over the border into Canada. They often had to hide in the room for days until a guide could lead them across to freedom."

"I'm glad we didn't go to Canada," Bobbie said. "I'm glad Mum and I are going to live here forever. We are, aren't we, Mum?"

"Yes, Bobbie, forever."

"After the fashion show tonight, we'll talk about the wedding." Alan reached for his glass and found it empty. "Bobbie, would you be so kind as to get the pitcher of water from the sideboard?"

She jumped up, almost overturning her chair in her eagerness to please.

****

"After some discussion, we've decided to

postpone the wedding until the first of March," Alan told Sam a few days later. "By then the custody issue will be settled, and Bobbie will be established at Arlington Hall. And there's the business of the unfortunate children at Greenfield."

"I don't follow you."

"I told the fire marshal that I'd see to having them buried, but by the time anyone got back to me, the remains had already been interred in the local potter's field."

"With no notice, of course."

"Nothing. They were expendable, I suppose, less money for the county to spend even if they had plenty. Lenore and I have discussed how best to memorialize them. Thomas Greer has offered to officiate, and I've been in contact with a local company about a marker with the names inscribed."

"Have you been able to get the records?"

"Between Bobbie and Lenore, all the names are accounted for. No one will notice or even care that three are missing."

"Bobbie, Rebekah, and Dick."

"The county thinks they're dead, too, and for now, that may be for the best, although since Lenore has temporary custody of Bobbie, she's in no danger of being reclaimed by the state."

"Ellen, Bea, and I would like to participate when the plans are firm."

"Thank you, Sam. I can't stop thinking that if the explosion had occurred twenty-four hours earlier, Lenore would have been killed, too. Somehow I believe she was kept safe...for me. I shared that with Thomas Greer. He's inclined to agree. He always said that I, too, was spared for a reason."

Sam put his hand on Alan's shoulder. "I'm sure you were, Alan."

\*\*\*\*

Alan scheduled the memorial service for Valentine's Day and circulated broad hints in Greenfield that county officials should feel obligated to attend. The marker, inscribed with thirty-seven names and topped with a weeping angel holding a child in his arms, was set in place two days in advance, covered with a canvas prior to being unveiled.

On the night before the service, Mrs. Swane called Alan from the dinner table to the telephone. "It's Mr. Bernard," Mrs. Swane said. "He says it's urgent."

"Go ahead with your meal while it's warm," Alan said to Lenore and Bobbie as he rose. "I'll be back as soon as I can."

When he came back, Lenore noticed his agitation. "Alan, what is it?"

"The notice of the custody hearing has reached Harcourt. His attorney contacted Sam a few minutes ago. Harcourt is willing to give up his rights to Bobbie for the sum of fifty thousand dollars."

Lenore put her hand to her throat. "Oh, Alan." Alan sat down again and picked up his napkin. "I could give him the money, but it would never end for Bobbie or for any of us. He'd come back for more, threatening to take her, and make our lives miserable."

"What did you tell him?" Lenore asked.

"I told Sam to remind the man that the buying and selling of human beings had been outlawed in this country for many years and that I'd not give Harcourt a cent. I will, however, spend any amount necessary to protect Bobbie."

Bobbie's voice was hoarse with fear. "Is he coming for me? Is Grandfather Harcourt going to take me away?"

Lenore realized too late that they'd forgotten Bobbie's presence.

Almost before the words were out of the child's mouth, her pale, frightened face disappeared beyond the edge of the table as she slid from her chair in a faint.

****

Sam arrived after dinner while Lenore was sitting upstairs trying to comfort Bobbie. "Alan, Harcourt must know that we've ferreted out his shady dealings and that he can't win in court. He's attempted extortion, and that's not only against the law but also the nail in his coffin."

"So what do you think he'll do next?"

"We know, or at least we're reasonably certain, that his man was in Greenfield with the intention of taking Bobbie on the night of the fire. I think he'll try to do it again." He looked up and saw Lenore standing in the door of the study, her face drained of all color.

"Alan, we have to get away. I have to take Bobbie out of here tonight. We can slip across the border to Canada before anyone knows we've gone."

Alan rose and put his arms around her. "Lenore, we've discussed the fallacy behind that reasoning. There are other ways."

"I can't let him take her."

"He's not going to take her. Sam, if you'd be so kind as to telephone Emory Roth and ask about the possibility of additional security here tonight..."

"I telephoned him before I came. He's sending four men within the hour."

Alan brushed Lenore's forehead with his lips. "You see, everything will be all right."

****

Alan persuaded Lenore that there was no need to postpone the memorial service. "We'll have the security guards accompany us to the cemetery. Bobbie will feel safer if she sees us going on with our daily lives as usual."

217

Rod drove them to Greenfield in the morning. The four security guards formed a tight cordon around Alan, Lenore, and Bobbie, but even so, Alan could feel Lenore's fear as he held her arm.

\*\*\*\*

Ellen, Sam, and Bea stayed to supper when they returned to Rumers Crossing. After dinner, Alan suggested that Bea and Bobbie go upstairs.

"May I show her the secret room, Uncle Alan?"

"If you stay out of the tunnel, and don't forget the door latches automatically when you close it. Prop it open before you go inside. Ask Mrs. Swane for some flashlights."

When the girls had gone, the four adults retired to the drawing room with their coffee. "I thought it was a lovely service," Ellen said.

Sam leaned forward. "Lenore, perhaps Harcourt won't make a move to get Bobbie. The state police in Texas are itching to get their hands on him if they can prove he's put even a toe across the line of the law."

"Doesn't that depend on how badly he wants Bobbie?" Lenore asked.

"I suppose it does," Sam admitted. "I've already made the authorities aware that he tried to extort money from Alan."

Ellen rose. "The little girls are occupied with lighter pursuits, so perhaps the big ones should be, too. Let's go upstairs, Lenore, and talk about the wedding."

In Lenore's sitting room, Ellen said, "You've looked ill all day."

"Ellen, I have to get Bobbie away. Did your husband explain..."

"Yes, and I understand that you're afraid, Lenore, but you can't run away."

Lenore twisted her hands. "I don't know what's wrong with me. I've never been so indecisive before.

218

I love Alan, and I want to marry him and spend the rest of my life with him. What's wrong with me?"

"It's called motherhood. The age-old story of the mother bear protecting her cub. I understand."

"Do you? I'm actually thinking of taking Bobbie and running away...leaving Alan behind. I've been afraid before, Ellen, afraid that I couldn't feed and clothe her when times were hard, but it was never like this. I was always able to make a rational decision and go forward. I'm behaving very badly, and I don't want to hurt Alan."

"He's been hurt too many times, you know."

"That's just it. He's been hurt, Bobbie's been hurt...they both deserve better, and somehow I'm caught in the middle trying to do the right thing for both of them."

"Sam feels reasonably certain that he can get permanent custody for you."

"Reasonably certain isn't overly comforting. I'm sorry, Ellen, I know he's doing his best."

"That's all any of us can do, including you. I hope you don't mind that he told me the situation."

"No, you should know."

"Bea only knows part of it, but we had to tell her enough so she'd understand that she's not to say anything about Bobbie in public."

"She's a good diversion for Bobbie right now."

"Perhaps you need a diversion, too. The first of March will be here before you know it."

"Ellen, I can't. I can't marry Alan and have him involved in this unsavory business any longer. I can't risk having Bobbie taken by her grandfather. Don't you see? I have to go."

****

Alan caught Lenore's arm as she started for the stairs after seeing the Bernards out. "Lenore, what's wrong?

"Alan, it's late."

"Tell me what you're thinking."

"That I have to go," she blurted. "I have to take Bobbie out of here."

He sighed. "You're back to that again."

"I don't see any other way."

"Obviously not. Lenore, we have guards round the clock."

"There were guards at the Home, too."

"Life is a risk, Lenore darling. You either live it or you don't. You've said that you love me, but if you can't trust me, then I wonder."

"I do love you, but you suddenly speak of faith and trust, and I don't think I have those anymore. I've lost everything except Bobbie, and I can't lose her, too."

"You haven't lost me, but you seem willing enough to cast me aside."

"It's not like that, Alan."

"Then tell me how it is. I'm not a fish to be hooked and thrown back for sport."

Lenore let herself look at the man she'd alternately accepted and rejected. The collar of his shirt lay open on the V of the soft blue sweater, and a few auburn hairs showed above it. She wanted to touch them, to put her face against them, to feel his heart beating against her cheek. She wanted to throw herself on his broad chest and feel his arms wrap around her like a blanket. She'd loved David with a girl's gentle heart, but her woman's heart loved Alan with a fierce, consuming passion that both intrigued and frightened her.

"One of the things I admired in you from the beginning was your confidence, your self-assurance that showed itself in taking employment with me, knowing it was best for you and Bobbie even if it meant a temporary separation. But all that has been stripped away from you and left you vulnerable to whatever storms of life come your way. That won't change no matter where you go."

"I always knew what had to be done," she agreed, weariness creeping into her voice.

"You've become so obsessed with protecting Bobbie that you aren't protecting her."

"What do you mean?" Anger replaced the weariness.

"You're making rash, impulsive decisions that may, in the short run, keep her from being returned to her grandfather, but in the long run they will also keep her from a life with all the advantages that her father wanted for her. Do you think he'd have left her behind if he hadn't felt that you and I could take care of her?"

"I don't know."

"He intended to take her. I'm convinced of that. I had hoped that he'd give her a choice, and then I realized that she was incapable of making such a choice at her age. I think he realized it too, so, as parents do, he made it for her. He made a decision in her best interest. You consider yourself her true mother, and you are. The mother who bore her made very bad decisions, ones that created this present situation."

"I don't believe that she left a will naming Robert Harcourt as guardian. She couldn't have done that, knowing what he was capable of doing."

"Perhaps she didn't, or perhaps she was coerced. We'll never know. At any rate, he'll have to produce the document in court, if we ever get there."

"Alan, I can't talk about this anymore tonight. It's been a wrenching day for all of us. It's not your responsibility to deal with Bobbie's situation."

"No, it's not. It's my choice."

"Out of obligation to me because you asked me to marry you."

Alan took his hand from her arm. "This conversation is getting us nowhere, Lenore. If you intend to leave, then make your plans and do it. I'll give you a letter of credit to a bank I know in Ottawa. At least then I'll know that you and Bobbie will never be in want. If things go badly, you can always come back."

"Alan, please try to understand."

"I do understand. Fear and pride are a dangerous combination. I remember the first time I ever tried to eat soup and dribbled it all over my shirt. I was mortified, and at the same time I was also terrified that I'd never master the skill. I went for twenty-four hours without eating until a determined therapist coaxed me to try again—and with the same results, I might add. Yet here I am, almost fifteen years later, at ease at the most elegant table no matter what the menu."

He started for his study. "I'll have Rod drive you to the station when your plans are finalized. Whatever you can't take with you, he'll carry up to storage in the attic."

She heard the study door close when she was halfway up the stairs. Her knees gave way, and she crumpled, sobbing into the carpet.

Chapter Nineteen

"We're going away," Bobbie said the next morning as Mrs. Swane set her plate in front of her. Lenore's place was empty.

"Yes, I know. I wish you weren't." The woman rested one hand on the child's shoulder.

"I like it here."

"Do you know about the security guards?" Alan asked.

"Yes, sir."

"How does that make you feel?"

"Safe, I guess, but Mum says it's like being in prison."

"We make our own prisons, Bobbie. A person can be free to come and go as he pleases and still be a prisoner of his own fear."

"I'm afraid."

"Of what exactly?"

"That if we run away, and Mum gets sick again, I'll be put in another orphanage. But if we stay here, Grandfather might take me away forever."

"That's frightening for you."

"If Papa hadn't taken Rebekah and left me, it would be all right."

"It would have been one solution to the problem, but wouldn't you have missed Lenore?"

"Maybe she could've come with us."

"I don't think so."

Bobbie sighed. "I was just thinking."

"It's good to think about things, Bobbie. Now I want you to think carefully about what I'm going to say. Apparently your father had been visiting

Rebekah regularly for several months. Lenore said that Miss Ervin told her about *Uncle Avram* who came after study hour and..."

"I knew about him. Everyone did. We were glad for her."

"But you didn't recognize the name. Your father immigrated from Russia with his parents. I know from Judge Sutherland's file that you remember them—your *Babka* and her scarf, your grandfather who always wore a little cap and let you play with his long beard. Their name was Rykovsky. Many immigrants anglicized their names, that is, changed them to sound more American. So your father, Avram Rykovsky, became Albert Rycroft."

"They died like Grandmother did."

"When I finished Harvard, I enlisted in the army and was sent to France. War is a terrible thing, Bobbie, and many of the young men I started out with were killed soon after we arrived. I was promoted several times, mostly because I was one of the original members of my company who happened to stay alive.

"One day Colonel Finch ordered me to hold the piece of land we'd managed to take between our lines and No Man's Land, land that neither side really held. I felt it was a hopeless cause and sent an enlisted man back to headquarters with the request that we be allowed to withdraw. Almost as soon as he was gone, the shelling began. I told my men to remain hidden in our trench and wait out the barrage, assuring them that we would be going toward safety very soon.

"Then a very large shell and several smaller ones found their mark. I caught one of the smaller ones in my arms. Fortunately, it was defective, but it still did much damage to my body and tossed me out of the trench and into No Man's Land, where I was an easy target for the German guns. Then I sensed that someone was near me and called out, *Who's there?*"

He paused. "And then a voice said, *Rycroft, sir.*"

"Papa?" Bobbie gripped the arms of the chair and leaned forward. "My papa?"

"Yes. At the risk of his own life, he carried me to safety. I never saw him again until one night just before Christmas."

"Papa was here? In this house?" Bobbie's voice fell to a whisper.

"When I opened the door to my room, I sensed a presence and called out, *Who's there*? And the answer came as before, *Rycroft, sir*. He had managed to trace Lenore here and knew that she would be able to tell him about you. "When he asked me to tell him where you were, I felt I had no choice. But I also told him how much you love Lenore and of my plan to marry her and adopt you. I asked him not to take you away before finding out what you wanted."

"I wanted to go with him." Alan heard tears in her voice.

"I know. Perhaps I shouldn't have made my home sound better than what he could give you. He must have felt it was true, Bobbie, and as parents who truly love their children do, he wanted the best for you." He took a deep breath. "So, if you want to be angry with someone, be angry with me, not your father. He wanted you, Bobbie. I'm sure it broke his heart to leave you behind."

When Bobbie finally spoke, she sounded very old. "He didn't take me because of what you said."

"I believe so."

"So maybe he would have taken me if you hadn't told him all those things."

"Perhaps."

"So it's your fault he didn't take me."

"If you need to place blame somewhere, you may place it on me."

She was silent for so long that Alan wondered if she'd somehow left the room without his being aware. "Bobbie?"

"Yes, sir?"

"Do you understand everything now?"

"I think so. Did Mum know? She acted kind of mad in Miss Ervin's office when you came in."

"I understood her feelings. I'll understand yours."

"I'm not mad at you," Bobbie said. "Maybe I'm not really mad at Papa, but he should have taken me. He promised." She slid out of the chair and stood beside Alan's. "I'd like to stay so you can be my Papa now."

He was about to say that he couldn't take Albert Rycroft's place when Lenore came in. "Bobbie, you need to come upstairs now."

"We were talking about Papa."

"I explained to her about her father coming here," Alan said. "I thought she should know that I might have influenced his decision to leave her behind."

"Come upstairs with me now, Bobbie dear."

Alan fought the urge to rise and take Lenore into his arms and shake some sense into her. Instead he finished his breakfast and went into the study to telephone Mrs. Fenton that he would be late coming into the office.

"Alan?" Lenore's voice came from the open door.

"Are you leaving today?"

"I've been thinking about what you said last night, about how I'd lost confidence in myself. And you're right, I have. I've been up there unable to make the smallest decision about what to pack, and what to leave behind. Nor have I been able to telephone for a train schedule. I feel as though I'm shattering into a million tiny pieces that can't ever be put back together again."

He waited for her to go on, hoping that she'd say what he wanted to hear.

"If I don't go, her grandfather may take her. If I do, he might still find her and bring charges against me as well, and I'd never get her back. Her father could come back for her. I don't know what to do or where to turn." She advanced farther into the room.

"I failed her once, when she was taken to Greenfield. Oh, I know I couldn't help becoming ill, but I didn't think ahead. I didn't think what it meant not having something to show that I was responsible for Bobbie."

He heard her begin to pace, the odd, muffled sound of her footsteps on the polished floor hinting at her still being in robe and slippers.

"I've hurt you, Alan, and I never meant to. It isn't you that I don't trust. It's myself I'm afraid of. I'm failing Bobbie, and I could fail you as well, if I marry you."

"Lenore..." He held out his hand.

"Don't, Alan. I can't touch you. I can't get near you, or I might..."

"Might let me back into your life?"

She stood still. "You'll always be in my life. I could never love anyone the way I love you."

"You must make a decision, my darling. Go or stay. What will it be?"

"Help me, Alan."

"All I can say is, stay with me, and we'll see this through together."

As she moved closer, he caught the scent of soap and bath powder. It stirred him as Elise Mayhew's expensive perfume never had.

"If I were one of the swashbuckling silent-screen heroes that I used to watch on Saturday mornings, I'd leap from my chair, crush you in my arms, carry you upstairs and...well, perhaps I'd better not go on. But I don't know how else to wipe away all your doubts and uncertainties."

He heard her gasp as she processed his meaning.

"We're both adults, well past the point of flirting and playing games, but it seems that's what we've been doing."

"I've never done either." The spirit in her voice buoyed him.

"Nor have I. I cannot make my intentions any plainer. I love you. I want to marry you. We seem to have reached an impasse."

Then he felt her fingers touch his outstretched hand as she said, "How did it happen? No, don't say it. I'm to blame. My obsession, as you called it, my irrational fear."

He closed his fingers around hers and drew her toward him. With little urging, she folded herself into his lap and laid her head on his shoulder. "Oh, Alan, forgive me. You've offered me the great gifts of your love and devotion. I don't want to lose those."

He searched for the pins that held her hair, removing them one by one until it flowed down her back. Then he pushed back the folds of her dressing gown and felt a tremor run through her body as he put his lips against her throat. His lips came down hard on hers, and she responded in kind.

He was still holding her when someone knocked on the door. Lenore almost went to her knees in her haste to remove herself from his vicinity. He took a deep breath. "Come."

Mrs. Swane opened the door but didn't come inside. "Mr. Bernard is on the telephone."

"What is it, Sam?" Alan heard a click as Mrs. Swane hung up the extension in the hall.

He listened for a moment, then laughed. "She told you that, did she? Well, I appreciate your concern. No, Lenore hasn't gone. In fact, you caught us at a rather inopportune moment." He wished he could see Lenore's face.

"No, I suppose nothing's settled completely, but we're discussing our options. It's all right. Never mind. We're in the study, actually, and perhaps this room is a bit more private for my dishonorable intentions. Yes, so early in the morning." He held out his hand and was surprised when Lenore took it immediately. "I'll keep you up to date. Yes. Yes. Goodbye, Sam."

He hung up and coaxed Lenore back into his lap. "Apparently Ellen told Sam that you were leaving, so he called to check on the situation."

"Are your intentions dishonorable?" She laughed softly.

"Quite. Are you blushing again, my dear Miss Seldon?"

"Not this time."

"If I asked you to lock the door..."

"Please don't ask me." Her voice was light.

He tilted her head back and kissed her throat again. "I've never seen you quite so full of abandon."

"I'm shocked at myself, but suddenly I'm so tired of being afraid, Alan. So tired of trying to do everything just right and never quite achieving the standard."

"Who are you, Lenore? The ever-efficient personal assistant...the terrified, uncertain mother... or this warm, responsive lover?"

"Perhaps a little of all of them." She removed his glasses and caressed his face.

They laughed together. "You haven't laughed in a long time," he said.

"I needed to laugh."

"Nothing's changed," he reminded her. "You know that. We'll have the guards until this is settled. I'll hire a tutor to come to the house. Roth suggested earlier that we not put Bobbie in school quite yet. Sam will file the custody papers on

229

Monday, and we'll be married on the first of March as we planned."

He half expected her to refuse but felt her nodding against him.

"Am I rushing you too much?"

" We've already put things off once for Bobbie's sake. I have my suit and a few other things."

"Somehow I think I'm going to be more interested in those few other things."

"I rather think you will be."

"What about Bobbie? What does she need?"

"She needs for me to stop behaving like a child myself. First we're going, then we're staying. Last night when you told me to go, I knew what I'd done, and I think that frightened me more than the threat of Robert Harcourt."

"I can deal with him, Lenore, but we both need a firm commitment."

"I want to marry you, Alan, if you'll still have me."

"I believe I will."

She leaned against him. "Half an hour ago I couldn't make the simplest decision," she said. "And I'm still afraid, Alan, but I realize now that it's better this way. Bobbie is safer here than on the run."

"Go up and tell her, then, and I'll telephone Sam and Ellen."

"I haven't liked myself very much these past few days. Bobbie didn't want to go. She showed more courage than I did, and she has the most to lose."

"We're not going to think of losing, Lenore, only going forward to a better day for all of us. Now go make yourself decent, and we'll go to the office and get some work done." When she didn't move, he added, "Unless, of course, you'd like to lock the door and..."

"Allow your dishonorable intentions?"

"Yes."

She went to the door. "Five minutes," she murmured.

He heard the key turn in the lock.

## Chapter Twenty

Emory Roth brought in a fifth man, Jerry Runyon, to live in the garage apartment and watch the house while the other men took care of the grounds. Ellen Bernard found Jonathan Evans, a struggling young law student who would be glad of the extra money for tutoring Bobbie five mornings a week.

Bobbie bonded with both of them almost immediately. Most of all, she developed an unexpected devotion to and admiration for Alan and talked incessantly about being adopted.

In short order, she also convinced Alan that, if she couldn't go to school right away and had to keep close to the house for an unknown amount of time, she needed a companion, specifically a dog.

"What kind of dog do you want?"

"A very small one—at least, that's what Mrs. Swane says."

"I always wanted a dog."

"You did?"

"Yes, but my parents wouldn't hear of it, and then I was away at school most of the time."

"Alan, you'll spoil her," Lenore protested.

"I will most certainly try to spoil both of you, my love."

\*\*\*\*

For the rest of the week, Bobbie talked of nothing else but the promised dog. Alan indulged her with pictures of all breeds from the book he had dispatched Mrs. Fenton to buy at the local bookstore. When nothing struck Bobbie's fancy, he said he'd heard that mixed breeds often made better companions. On Saturday, they drove to the animal shelter in the next town.

The selection was large and varied, but Bobbie kept coming back to one, a large, lumbering, shaggy black animal who worshipped her with luminous brown eyes, pink tongue, and thumping tail.

"Bobbie, Mrs. Swane agreed to a small dog," Lenore reminded her.

"But he isn't going to be *her* dog, Mum. He's going to be mine."

"Exactly how big is he?" Alan asked, pushing his fingers through the wire to feel the dog's head.

"He's half as tall as Bobbie and probably matches her weight. Alan, he's really unsuitable."

"But the important thing, Lenore my love, is if they're a match."

"He loves me already," Bobbie insisted. "Don't you?"

The long, plumy tail beat the floor vigorously.

"Could we have this dog out of the cage for a few minutes?" Alan asked the attendant.

Lenore braced herself for an attack, but to her surprise, the dog rose from his haunches with unexpected grace, walked sedately from the cage, and sat down at Bobbie's feet. She put her arms around his neck. "You want to come home with me, don't you?"

"Where did he come from?" Alan asked.

"He was picked up on the road south of Rumers Crossing about three weeks ago. No one's come to inquire about him."

"Is he healthy?"

"The vet who examined him said so. He'd missed a few meals, but you can't tell that now."

The dog turned his massive head in the direction of Alan's voice.

"Alan, he's simply too big," Lenore said.

Alan ran his hands over the dog's head and neck, then down his flanks. "He *is* rather large, but...are you very sure he's the one you want, Bobbie?"

"Oh, yes, sir, I really do."

Alan laughed. "Then you must have him."

"Alan, Mrs. Swane said..."

"Then Bobbie must convince her otherwise. Can you do that, Bobbie?"

"Maybe."

"It will be up to you, and, of course, to the dog."

"Prince," Bobbie said. "His name is Prince. He has a royal walk, like the one in *King George's Dog*."

Lenore sighed. "Oh, Bobbie, you read too many books."

\*\*\*\*

"I said a small dog, not a horse!" Mrs. Swane exploded when they walked through the front door with Prince.

"His name is Prince, Mrs. Swane, and he'll be so good, I promise."

"He looks more like a *pauper* than a prince," Lenore murmured to Jerry who was standing nearby in amused silence.

"He's a *horse*." Mrs. Swane put her hands on her hips. "With that tail, he'll have every lamp in the house swept off the tables in a day."

"I'll watch him, I promise I will." Bobbie grasped the new collar and leash purchased for more money than the dog cost.

"You'll do more than that, missy. There's feeding and watering and running the carpet sweeper every blessed day." She stalked off toward the kitchen.

"I thought you were going to get a small dog," Jerry said, reaching down to scratch the animal's ears.

"His name is Prince," Bobbie repeated. "He wanted me to take him."

"No doubt he'll rule this place like a king, won't you, boy?" Jerry winked at Lenore.

"I'm going upstairs to pack," she said. "I'm sure Mrs. Swane will throw all of us out before lunch."

****

Prince proved to be an intelligent animal who seemed to understand that he must stay out of Alan's way. He attached himself to Bobbie with a slavish devotion, even growling menacingly when the milkman made his regular delivery while Bobbie happened to be in the kitchen.

Lenore reflected that the dog was as attached to Bobbie as Bobbie was becoming to Alan. She encouraged the relationship, but Alan was more cautious. "I want you to always remember your father, Bobbie," he said one evening shortly before the wedding, while he was helping her with the advanced math lesson that Jonathan had assigned. She'd interrupted his explanation with the pronouncement that he could see numbers in his head better than she could see them with her eyes and that everyone would think she was smart just like him, like her father.

"Papa's gone," she said in a flat voice that still betrayed some vestiges of anger.

"We discussed that, I believe. He loves you so much that he gave up what he wanted, which was to have you with him, so that you would have the best life possible. I'm going to adopt you and be in the place he wants to be, but you must never forget to think of him with respect and love."

Bobbie was undeterred. "Will I be your best little girl and your shining star?"

"No, Bobbie, that is reserved for another. Now, about this mathematical puzzle we're solving. Before you begin to divide with a decimal, you must move the decimal point to the right and create a whole number in both the divisor and the dividend. Do that now."

Bobbie bent over the paper on the library table that Jerry had moved into the drawing room at Alan's request. "I've done it."

"Now divide as you would any other long division problem."

She laid down her pencil. "Are you going to be very strict?"

"Yes, very."

She sighed and picked up her pencil again.

****

"Alan, she adores you," Lenore chided him when Bobbie went upstairs, followed by Prince, who had his own bed on the floor beside hers. "She wants to feel like other children, with a real mother and father."

"I will be her father in every sense, Lenore darling, but I won't take Albert Rycroft's place. He saved my life at the risk of his own, and without knowing it he saved Bobbie's life, too. She will understand and appreciate that more as she grows older."

Lenore closed the door that Bobbie had left ajar and curled herself into Alan's lap. "I can't believe we'll be married in two days."

"It can't be soon enough to suit me. You're sure that you aren't concerned about leaving Bobbie here while we take our wedding trip?"

"A little, but there are the guards, and Mrs. Swane and Jerry will look after her."

"Oh, yes, they both have her well in hand."

"Her riding lessons begin the day after the wedding. She takes out her boots and polishes them at least once a day. I'm afraid she's getting quite spoiled."

"The lessons will be good for her. She's cooped up in the house too much, but that will end after the custody hearing when we get back."

"I wish it could have been scheduled sooner."

"Harcourt's attorney was granted the postponement, but I think that's the last Judge Merrill will allow. Frankly, I don't understand why the man is pursuing a hopeless case."

"I just want it to be over."

Alan stroked her shoulder. "I just want you."

"The conversation seems to end up this way every evening, doesn't it?" She removed his glasses and set them aside. "Ellen says you need to replace these with more stylish frames."

"What do you think?"

"I agree, and perhaps they shouldn't be so dark. Your eyes don't need hiding, Alan."

"I don't think I was hiding my eyes so much as I was hiding my soul from the world."

She smoothed his eyelids with the tip of one finger. "Who said that the eyes are the window of the soul?"

"I don't remember, but it's apt, isn't it? Enough about eyes. I should like to discuss lips."

"You would." She gave herself up to his insistent mouth.

****

It was later than usual when they went upstairs that evening. Alan fell asleep immediately. He wasn't sure what woke him, Lenore's screams or the terrible snarling of the dog. Sliding open the drawer of the bedside table, his hand closed around the cold steel of the gun he'd kept there ever since his return from the war.

At first the sound of several sets of feet in the hall confused him, but as he listened more closely, he recognized that the lighter steps were behind him and the heavier ones seemed to be moving toward the stairs. He waited a moment, then stepped out of the bedroom. "Prince."

Almost at once the snarling and barking ceased,

and he felt the solid bulk of the animal pressed against his leg. Grasping the dog's leather collar, he took a few steps. The heavier footsteps seemed to be going down the stairs now.

"Alan!" Lenore stepped from the room she shared with Bobbie.

"I'm coming, Lenore. Don't move." The dog tried to pull him in the opposite direction. "Prince, no. This way."

"Bobbie's gone! Her grandfather's taken her."

"Did you see him?"

"She's gone!"

"Then go and call the police on the upstairs extension. Just dial the operator, and she'll connect you. Quickly, Lenore."

"But Bobbie..."

"Do it now. And don't turn on a light."

He followed her to the table with the telephone and listened as she made the call. "Now tell me what happened."

"I heard someone in the room and reached to turn on the light, but someone struck me and knocked me back onto the bed."

"Are you hurt?"

"I'm all right. Alan, we have to go after Bobbie!"

"We have to think first," he said sharply, his own fear escalating.

Prince began to growl again. The sense of knowing that someone was near, developed soon after he became blind, made Alan tense. He pulled Lenore closer to him. "Go back in your room and lock the door," he whispered.

"I've got to find..."

She clutched at him, but he shoved her roughly in the direction of her room. "Hurry."

The low, savage growl from Prince boded ill for whoever else was around. "Prince, no," Alan said. "Stop it."

"Get the dog out of the way or it's dead, and so are you."

Alan strained for some recognition of the voice, but there was none. "I'm holding him," he replied.

"Where's Bobbie?"

"You don't have her?"

"Would I be asking if I did?"

Alan moved the hand with the gun in line with the pocket of his robe and dropped it inside. "Who are you?"

"You don't need to know. Where is she?"

"The police are on the way."

"That was a mistake."

"How did you get around the guards?"

"I figured it out."

"How?"

"Stop wasting my time. I want the girl. I want her right now."

"Why do you want her?"

Alan heard the man curse under his breath. "I'll kill you and the woman, too, if I have to. Where's the girl?"

Alan's ears picked up the faint sound of footsteps coming in the opposite direction. "Is there someone else with you?"

"An army. Are you going to tell me where she is, or do I have to tear this place apart?"

Alan felt the presence move closer and tightened his grip on the gun. The footsteps behind him stopped abruptly.

"Downstairs," he lied. "She sleeps downstairs in a locked room."

"Show me."

Alan took a step forward. "I'm blind," he said. "You'll have to help me down the stairs." As soon as the man touched him, Alan stuck his foot to the side and at the same time jerked back. He heard the man cry out as he tumbled, and then he felt someone else rush past him.

At the sound of a gunshot, he whipped his own gun out of his pocket, listened, took aim, and fired. Behind him, Lenore screamed, and he was somehow aware that, outside of his own darkness, there was light around him.

"Mrs. Swane?" Lenore called out. "Don't shoot again, Alan. Mrs. Swane is down there!"

He grasped the banister. "Mrs. Swane, are you all right?"

"She has a gun," Lenore whispered in disbelief.

The woman turned to look up at Alan and Lenore. "Did I kill him?"

In the distance, police sirens wailed loudly.

****

The police chief placed the two guns side by side on the foyer table. "This one is yours, Mrs. Swane?"

"Yes." She turned her face away from the body sprawled at the foot of the stairs.

He picked it up, smelled it, then spun the barrel. "One bullet missing."

"I fired once."

"In the dark?"

"I could see his shadow."

The chief laid the gun down and took up the other. "And this is yours, Mr. Ashley?"

"Yes."

"There's one bullet missing from this one, too."

Jerry held out his weapon. "This is mine. It hasn't been fired."

The officer nodded and turned his attention to the four security guards prowling nervously about the foyer. "All right, let me check the rest. You two were in a car down by the road?"

The older man nodded. "That's right. No one came in through the gate."

The chief smelled their guns briefly, checked the chambers, then returned them. "Now the two of you who patrol the grounds."

It took even less time to know that their weapons hadn't been fired, either. "All right, now give me the story again."

Harold glanced at his partner. "We check all the doors every hour on the hour. We'd just made our two o'clock rounds and were on our way to the back of the house. We have a key to the kitchen, and the housekeeper always leaves some sandwiches and a pot of coffee for us. We were about to go in when we heard all the commotion."

"And you never saw or heard anything outside?"

Harold turned to Alan Ashley. "Mr. Ashley, there was no one—*no one* out there."

Another policeman came back from checking the French doors by the porte cochere. "This lock's been jimmied from the inside."

"No!" Harold exploded. "We'd just checked it. He couldn't have opened it that fast."

Alan shook his head. "Harold, no one's blaming you and Larry."

"I said it's been jimmied *from the inside*," the policeman said. "Someone in the house got out through this door, not in."

The police chief stepped over the body still lying face down. "There's a bullet in the wall behind him. I'm going to have to dig it out."

"That can wait," Alan said. He put his lips against Lenore's streaming hair. "The most important thing is finding Bobbie."

Mrs. Swane swayed slightly. Jerry caught her arm, then took his hand away and saw blood. "She's been shot."

"Then I must have hit *you* when I fired. I didn't know you were there, Mrs. Swane."

"Serves me right for trying to play Sherlock Holmes," she said, her voice shaking. "I believe I'll sit down."

"Dr. Sims has already been called," Alan said. "Take her into the drawing room."

"I'm all right. It's only my arm."

"She's bleeding," Jerry insisted.

"Oh, Bobbie," Lenore moaned.

Alan caught her before she fell. "Someone please get a chair for Lenore."

\*\*\*\*

Rolf Sims saw to Mrs. Swane's injury before, as the assistant coroner, he inspected the body. "She's all right, Alan. The bullet just grazed her upper arm. I dressed it, and she's lying down on the settee."

He bent down to look at the body. "Who is it?"

"I'm assuming it's Robert Harcourt," Alan said.

"There's no identification on him," the police chief said.

"Jerry has already called Emory Roth. He'll be able to tell us." Alan bent over Lenore. "It will be all right," he murmured.

Sims turned the body on its back. "This man wasn't shot. His neck's been snapped. Somebody came up behind him and used that maneuver we learned in army training. He's not a small man, so whoever did it was at least his size."

Harold bent down and retrieved a bullet from under the table. "This must have been what grazed Mrs. Swane." He passed it over to the police chief, who confirmed that it matched those in Alan's gun. Then he compared the one he'd just dug out of the wall. "Might match the woman's gun. You sure there's no bullet in the body?"

"There's not a drop of blood on him anywhere. See for yourself. Look at the head and neck. You can see what I'm talking about."

The chief nodded. "You ever kill anybody like that, Dr. Sims? In the war, I mean?"

"No, thank God."

"Mr. Ashley?"

242

"I was taught the maneuver, but I never had occasion to use it."

"Mrs. Swane said that Mr. Ashley never came downstairs," Jerry spoke up.

"And he'd have gotten me before I could've positioned myself behind him," Alan added. "I've perfected a number of skills without being able to see what I'm doing, but I'm afraid that isn't one of them."

"Whoever did it knew what he was doing," the doctor said. "He meant to kill him."

"And you say that this might be the grandfather of Miss Seldon's niece?"

"Or one of his people. We were involved in a custody dispute. His attorney kept postponing the court hearing, and he tried to extort money from me several weeks ago."

"What were his chances of getting the little girl?" the police chief asked.

"Almost nil, despite the fact that he said he had a will, allegedly written by her mother, giving him guardianship. We've actually been expecting him to try to take her. That's the reason for the guards."

"Allegedly?"

"It's a long story," Alan said. "Rolf, if you'd be so kind as to see Lenore now."

"I'll take her upstairs and give her a sedative," Rolf Sims said.

Alan kissed Lenore's forehead. "We'll find her, my love. It will be all right." Then he turned to the police chief. "Are your men searching for Bobbie?"

"There are tire tracks out back but no sign of a car."

Lenore roused at that. "I've lost her. She's really gone forever this time."

Rolf Sims lifted her to her feet. "Come, Miss Seldon."

\*\*\*\*

Emory Roth arrived and identified the body as Robert Harcourt, then went out to look at the tire tracks. "I agree with the police that there was an accomplice, perhaps the one who got out through the French doors," he told Alan when he came back. "I don't understand how anyone got in here with the guards. They're my very best."

"The main consideration is finding Bobbie," Alan said. "We'll worry later about how they got in."

Jerry came out of the drawing room where he'd been sitting with Mrs. Swane. "She's very worried about Bobbie."

"Harcourt didn't have her, I know that much," Alan said. "He kept asking me where she was hidden."

"Then if he didn't have her, how could his accomplice have gotten away with her?" Jerry asked.

Roth moved closer to Alan and spoke so that he couldn't be heard by the police as they finished gathering evidence. "Could she be hiding in the house?"

Alan sucked in his breath. "Of course! That's what the dog was trying to tell me when he tried to lead me away from the stairs. Where is he? Where's Prince?"

As if he'd been waiting for his cue, the massive dog rose from behind the rounded newel post at the top of the stairs and whined softly.

"Where's Bobbie, Prince?" Alan asked, taking the stairs two at a time. "Where is she, boy?" He grasped the dog's collar, almost losing his balance as Prince hurtled down the hall in the direction of the stairs leading to the attic. "The secret room. Why didn't I think of it?"

Jerry took his arm. "Because you're not a dog or a terrified little girl."

They found Bobbie huddled against the door inside the secret room. Barefoot and clad only in her nightgown, she sat shivering in the damp darkness. Prince refused to let the men near her until he'd nuzzled and licked her from head to toe.

"I knew you'd come, Papa," Bobbie wept as Alan folded her in his arms. "I knew you wouldn't leave me again."

****

Rolf Sims was still trying to persuade Lenore to accept a sedative when Alan, accompanied by Jerry and Prince, carried Bobbie into the room.

"Bobbie!" Lenore almost tore her from Alan's arms. "Oh, Bobbie, I thought you were gone." Snatching a blanket from the bed, she wrapped it around the child and sat down, holding her like an infant.

"The police are going to have to talk to her," Alan said.

"Not now." Lenore leaned over Bobbie as if to shield her. "Not now."

"I'm afraid they're going to have to hear from her exactly what happened. Come, Lenore, she's all right."

"I'll never let her out of my sight again."

Alan sat down beside her. "She's safe, Lenore. Harcourt is dead."

Bobbie stirred, then sat up. "Grandfather's dead? Did you kill him?"

"He fell down the stairs," Jerry said quickly.

"But he's really dead?"

"He's really dead, Bobbie," Alan said. "He can't hurt you anymore."

"I thought you were Papa."

"Yes, I know. Why?"

"Because he was here." She slipped out of Lenore's lap and huddled in the blanket on the floor at her feet. "He was right here in this room. I woke up and saw him, and he told me to be quiet and come with him."

"Didn't Prince bark?" Alan asked. "It was his barking that alerted me to the fact that Harcourt was in the house."

"Prince didn't bark. I don't know why." She reached for the big dog standing guard nearby and put her arms around his neck.

"Dogs know who's a threat and who isn't," Jerry observed.

"Did your papa take you upstairs to the secret room?" Alan asked.

"Yes, sir."

"Did you tell him about it?"

Bobbie shook her head, then remembered to speak. "No, but he knew where it was. He just put me inside and closed the door, and then I remembered that it locked, and I was so scared no one would find me...and I was so cold..."

"Are you quite sure it was your father, Bobbie?" Alan asked.

"It was Papa. I know it was. He called me his best little girl and his shining star and said he wouldn't let anything hurt me, and..." She buried her face against her knees and began to sob. "He left me again. He left me again."

****

The police chief agreed that it wasn't necessary to talk to Bobbie in order to make his report. "Mr. Roth filled me in on the rest," he said. "If the state police in Texas wanted Robert Harcourt any way they could get him, well, they won't have to bother now."

When the police had gone, Lenore went with Dr. Sims to check on Mrs. Swane and saw her back to bed with instructions not to think of getting up to prepare meals the next day.

She came back in time to hear Alan asking for an explanation of Mrs. Swane's gun. "She bought it and asked me to teach her how to use it," Jerry said.

"I didn't think it was a good idea, but I decided that, if she was going to keep it, she should know how to handle it safely."

"It was equally ridiculous for me to keep that gun in the drawer beside my bed. The police were discreet enough not to come right out and ask why a blind man would have a gun, but I'm sure they wanted to."

"Why *do* you have it, Alan?" Lenore looked through the bedroom door to reassure herself that Bobbie really was all right, then sat down beside Alan.

"Pride, I suppose."

"I'm glad you didn't kill him."

"I might have. I was willing to do it to protect you and Bobbie."

"I don't want Bobbie to know that her father killed him. He did, didn't he?"

"Oh, yes, that seems certain."

Lenore leaned against Alan's shoulder. "We'll have to make her understand that he didn't leave her again, but we can't tell her what he did."

Jerry stood up. "The police shouldn't know either. I gave them the idea that hiding in the secret room was her own idea."

"Thank you, Jerry. Involving Rycroft would be unkind, at the very least. Tell Harold and the others that the men must have come through the tunnel and that they couldn't have prevented it."

"The tunnel?" Jerry asked. "I thought that was it. But how..."

"I'll call tomorrow and see to having it closed up permanently. Goodnight, Jerry."

Lenore moved closer to him. "It's over, then."

"I'll call Sam in the morning. I'm sure the judge will sign the custody order as soon as he sees proof of Harcourt's death. Then, after we return from our wedding trip, I'll petition to adopt her." He lifted

Lenore's face toward his. "There is going to be a wedding, isn't there?"

"Yes, Alan, there is." She was silent for a moment. "What will happen to Albert Rycroft?"

"He has to be found first, and somehow I don't think he will be, especially if no one knows about him. I rather expect he'll be on his way back to Palestine tomorrow. His business here is finished."

"Will he be back?"

Alan shook his head. "I don't know, Lenore. He's left her behind twice now, but he's still her father."

Chapter Twenty-One

The Bernards hosted a dinner for Alan and Lenore on the night before the wedding. Bobbie wore her favorite pink taffeta dress from the *Bea Box*. "I've been wanting somewhere to wear it for a very long time," she told Alan while they waited in the drawing room for Lenore.

"You might have had a new dress, you know."

"All of my clothes from the *Bea Box* are new. And Bea says she'll bring me more in the summer. Besides, my wedding dress is new."

"Ah, yes, your dress for the wedding, Miss Maid of Honor."

"I knew it was perfect the minute I saw it. Mum's is perfect, too. You'll see tomorrow."

Alan considered Bobbie's casual *You'll see tomorrow*. Like Lenore, she now took his blindness for granted. He was blind, but he wasn't a *blind man*.

"You'll describe her in detail for me."

"But not until tomorrow. It's against the rules or something."

Alan filled his pipe but didn't light it. "It's traditional for the groom to catch his first glimpse of the bride as she comes down the aisle."

"But she's not coming down the aisle, is she?"

"No, we'll just stand together in front of the altar."

Bobbie smoothed her dress, enjoying the feel of the material under her fingers. "Someday I'll walk down the aisle, though. I'll wear a dress that swishes like this, only long and white, and a veil, and carry pink roses." She leaned against the arm of Alan's chair. "And you'll walk with me and give me away, won't you?"

"To be sure."

"Because that's what fathers do."

While Alan was still formulating his reply, Lenore joined them. "I'll go tell Jerry we're ready," Bobbie volunteered.

"She was planning *her* wedding," Alan told Lenore. "It seems I'm to give her away."

Lenore put her face against his. "You've won her heart completely."

"And *your* heart, my love?"

"It's yours forever, Alan dearest."

****

Bobbie fastened the pearls around Lenore's neck. "I still can't believe that Alan found Mother's pearls in that pawn shop after so many years." Lenore touched them lovingly.

"Mr. Ashley can do anything, can't he?"

"No one can do everything, Bobbie dear."

"I helped, you know. I told him about Poole Street."

"He wouldn't have known where to begin without you." Lenore turned and gathered Bobbie into her arms. "Oh, Bobbie, everything really is going to be all right now!"

Downstairs, Bobbie described Lenore's cream-colored silk suit and hat in minutest detail. "She's beautiful," she finished, almost out of breath.

"Yes, she is." Alan fingered the collar of the silk blouse worn under the suit. "She's a breathtakingly beautiful bride. Now, Bobbie, Lenore has had her wedding gift, the pearls, but you haven't had yours."

"I'm not getting married."

"No, but in way, our wedding is yours, too. Today the three of us are committing to be a family." He drew a blue velvet jeweler's box from his pocket.

"So this is for you, Bobbie, with our love."

He heard her sharp intake of breath as she opened it. "She's totally shocked," Lenore whispered to him.

Bobbie lifted the gold chain from its satin bed. "It's beautiful. Is it really for me?"

"The pearl in the middle was taken from Lenore's strand, at the end, where it wouldn't show. The diamonds on either side came from a very old necklace that belonged to my great-grandmother." He held out his hand. "Let me put it on for you."

Lifting the hair from her neck, he realized that she was wearing another necklace. "What is this?"

Bobbie stood very still. "It's the locket that Papa gave me just before Mama took me away. I never take it off."

"I see."

"But please, may I have this one from you and Mum, too?"

"Of course. Would you like to put it away for now?"

"No, I want to wear it, please."

Alan fastened the clasp as skillfully as if he could see it. "It's so wonderful," Bobbie whispered, arranging the delicate chain on the outside of her dress, while the locket remained hidden. "I'll wear it always."

****

During the brief ceremony, Bobbie stood with Lenore and held Alan's ring, while Sam Bernard did the honors as best man. Le Monde catered the wedding breakfast that followed in the employee cafeteria of Ashley Enterprises. Just before noon, Rod drove Alan and Lenore to the station to catch the train.

****

"Are you sure you're all right with leaving Bobbie for a week?" Alan asked again as the train

251

gathered speed.

Lenore settled back into the seat and reached for his hand. "I feel as though a huge weight has been lifted."

"I feel the same way."

The conductor stopped at their seats. "Tickets, please," he said to Lenore, taking note of Alan's dark glasses.

"My husband has the tickets," she said.

Alan produced the folder from his inside pocket. The man punched them without comment and returned them to Alan's waiting hand.

"Did you enjoy saying that? *My husband?*" Alan asked.

"For several reasons."

"I think I realize now that all the confidence I tried to show the world was completely false."

"What do you mean?"

"I mean that I appeared to have things well in hand, but I didn't really, and everyone knew it. They stepped in to pick up the slack, and I let them. You make a simple statement like *My husband has the tickets*, and I don't even care that the conductor thought a blind man couldn't be responsible for something like that."

She leaned over. "Just don't forget that you have the baggage claim tickets, too."

"They're quite safe." He patted his pocket. "Perhaps we should have gotten a compartment."

"For a four-hour trip?"

"There's not much privacy here."

"You're holding my hand."

"I'd like to do more." He leaned over and kissed her cheek.

"Did you hear Bobbie giggle when you kissed me in the church?"

"She's settled in much better than I ever expected."

"Was it only two nights ago that everything happened?"

"It seems longer. Jerry has disposed of my gun and Mrs. Swane's, by the way. Neither of us had any business with one." He shook his head. "I might have killed her."

"You didn't."

"Jerry will supervise the closing of the tunnel while we're gone."

"I still don't understand how anyone knew it was there."

"The secret room and the tunnel were the subject of a magazine article some years back, so their existence wasn't unknown. It's how Rycroft got in and out of the house the first time, I believe. How Harcourt found it, I don't know, but it doesn't matter now."

"I'm relieved that Mr. Roth was able to find out that Bobbie's father had used his passport and is safely out of the country."

"The police don't even know about him."

"I'm glad you didn't tell them he was there."

"I told them there was a second person in the house, and there was—Harcourt's accomplice. I saw no reason to bring Albert Rycroft into it. He accomplished his purpose and now he's gone."

"To Palestine."

"Roth believes he's involved in undercover work there."

"I can't imagine what he has that Bobbie's grandfather knew about and wanted."

"It doesn't matter now."

She moved closer to him and put her head on his shoulder. "I do love you, Alan."

****

A driver from the hotel met their train and took care of their luggage. Alan signed the register using the smaller straight-edge, made to fit in his pocket, like the larger one he kept on his desk. "My wife invented this," he said to the desk clerk.

"It's...uh...unique."

"The only one of its kind. So is she."

The bungalow to which they were shown was on the far end of the hotel property. "I asked for the accommodations with the best view of the mountains. That's what I enjoyed most when I came here during college. I still remember how they looked in the early morning and at sunset."

Someone had turned on the lamps and lighted the fire in the main room.

"I asked that the kitchen be stocked," Alan said. "I even arranged for champagne. Surely your mother wouldn't mind on this occasion."

"It's not legal, and Ellen said it made her tipsy."

"I don't mind a tipsy bride at all."

Lenore walked him through the bungalow twice until he said he had the layout firmly in mind. She unpacked for them and changed into the expensive negligee that Ellen had urged her to buy. Alan was sitting in front of the fire when she came back.

"The champagne is just right," he said, indicating the bottle in the ice bucket.

"I'm very uncertain about this, Alan."

He felt for the corkscrew and in seconds had the bottle open. "I'll let you pour. It was quite expensive, and I don't want to waste a drop."

She filled the two glasses and handed one to him. "Just the idea makes me rather giddy."

"What are you wearing?"

"The negligee that Ellen convinced me to buy. It's blue satin."

He smoothed the sleeve. "I like it. Is your hair down?"

"I thought I'd let you do that."

"First we'll toast each other." He lifted his glass. "To us. To Bobbie. To the love that we share."

"To love," she said, moving her glass to touch his, then sipping cautiously. "It has no taste, but there are bubbles."

"It will come to you." He emptied his glass before unpinning her hair. "Never cut your hair, and always wear satin."

\*\*\*\*

When the fire burned low, Alan sat up. "Lenore."

She stirred drowsily. "Am I tipsy?"

"A little, perhaps." He stood and lifted her in his arms. "We'll see how much I remember about this room now," he said. "I'll try not to drop you."

She touched his face. "Once you said that your body ached for mine," she whispered.

"I remember."

"Now I...I understand."

"Then we're of one mind."

"I love you, Alan. I love you so very much."

\*\*\*\*

Alan woke in the night and reached to touch Lenore's hair, spread across the pillow beside him. He breathed deeply of its scent and thought of their earlier lovemaking. He smiled, remembering how she had responded to his gentle touch in the warm darkness. Finally, she had fallen asleep in his arms, one hand resting on the tangled scars that covered the slight depression in his chest from armpit to nipple. He reflected that, like his blindness, she'd accepted this additional inescapable reminder of the horror that had changed his life forever.

Beside him, she stirred and turned over. Being careful not to wake her, he touched her bare shoulder. He had despaired more than once that this night would never come, and yet it was here and past, but there were more to follow.

In a week they would return to a child whom they both loved and who adored them as well. He wanted her adoration, too, needed it as he needed

255

Lenore's, but he couldn't forget Albert Rycroft's sacrifice.

He knew that Bobbie was still struggling and might always struggle with what she saw as her father's rejection. The man was a mystery. He had left his daughter behind twice. Would he change his mind someday? Would Bobbie go with him?

Alan considered how she had slipped her hand into his after the wedding and said, "Mum is happy now, and so am I." Already, any thought of losing her was unbearable.

Lenore stirred again and spoke his name. He gathered her in his arms. "Go back to sleep, my love."

She murmured something unintelligible, patted him, and fell asleep again.

****

The weather was unusually mild for early March. They walked on the hotel grounds and ventured to the foot of the mountain he'd climbed in his college days.

A hired car took them into town to shop. Alan insisted that Lenore buy whatever she liked, but she told him that she'd never seen so many things she could live without. They settled on a pink and white hand-knitted sweater and matching cap for Bobbie.

At night they sat in front of the fire until it burned out. "I can't stop talking, it seems," he told her on their last evening. "I have a lifetime of thoughts and feelings stored up, but there was never anyone to listen, before. I hope I'm not boring you."

"You could never bore me, Alan. Even in the days when I didn't like you very much, I found your conversation interesting."

"And now that you love me, I must be totally fascinating."

She laughed. "You might say that." She reached for his glasses. "We're going to have to do something about these as soon as we get back. They're quite scratched and somewhat bent out of shape."

"You're going to make me over?"

"Not really."

He traced the outline of her face. "I wish I could see you. Ellen says you're very beautiful."

"Ellen is kind."

"Bobbie says so, too."

"Bobbie thinks everyone she loves is beautiful. I hope Mrs. Swane isn't petting her to death. For all her talk of being strict, she dotes on Bobbie. Think of her making that bed for Prince after she declared he was a horse and didn't belong in the house."

"I think we needn't worry about Mrs. Swane. She set limits for me as a boy and will do so for Bobbie. Come to think of it, she still does. I may have to teach Bobbie to hunt for the butter cookies."

"And turn her to a life of crime, too?"

"Perhaps."

"It's been a lovely week in every way."

"We'll come back here next year on our anniversary, if you like." Alan began to remove the pins from her hair. "I'll reserve the room before we leave."

"Alan, the adoption will go through, won't it?"

"Sam believes so."

"It's only been a week since..."

"It's over, darling Lenore."

"I hope so. I do hope so."

"We'll be a very special family."

"Perhaps the doctor was wrong, Alan. Perhaps you'll have a son someday."

"I'm content with you and Bobbie."

"I can't help thinking about her father."

"He made the decision he felt was best for her." He rose and held out his hand. "You came into my life so unexpectedly, out of breath and smelling of damp talcum. I believe I fell in love with you at that very moment."

"Did you?" she murmured.

"Yes."

"You didn't care for Pollyanna."

"Not altogether."

"She's gone. Perhaps she never really existed."

"But you are here, darling Lenore. Here in my heart forever." He lifted her in his arms and stepped forward with a clear vision of the path ahead.

**Look for the sequel to this book,
FINDING PAPA'S SHINING STAR**

In the dark days of the Great Depression, when eleven-year-old Bobbie Rycroft became Annie Ashley, cherished daughter of Alan and Lenore, she left behind a life of fear and deprivation. Or so she believed as she grew to womanhood, sheltered in an affluent home with every material possession and opportunity.

Graduating from Vassar just as America—and Ashley Enterprises—gears up for war, she goes to work for the family business and meets David, such an annoying man, one with an unusual past of his own.

As they make decisions for better or for worse in the midst of World War II, Annie finds the conflict impacts her life in ways she never could have imagined, and when David's own tangled connection to her past puts Annie in danger of losing her life, she must face her past instead of hiding from it.

\*\*\*\*

**A word about the author...**

Judy is a retired teacher who has written stories and poems since she could hold a pencil, always promising herself that someday she would pursue publication.

Grandparents and older friends gave her a passionate interest in history and genealogical research, from which she draws many of her characters and plot ideas.

Widowed for many years, she has two grown sons and a granddaughter whose smile lights up her life.

Thank you for purchasing
this Wild Rose Press publication.
For other wonderful stories of romance,
please visit our on-line bookstore at
www.thewildrosepress.com.

For questions or more information,
contact us at info@thewildrosepress.com.

The Wild Rose Press
www.TheWildRosePress.com

## Other Vintage titles to enjoy...

SHE'S ME by Mimi Barbour: A spoilt model pricks her finger on a rose thorn and is transported back to 1963 and into a chubby librarian's body. As "roomies" they learn a lot from each other and each finds the man of her dreams. HE'S HER by Mimi Barbour: Same rosebush, different victims! WE'RE ONE, third in the series, gives us a new angle on the uses of that rosebush as the hero and heroine travel from Las Vegas to escape a death threat. All three are available together as THE VICARAGE BENCH.

DON'T CALL ME DARLIN' by Fleeta Cunningham: In Santa Rita, Texas, 1957, Carole the librarian faces censorship and a pyromaniac. Will the County Judge who's dating her protect or accuse her?

BLACK RAIN RISING by Fleeta Cunningham: Another in the Santa Rita series, starring a country singer accused of murder, the courageous daughter of a radio station owner, and a little girl who needs an operation in order to live.

SOURDOUGH RED by Pinkie Paranya: At the end of the Klondike gold rush, Jen and her younger brother have the aid of a sea captain and a doctor in the search for her twin, lost in Alaskan wilderness.

SCHERESADE by Ronit Lèvy: Erika's new life in America is full of promise. So why have nightmares returned? A passionate young neurologist and an embittered Holocaust survivor help her unravel the mystery of her past and discover true love.

A TRAIN THROUGH TIME by Bess McBride: On a sleek modern train heading to Seattle, Ellie awakens in the midst of a Victorian-era re-enactment. Handsome, green-eyed Robert Chamberlain, leader of the group, finally convinces her the date is 1901....

SHATTERED DREAMS by Margaret Tanner: Three World War I soldiers leave a shattering legacy as they pass through Lauren's life. Which is killed? Whose child does she carry? Who does she marry?